ARE SOULS MADE OF ZINC?

A SAGA OF LOVE, LOSS & ACCEPTANCE

TRISHA RAHA

Contents

Contents

Preface

Have you ever been in love with someone (romantically)?

If you said "yes," I want you to think about the person who exposed you to the importance of romantic love and ask yourself if you could keep your heart safe with it. To you, how pure was it?

So..?

Did you ever think that love is eventually essential to fully comprehend a soul? How wholesome right? Yet,
can you believe that the feeling of love can be malleable, just like zinc is—strong, adaptable, and yet susceptible to the wear of life, and contains hidden properties – so does our souls. It is waiting to be discovered while they bond with another soul (element), tested by the fire called time, and shaped by the hands of fate.

But why only zinc?

I'll leave the 'why' in this book...

...Wait, Fancy a hint?

What if I tell you that our souls feel more connected to emotions like love, sadness, and unexpected moments of destiny, much like zinc that fuses into alchemical changes? Every interaction alters its makeup, bringing to light aspects of our inner selves we were unaware of. The wonder is that although some ties break and just leave wounds behind, others shape us into something unbreakable. But what drives these changes? Maybe we have more agency than we think, or maybe it's the invisible chemistry of fate.

So, this romantic mystery invites you to unravel a saga, based in India and felt across the skies, must do is a - paying attention to every word, cause the climax could lead you to zone out. Perfectly, like hidden alloys, the secrets in this saga are layered and just waiting for you to be discovered. Heartache, doubt, and pieces of answers may be strewn about like ash but you will feel the reality.

Have faith in the process, despite everything in or around your time, I hope you look back to the 20th-century romance when the digital life was less engaging as compared to today and feel free to feed your imaginations with lots of curiosities.

Are Souls Made of Zinc? A Saga of Love Loss and Acceptance is not just a saga of love, loss, and letting go; it is a journey of a character who learns to explore his heart's resilience and entangles himself with the spiritual journey of self-discovery at its core. This saga does not just capture the love and belongingness but it delves through the heartbreak of separation, loss, growth, and the unspoken truths that linger between all of us.

Ishan, a boy who grew up accepting the biggest losses in his life and was healed by strong faith, carries the quiet strength of someone who has faced life's deepest shadows. When Nysa, a low-maintenance companion, enters his world, she becomes both - a mirror and a mystery to him—reflecting his hopes and challenging his understanding of love. Together, they navigate a world riddled with expectations and cultural norms, testing the limits of what they can endure as time tests their bonding.

This book is as much about their beautiful journey as it is about the readers'. It's an invitation to delve into the philosophies of love, spirituality, and growth, to question the intersections of human connections, love, and maturity, and to ponder the bittersweet art of letting go.

As you turn these pages, you may find echoes of your own story—a first love, an impossible choice, or a moment of transformation in a man's life and the heartache when someone leaves you despite your efforts. I hope you will embrace the emotions, and contradictions, relate as much, and absorb the lessons that come with each step of their journey before it halts with an unexpected mystery.

Acknowledgements

A warm thank you with all due respect, to my world - my dear parents,
Mrs. Sanjeeta (Rubi) Sen Raha, Mr Tridib Raha, and my sister Ms. Tamanna Raha, for their unconditional love and support.

Thanks to Ms. Naila Vasquez for their immense efforts, encouragement,
Ms. Debasmita Choudhury for her creative support-helping me start and Ms. Priya Mandal,
Mr. Abhinand Dhandapani and Ms. Bushra N. for their illustrative ideas.

Special thanks to Mr. Arnab Kumar Pal for their immense love and inspiration.

Additional gratitude goes out to my online family and everyone else who has helped me throughout my journey, validated my efforts, and stayed friends with me, unconditionally throughout my writing career.

ACKNOWLEDGEMENTS

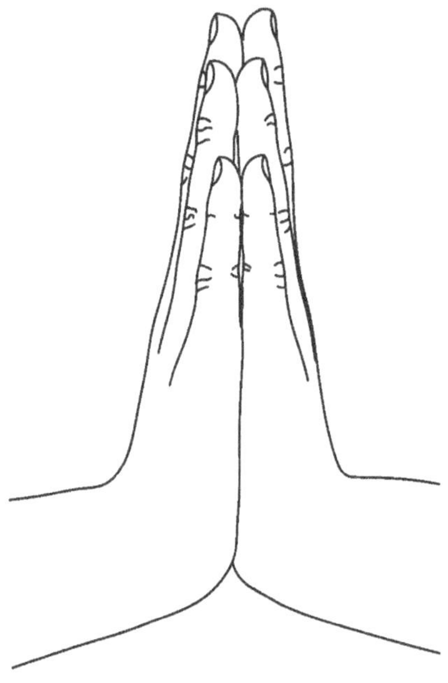

Don't Miss The Mandatory Spoiler:

To make this book more engaging for non-readers, the author has added a secret recipe.

While you turn the pages, Ishan's roller-coaster life has left him confused at times, where he questions, he communicates his true feelings with his heart in search of consolation; thus, right before each chapter, a few phrases allow you to understand Ishan as a growing man more deeply and also to get a slight taste about the chapter's context.

But, trust me! A lot is happening...

Welcome to *Are Souls Made of Zinc?*

Message From The Author

Dear Readers,

The core inspiration for writing this book represents a deep personal spiritual journey, crafted with sincere intention and profound inspiration. These pages reflect my learnings, spiritual insights, and personal transformations, gathered through deep contemplation and guidance.

I invite you to read these words not with defensiveness, but with an open heart and a spirit of curiosity. Spiritual understanding is inherently personal and subjective. What resonates for me might differ from your experience, which is perfectly valid. My ultimate goal is not to challenge or provoke anyone/ anything but to share existing insights (incl. Religious references) that might inspire your inner exploration. If any part of this work inadvertently touches a sensitive area or seems to conflict with your beliefs, I sincerely apologize.

These reflections come from a place of respect, love, and genuine seeking. May they serve as a gentle invitation to reflect, explore, and connect with your spiritual understanding.

With compassion and humility,

Trisha Raha

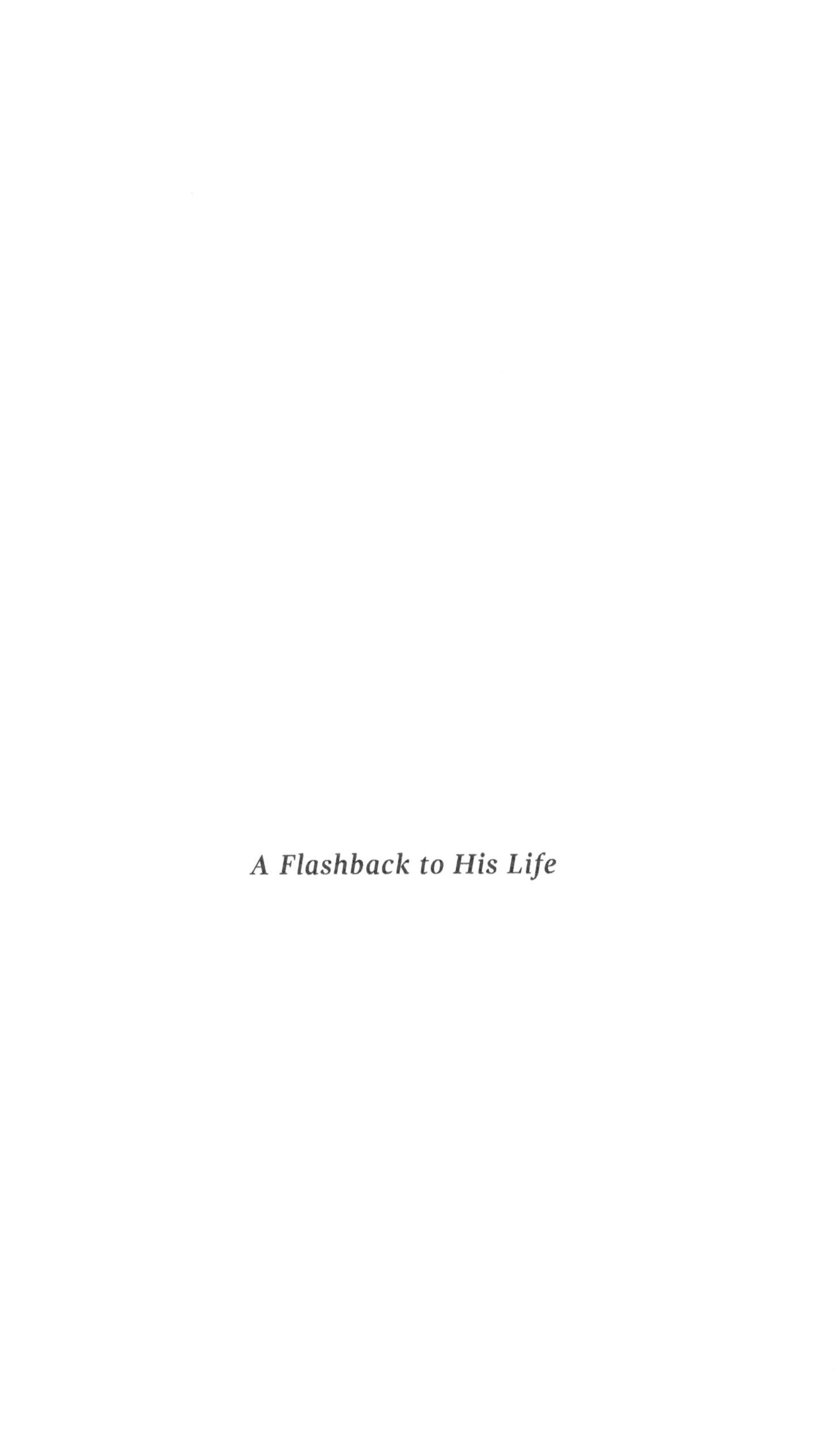

A Flashback to His Life

CHAPTER ONE

Dear Heart,
This soul of mine is trapped inside my temporary body,
It has lost someone.
Someone? Who?
Someone,
whom we cherished and loved till fate did us apart...
Why?
Because we begged 'Could you still love me?'
Until she left me,
Left?
But she loved you, right?
In this world where white was hers and black was mine,
Was it too hard to find this love and define it?
The fire was her and the ashes were me,
I sunk,
I sunk in her absence,
cause all she left in her memories is my beating heart.
No fate, no efforts and nothing in the world did us fair,
The true man in me prayed for her best,
Unaware of the animal who left you at the doors of death!

Ishan dusted over a cardboard box full of crinkled, dusty papers with an antique invitation envelope, one of the papers he held read 'Fate'. He wanted to clutch the journal, but his mind interrupted, "The pages smell of her." Even though he could not comprehend a word in the papers, he read the small letter in English below 'Fate', which was kept safe for him in the box, and he kept flipping the pages with weeping eyes. Hours passed while he stood outside crying in the rain as her memories filled his head and her scent made him weaker. He felt guilty and his heart wrenched at the prospect of her being gone.

With this, Alia lets out a deep sigh.

"Alia, what happened then?" Vani inquires.

"I believe it was her, but I'm not sure, Vani. That was the last time, I saw him."

A booming voice echoes into the room. "You know! What became of him?"

Everybody turns around in disbelief to notice the person behind the voice, and there we go...everyone screams with a friendly approach, "Oh Ayush! It's freakin Ayush! Ayush?" Strangely the room has a reassuring atmosphere now. Ayush grabs a chair noticing Vani's silent gaze. He sits beside Vani, as she orders a filtered coffee for him.

"I'm sorry, guys I wasn't there that day," Ayush confesses as the coffee arrives.

"I had a minor accident on the way to her funeral, but I still wanted to be there for him. I attempted to contact him, but he answered very late."

"Where is she, then?" Alia queries.

"I'm sorry Alia," Ayush replies softly, "she's no more.'" He hands Alia a black cardboard box full of a few invitation cards and a journal. The box moves to everyone on the table. As the conversation goes on, the three of them decide to walk away from the café and spend their time in the old college classroom, away from the chaos. Vidur, another friend, soon joins the three at their old college classroom as they continue to converse there.

"I know what you are all interested in now, but I assure you that it will not be that simple. However, we must discuss them; it's not only a privacy issue; there is more about him that we are unaware of..." Vidur had spread a silence and everyone felt the seriousness in his voice.

He fumbles, "I...I wish the two of you had met...them...them. Moving on is not impossible, but it makes a big difference to forget and go on when you lose someone you love deeply." Vidur adds on.

"But from someone's death? Are you serious? How broken Ishan must have been, he's not here yet and none of you care about it?" Vani blurts out.

"I understand." Vidur continues as Vani calms down. "The grief of someone leaving you lingers in your head until you let go of it. The reason becomes the biggest killer in this, though; even a small thought of it can consume you for the rest of your life." Everyone becomes more curious and looks toward Vidur as he keeps speaking.

"I've known Ishan since the little boy in him set his goals for life, lost those around him, and chose spiritual enlightenment as a path to learn about life. He has never looked back since then. I can recall when his parents abandoned him during the summers of 10th grade, and he was living with his old grandmother and Giriju Uncle (her caregiver) in their flat near Government Press Road in Guwahati. Although he was born and raised in Guwahati, his family was originally from Delhi. His Grandmother and Giriju Uncle played chess with little Ishan, taught him about the world, and recited poems and stories from ancient India. Giriju's Uncle loved to teach him cooking on the weekends, they raised the boy very well, no doubt. As he grew up, he took some responsibilities to balance the household and learned a lot of new things about life. He used to tutor some of his juniors for free, their family was barely getting by, and Ishan focused a lot on his grandmother's health. It continued to deteriorate until she left the world one day. The small child broke his heart, his only parent, the storyteller he loved, one of the first love embraces he received, everything vanished one day, he loved her so much, and his shattered heart just learned to shut down as every eye in society was pitying him. His grandmother's funeral was more than a shock to him, and by this time his parents had arrived to handle the funeral. As they decided to stay with Ishan, he had completely isolated himself, going days and months without speaking to anyone much; we (I and Ayush) kept visiting him, asking if he wanted to play, but he never listened. After he went through all of this, he questioned me once:

"Why is it so hard to love people? Why do they keep leaving, keep changing their minds, it is easy, right?"

I bet I could not answer him but that day, we both grew up a little, with this thought that a lot of things in the world are temporary, including the types of relationships. I knew he only needed time, and after a few months of trying hard to convince him, he was ready to hang out with me. I still believe that he holds some negative feelings about his parents because of this. When we started going to college, Ishan was never afraid of facing life or taking risks and had a limited zone of his own. He always cared about the world he was living in, irrespective of his strong intellectuality, and his great physique, this dude never listened to anyone and never stopped in life after then, whereas generally, humans do. I would have given up if I were him. Our guy ended up losing most of his friends ever since he got into college. Yet apart from everyone Ishan knew in his college, there was this girl called Arushi.. (not the only girl he knew — Definitely, dudes today who just know one girl and marry that girl are emerald ores—THEY RARELY EXIST, sorry!). Arushi was an oddball to him. Arushi had recently shifted to Guwahati; she and Ishan shared the same communications course. They were so focused on their classes that they only spoke during group discussions, where they challenged each other's intellect and it was fun to watch them debate over opinions. Ishan and Arushi took a few communications assessments together to negotiate the differences between them, and indeed they had other friends who knew these competing bugs, including me, Alia, and Ayush. While they were both equally invested in the classes, there's nothing unusual about a teenage boy fuelling his ego to win, it did appear immature but he never cared. Apart from all of this, Ishan always respected Arushi, so there was a mutual understanding between these competitors but Arushi never cared about competing seriously, all she cared about was studying. Her marks and skills were simply a stacked mound waiting for abroad universities to accept her!

Arushi was indeed a beautiful soul with a dedication towards her future career, she was always picturing big things and was never afraid of challenges in life. So, this may have begun with their late nights in the library, as they were exploring a project based on the Sixth Schedule of the Constitution, it was an interesting one! What was more interesting was that I used to find their heads bowed over heavy textbooks on the same table, the gentle hum of their common coursework drawing them closer through little debates, close clashes, and touches of sarcasm. Arushi had always been the serious one, taking detailed notes and maintaining an unflinching focus. Ishan, on the other hand, added lightness to their study sessions, making jokes to relieve the stress of never-ending deadlines. They effortlessly balanced each other and connected so well, creating a subtle beat in the pauses between words. One evening, while sitting in a quiet area of the college café, their conversation shifted from coursework to teenage fantasies. Arushi asked Ishan, as she rested her chin against her hand on the table,

"What would you do if you weren't stuck here studying?"

"Travel," Ishan replied. Arushi frowned and looked at him with a weird expression as if she wanted to know more,

"I just want to see the world, explore cultures, learn how different people live, and enjoy different cuisines. I want to know what keeps them going. Of course, I can take you with me. Someone needs to make sure I don't get lost, " he added with a smile.

Her chuckle was gentle to this, and her gaze lingered on him for longer than usual. Some feelings moved inside her, unguarded. She moved closer to him, her palm brushed across his while reaching for a notepad, and neither of them moved away. The stillness stretched, and their gazes locked. The line between friendship and something more blurred, leaving them both breathless, uncertain, and unmistakably pulled to one another.

"What's on your mind Aru?" Ishan whispered, his tone firm and welcoming.

"That you're too smart to be existing...handsome...but. sharp..." Ishan stopped her right there with a strange expression and blushed as he stared away from her eyes.

"What?" Arushi asked in shock.

"Nothing looks like my first time..." Ishan fumbled,

"Hearing so high about yourself or spending time with me like this?" Arushi giggled softly as her dark brown eyes sparkled and Ishan cherished noticing her appearance for a few seconds.

"No, someone complimenting me and the bonus is someone observing me, it's the first time!" They both blushed but Ishan sensed there was still something wrong.

The next day when they met, it wasn't at the library or over coffee but at her house. Arushi had contacted him late at night, and her voice sounded hesitant as she advised him to sneak in from the balcony, causing Ishan to feel nervous. He sneaked into her house and climbed up the balcony with the help of garden stairs, as Arushi was waiting for him in her room,

"I just needed to talk," she expressed softly. Without asking why, he grabbed a chair and pulled her close to him. Ishan felt that he might lose her before anything started, he was insecure and scared. On the other side, she appeared exhausted, her sparkling eyes were shadowed with a darker tone, and he felt a little stress hiding behind the shade. Ishan didn't ask much, as she handed him a steaming cup of chai and sat across from him.

"What is wrong, tell me?" He tried to converse with her like a friend.
She sighed, her eyes locked on the swirling tea in her hands.

"Do you ever feel like you're participating in a race you never signed up for? Like studying, working, and getting married to live, in between all these, you must grow, learn, and balance because your boss or family might expect it and your lover will, too. Why are we in this race?" she enquired, her tone tinted with discomfort.

"I feel that every day," he expressed with a tiny chuckle, but his expression softened when he noticed her lips twitch in a faint smile.

"But, hey, I am quite excellent at cheering from the sidelines, especially if it's you, let me be your loudest cheerleader. And see, everyone does it, you don't have to run it alone, you understand, right?" Ishan assured.

Arushi's expression was still the same and for a moment, the silence between them spoke louder than their words. As they sipped the chai simultaneously, the vibe was not uncomfortable, rather it was quiet like the soundness before a storm. The conversation continued as they both zoomed in on their perspectives of life and thought over from their childish-selfish sides. Ishan found it normal to be himself and to fall for her, but it bothered Arushi. Eventually, she concluded that Ishan may not see what growth is, what an independent woman's future is like, and how it is important for oneself to navigate everything in life – as much as one can, while Ishan appeared limited to her. As she cries her heart out, they figure out that these differences can cause them to struggle or take risks in the future. There was no kind of confession between them but Arushi and Ishan's blurred friendship led to this confusion and complexity, stopping Ishan from trying hard to get her and she rejected him even before he could prove himself to her. It was maturely weird but she had seen the world more toxically, she started to rely on herself instead of what Ishan concluded for them, in his mind. She finally replied, looking up at him,
"You always know what to say." Her voice was calm but confident.

"Not always," he confessed with a rebellious tone.

"But I know when you need someone to listen, and I also know that women are more likely to seek a solution first, but they don't always need one, right?

You would not have shared this with me if you wanted a solution. I know you want me to be there, but I'm still not a mind-reader, so if you want to talk about it further, I'm here for you." Ishan paused and added with a calm expression.

Their eyes met briefly, Arushi nodded with a no as she was leaving and in that moment of their unsaid connection, there was trust, understanding, and a type of intimacy that didn't need to break any lines because Ishan feared she wouldn't like him back anymore. That day she left as she realized Ishan knew her well, and likewise as time passed, she dodged spending time with him. As the classes came to an end in a month. Arushi decided to move abroad where in the meantime Ishan had grown feelings for her. His little self could not get on his knees and say to her "I like you" as that might bother her before she leaves. Ishan and Arushi spent very little time together but as the course end came closer, he started making more excuses to sit and study with her, although he could never muster up the courage to ask her out on a date.

He stood on the edge of expression, his thoughts like waves of feelings crashing against the shore of time and leaving, the same waves might never return. He wrote a letter, a frail vessel carrying his reality, his feelings, which grew heavier with each fleeting moment. Should he hand it to her? Will she take out the time to read it, and feel it, amid the hurry of the journey? Or Will it be lost in the shuffle of life's demands? Am I worthy enough for her? As the time arrived, they had to part ways, Ishan took a long breath, the words in his heart drowning in the silence of opportunity slipping by. He saw her board the bus, and his mind captured her silhouette dress against the horizon, he felt the weight of his inaction in a parallel mind, and finally, he questioned himself, "Who am I then? Why am I living, living for some mere ages, someone to love me back that is so calculative and why would I be dying? What is even death? How can I give my love to someone when I don't know what the purpose of my/ their life is? Why am I bound to certain rules and why am

I built with a skin, so perfectly, how?" Life it was, he reflected. Perhaps some truths are designed to be carried rather than stated, as a reminder that love, in its purest form, is frequently found in an enduring manner. He realized that separation after falling in love is like a paradoxical language, serving both the wound and the teacher. It is a process that requires both to carry two truths at once: the strong desire to remain connected through reality and the importance of letting go.

So Ishan decided to give it a chance for the final time, he knew where she was headed, so he mailed the handwritten letter to Arushi, expressing his one-sided feelings towards her. With this. Vidur's eyes scanned the room cautiously as he leaned in and lowered his voice to a conspiratorial whisper.

"Listen," he said in a serious tone, "this isn't just idle talk that we're going to talk about. This gossip is...super-important."

Alia smirked and everyone looked at Vidur with a weird expression, he hesitated, making the quiet tense. "Alia and Vani have known Nysa since school. Ayush and I are here to support Ishan, not to spread this gossip. It's a mission, every phrase, every detail. Consider this to be classified intelligence. One bad move, one misstep, and everything might unravel."

"Why are you calling it gossip? Idiot! We are here to help them..." Vani interrupted with a straight tone.

"Makes sense...it's strategic planning...haha," Vidur replies.
Ayush's fingers subconsciously pounded a rhythmic code on the table, reflecting the urgency of their speech. Every word that was muttered seemed to bear the weight of a secret that might alter everything, and the room seemed to shrink around them. Vidur takes out his phone and after surfing through something, he reads out the letter that Ishan had sent to Arushi.

<u>ISHAN'S E-MAIL LETTER:</u>
<u>Subject: Dear Arushi!</u>

Hey Aru,
First of all, I have a minor confession to make – I did not choose to like you, my heart did!

Keeping this in mind, I'd like to share something with you, so please stick with me until the end: I used to believe that love was something unreal, something that only gives us teenage adrenaline and might make you regret it later on, but when I met you – I know, I was childish, but you left an imprint on my heart that may never fade. You are my first romantic interest, Aru. Being a man, I know what it means but for now, whatever words I can think of are - *I feel so special with you!* It hurts me to let you go. I would be a fool not to tell you that I liked you and I fell in love with you. All I need from you is to be with me. But perhaps fate has written something much greater for you than I could ever give you. I cannot stop liking you; it's like breathing for me now! I breathe and think about you!
I know I am hopeless, but if I can, I'd like to spend my future with you. Perhaps I'll miss our old days in class, our reckless laughs and happy tears, always. I know it's difficult, unbearable, or even stressful for you because we had our disagreements and differences till the end, but remember, it's only today or tomorrow, and there's always hope. I simply want to be by your side through whatever it takes. With this, I promise to work hard and never give up until I reach you. Hold on until I win you over and over again! This may be a bit cliché, but my feelings are overwhelming with care and love for you. The rest I can tell you in person, hehe, but remember that you are worth every mile!

Love,
Ishan

As the departure day arrived, Ishan was expecting to meet and ask her about the mail, but Arushi was busy packing her things up, and they missed the chance to catch up. His unsaid feelings, awkwardness, and that breath of relief that he felt with her remained in her inbox, which never found a reply. Ishan pretended as if something in the universe that had stopped him from reaching out to them or embarrassing his feelings in front of them explained a caution indeed! Parting from someone you love means confronting the illusion of permanence as love frequently weaves itself into the fabric of our identity, and separation seems like unraveling that thread, but Ishan had just started to fall for her, this wasn't a great time. He should have realized that this unraveling serves as a type of creativity, providing an opportunity to rediscover oneself outside of the confines of togetherness, but here Arushi was never a part of his so-imagined bond. He was making himself miserable with this web of feelings! As he witnessed her leave, his shattering heart diverted his mind by focusing on a familiar song that was being played on a tea stall radio, nearby – the old classic *Aaye ho meri Zindagi mein...*by Mr. Sanu! Indeed, crazy timing.

In love, separation is more than just a physical distance; it is an emotional journey towards acceptance. It will advocate letting go of your expectations, unlearning the impulse to possess, and accepting the bittersweet reality that the beauty of love is frequently found in its vulnerability or its one-sided nature. To let her go was not to ignore or devalue what they shared, but it was to honor his feelings with kindness, allowing them to transform rather than remain stagnant. The art of separation holds a lot of patience, endurance, and the fortitude to sit with nothingness. It demonstrates that love can evolve, taking on new forms in recollection, gratitude, and, in some cases, silence. All Ishan did was surrender to love's potential to live beyond borders, and he was still in his teens, clinging on to his feelings for longer than enough made him way mature, though. Her memories protected him from the changing world and the part of societal negativity that had corrupted the literal meaning of love. This was unusual!

Even I assumed Ishan was going through the same embarrassing lost-his-girl moment, and we were having fun spotting him like that: vulnerable! All the dudes used to tease him as he passed through the streets of the college like a sadist, and we were friendly to him after Arushi left. He used to read a lot of books, so Ayush and I used to knock on his door every evening and drag him out to play football with us until Ayush joined a restaurant-based business, not sure much about that, though... and our routines were doomed. I used to contact Ishan for night walks, but weeks passed by, and I began to believe that he had forgotten about her until we all received Arushi's invitation letter.

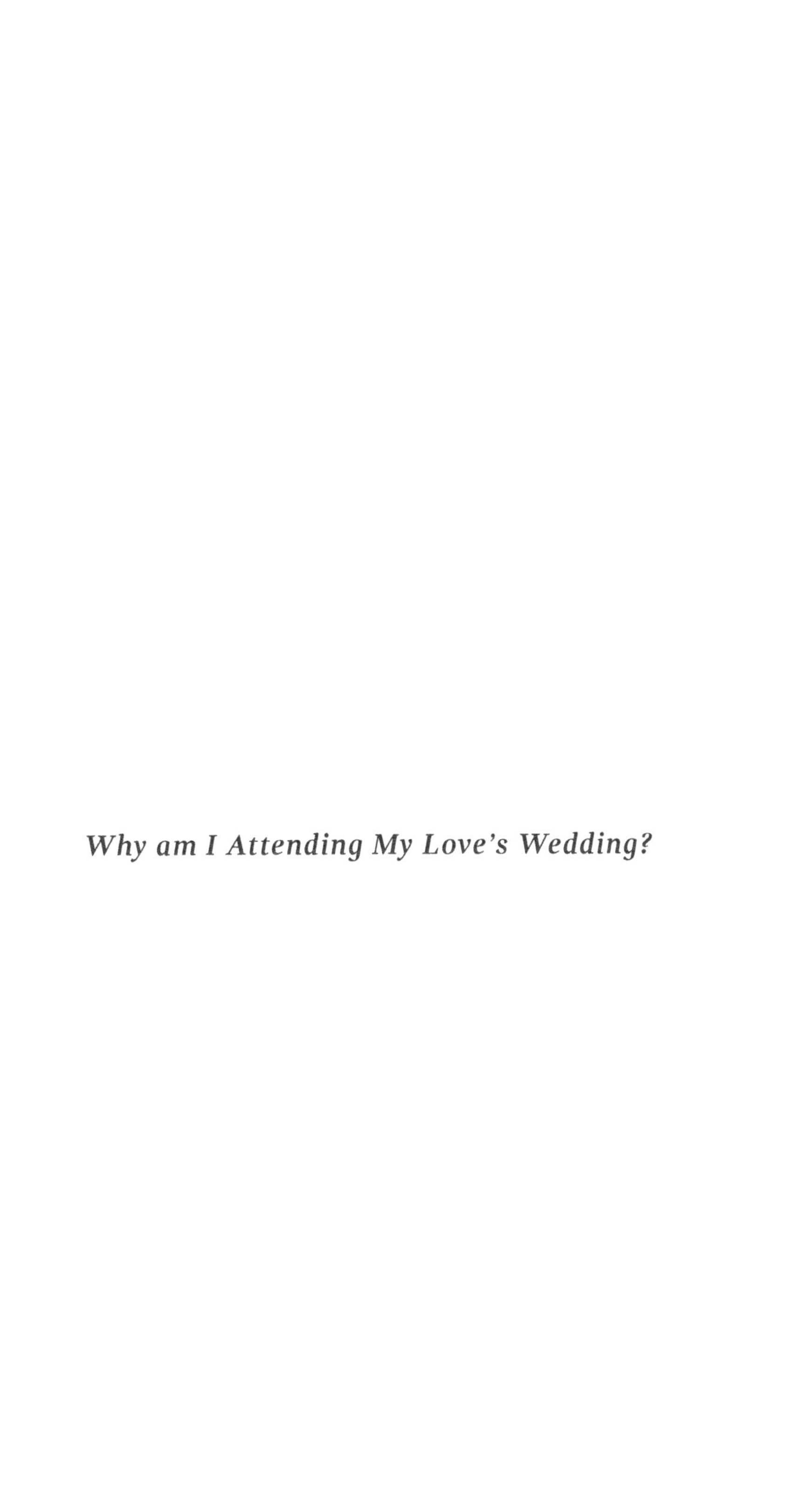

Why am I Attending My Love's Wedding?

CHAPTER TWO

Dear Heart,
I heard this somewhere,
Nizami Ganjavi painted me as a tragic lover,
A lover who is constrained by conservative societal traditions,
Imtiaz Ali's film came out, and everyone started searching for me,
Am I called MAJNUN ? Am I called SHISHUPALA? OR Am I called
FRANCIS?
The next moment I found myself wondering, who am I?
A person who knows the madness that is close to love, feels it,
wishes to practice it but is fated with uncertain boundaries,
boundaries of yearning, insecurities, loss, pain, and heartbreaks.
They could be right, they could be wrong, yet they love someone
they must have read love, understood it, felt it or thought deeply about
it.
But when they love a person, they do not expect but give,
give their heart, their feelings, their true self and soul which is above
humane to do..
..Even if you do not declare or realise, they are the best of all lovers,
what they speak does not exist, what they feel is unreal
but just them finding their love is reflected, suffices them forever makes
them a Majnun.
Sadly, today, Majnun will not wander for you in the jungles, hills, cities
or the highlands,
They will not cross borders for you, but they remember they might be
waiting for you...
until death do you's part

As time ticked, Ishan started to believe that he was unlucky because he was alone and Arushi might have felt something about Ishan, however, she chose to be a realistic person and let go of such vain feelings as a bright future was awaiting her. She chooses her future over him indeed! Time went on and a lot of differences occurred in both of their lives. Ishan had changed but he was a better human being now, finding answers about and from life, growing up as a kind human, he was living his delusion with the confidence of asking Arushi out, and once it was time for her graduation, he kept scrolling her Facebook timeline and Instagram memories with his anonymous ID.. until one day, a post mail arrived where he learned of Arushi's marriage abroad. Damn! The only thing that could have moved his smooth monochromatic focus from life was this freaking news! Ishan had waited four years to win her, but everything fell apart for him in a matter of seconds, all with a single post mail. How did she even learn about his address? Weirdly interesting! The invitation was for two months post that time, I guess it was July 2013 when we received that post. He kept trying to contact Arushi, but all he had was her wedding invitation and an unreachable phone number. Ishan decided to attend her wedding and we kept stopping him, but he felt some intuition. I and our other friends were not going to attend as we couldn't afford it but his case differed.

Even though he had no money and no income source because he had just graduated from college, all he had was determination, he began looking for jobs, but time was running out, after days and nights of failures for 2,3 weeks, Ishan's mother realized the depth of the situation, she always had a feeling to make it up to Ishan as they had left him home alone before and it was somewhere a hurtful gap in their relationship which she could make-up now. His mom was aware of the issue throughout, so she communicated with him about it. Ishan was already discouraged from failures and he communicated his feelings. His mother felt horrible about it and decided to help him apply for a visa to Istanbul, Turkey. I remember how he and his dad were sitting on the roof and they were discussing his visit to Arushi's wedding. Lucky guy! Ishan told me, his dad is a computer engineer and he never wants him to leave his life decisions into regrets. It's because he says none can fix real-world issues by learning code fixing, none can fix relationships by learning theories and none can fix reality with dreams. But what one can escape is regret and absorb is hope, hope to run themselves ahead and give it a try. His parents were convinced to back him up as he wanted to go this far for his love, the last time. After some more advisory pointers and regular nagging, they encouraged Ishan to fly to Turkey. Arushi was planning to marry her spouse Zeeshan. Ishan kept feeling nervous and googled about Zeeshan, texting Arushi as much as he could and finally, he arrived at the address mentioned on the card. A load of web pages and Facebook links popped on the Google screen as he got to know that Zeeshan comes from a highly progressive family where his dad owned a great business of dry-fruits supplies. He and his dad worked over the years, ever since Zeeshan turned 19, he joined this business named *Al-Tamr* which grew into a global sensation. He was not sure if she would turn up but a gentle voice, as melting as ice, addressed him from behind.

'Ishan? Ishan...Welcome..!'

The sweetest voice on the planet, as the intensity of the voice dug a hole in his heart, he heard footsteps heading towards him from the back. The footsteps were not alone, as the jingling anklets added melody to them, and Ishan knew it was her. As she approached, he came to a pause and turned to see her: her face, the scent of sandalwood, those brown sparkling eyes twinning with brown lipstick, the everlasting dark-green bindi, the extra large earrings, and the same solemn smile.

IT WAS HER! Arushi...

But Ishan's eyes were filled with disbelief as he realized something appeared very different in Arushi, and he looked towards her anklets. She nods with a smile and directs her eyes towards a broken phone. Ishan realizes how his every message or calls were missed and this was none's fault. He walks closer to her, he takes time to look at her, as he forces himself to accept that the Arushi he loves was pregnant now. Ishan had never imagined in his wildest dreams that his decision to visit her would be so difficult for him. His heart felt a thud, his hands shivered with sweat dripping from his forehead, and every sound around him got inaudible.

He waited for her for four years, four hurting years with spinning hopes and there she was, a perfect beautiful woman with a new life in her womb which was hard to hate or ignore and yet she wore a smile with a little blush, standing in front of him, always smelling as comforting as ever. He realized, what he planned with her was just in his mind, nor she ever saw the mail, it was all just about him, she was never a part of any of this, she might or could have felt for him but her major decision had drifted him so far from her life that he was 'just a mere friend' to her. So, he decided to accept the fall knowing this would keep on hurting Ishan in and out for a long time. Soon, in the end, one of the fine post evenings when everyone knew it was time to leave, Ishan was way more heartbroken and Arushi could see that. Ishan stood outside the grand hall, his heart a storm of emotions. Inside, the soft hum of prayers and the recitation of vows filled the air, a reminder that Arushi was moments away from committing herself to be someone else's forever. His feet halted, away from the spectacle and holding on to the love that was still burning within him. As the Nikah preparations were going on, after a couple of hours, he turned to leave but the voice of an old Maulavi boomed from the speakers outside the hall, he became curious, the old man was addressing the gathering about "Life," the Maulavi said, his tone steady and profound, "Life is defined by what you give rather than what is taken from you."

Allah tests our patience, ability to surrender, and willingness to trust what is meant for you will be with you.

Ishan hesitated, his steps slowing. The Maulvi went on to say, "My friends, suffering is not the end.

It opens the door to a deeper awareness of our humanity. It teaches us to seek strength in faith, to discover meaning beyond our suffering, and to walk with humility."

A little boy from the gathering questioned the Maulvi, "Sir, where did this come from?"

Everyone laughed at him as the Maulvi closed his eyes and expressed, "When you go home, open the Qur'an and learn about what Surah Al-Baqarah, 2:155 says, you will find the very answer there." As the Maulvi continued his speech, Ishan felt a strong connection with the words. He realized that, while his anguish was severe, it was not insurmountable. Love was not intended to shatter him, but rather to shape him into someone stronger, wiser, and more compassionate. He noticed another person in the crowd holding a Qu'ran with English translations, so he switched seats beside him and borrowed the Qu'ran to confirm what Maulvi had just said. He asked the individual to assist him as he found the Surah Al-Baqarah, 2:155, which simply meant, *Allah will surely test you with something of fear and hunger and a loss of wealth and lives and fruits, but give good tidings to the patient.*

The text strengthens the idea that challenges, including heartache and loss, are part of life's path. It encourages one's patience and trust in divine wisdom, it serves as a reminder to all that facing adversity with faithfulness and kindness results in inner growth and increased strength. Ishan gathered himself and chose not to leave. Instead, he chose to stay—not to battle for her, but to accept the situation gracefully. He observed her from a distance, his heart sorrowful yet filled with quiet determination. Maulavi's words stuck with him, a gentle reminder that every ending is also a beginning. The following evening, when Arushi was making chai, she called Ishan into her room, she thought he might be leaving soon and Ishan arrived. He pulled a chair and sat next to her, Arushi smiled and initiated, 'I have never wanted you to be this way, I am not happy but you can be happier, live in Ishan!.'

This perplexed Ishan, and before he can say anything, he looks at her with a blush-red face, gulping his tears down his throat, as if someone had struck a chain of nails on his throat, but his love needed all of his emotional strength to empower her. Before he could reply to anything, Arushi slowly lifted her dupatta that was covering her backless kurta.

The dim lighting in the room followed by the crimson shade of sun rays touching the beige walls of the room, highlighted a few shadows on Arushi's back, displaying the sharp contrast between her radiant skin and the untreated, purplish bruises, long scratches, two stitches taped perfectly down near her waist, all concealed beneath a thin layer of foundation. Ishan's breath caught up as he saw what she had fought so hard to hide. Each scar revealed a quiet story of suffering, betrayal, and perseverance from a past he could only begin to comprehend. He moved closer to her, his firm hands quivered as he stretched out. His chilly fingertips softly brushed against the marks on her back with a passive touch lining on them, she flinched her back and hardened the skin before it could melt beneath his soft touch. She closed her eyes as he continued to touch her scars on the warm skin with his icy fingertips just to accept that it was real, and tears streamed down her quiet cheeks. Ishan's heart was crushed under the weight of the wordless pain inscribed on her body. His frigid eyes glistened with unshed tears, his ego, his manhood, his heart, everything halted for seconds to realize as the shock gradually gave way to agonizing anguish.

"Wh..what is all this? Do you want me to believe..this? I am furious, furious..as..hell, why? Why are you still..?" he fumbled in a quivering murmur.

"Yeah, but in front of you, I am the most miserable person ever. I know..come to me, Arushi. Please." He sobbed like a kid who lost their loved ones. His arms opened slowly, fearful of shattering her further. Arushi hesitated, tears welling in her eyes as she turned to face him. Her defence gave way, and she moved into his embrace. His arms closed around her with a tenderness that held a blanket of safety; her warmest hug. After few seconds, Arushi slowly moves away from him, Ishan urges,

"Come with me, Arushi.."

Arushi interrupts with a teary smile "And what?.. What plans do you have, Ishan?"

Ishan replies with a soft sobby voice, "Let's first run away! I cannot stand for your choice but you can still choose me. Think again, please?"

"And let the world point at me right? Look at her, she chose her destruction and is now damaging his life, I have a baby with me, and the entire world will question her/him as a father. I am about to vow for him. It's best for everyone if I stay here and you keep away from all of this; I created this hell for myself. The world already looks at me in that way, and the comments from my family, in-laws, and strangers online drain my vitality. My in-laws want me to be an all-rounder, pressure me to spoon-feed them, my family wants me to keep performing better, and so on. I look at myself, and my baby and go through each day without any dreams. You're my only close friend Ishan. I know about everything, what we had was a past, you might have a dream now, correct? Why plunge with me!" Arushi sobs.

"Arushi..I am really sorry..sorry that I..I as a man, should have put all my efforts and sorry..that a man made you feel this way, treated you this way, made you feel that you cannot be loved! But, see we still have time, only if you understand. It is the best for both of you." He teared up, "How could this happen to you? ...Allah!" his voice breaking as if every syllable tortured him.

"When all you ever desired was love...when all you ever imagined was growing old with someone...when all you ever wished giving was pure love and care?" His lips quivered as his jaw tightened, attempting to contain the wrath that was rising within him. But his rage was turning into pity as he noticed the fragility in her stance, the way her shoulders stooped as if bearing the weight of a thousand storms.

With this, Ishan feels deeply guilty, cries and passionately holds her hand. Arushi remains persistent with her rejection as she points towards her belly, and Ishan understands. Even Arushi feels as if something entangles her neck with sharp nails from inside.While deep down they both knew the reality, Ishan draws Arushi closer to him as he gulps his emotions, unzips her kurta's back chain as she is still in tears. Ishan waits for her consent and she nods expressing acceptance, Ishan softly touches her scars again with his cold fingers and hugs her from back placing his chin on her shoulder as he consoles her, "You deserve love not scars, I love you, Arushi, please, don't leave it here."

She cries as she grabs one of his arm folds that rested down her shoulder, her grip tightened on the creamy yellow kurta he wore, which continues to wrinkle with her grip. The sun rays begin to fade from the wall, and the room dims, with a small radium lamp blazing in the opposite corner. His heart refuses to leave her. As she softly pushes him away and continues to sob, "Ishan, why is it that a girl has to take off her clothes and cross her thin borders of respect to find love in this era? Why is it that a man exposes his weakest emotions to the woman he loves and loses her forever with those emotions of his? Tell me what scriptures teach us this? What the world has become, what true man accepts this? None, correct? Leave it, dude, I've been with Zeeshan for a few years, and sometimes I feel ashamed to look at the images he has of me, he just looks at me with lust and objectification. I did not realize all this until I was pregnant. If you look at the pictures I have of him, zero nudity, and everything is so pure, just us. Even if I had something like that and we had broken up, I had not kept any such images of him. For all the time I have been manipulated despite my best efforts and respect, he continues to question my love, torture me and break my trust to date, I'm tired of proving Ishan. He cares about how the world will look at me, who is having second thoughts and secondary emotions about me, but not what I feel for him or not what 'us' means. I feel like if I choose to do something wrong in this heat of the moment, he is one of the reasons apart from my control, I am tired..."

Ishan's heart was crying as a man who loves her but the boy within him who was looking at her with his incapable limits, questioned her, "How can you be with him? He isn't a good husband nor could be a father and you are risking your life now, just for the baby to grow up like him or see you both like this, do you really want this? Arushi, please?"

"Are you..?" Arushi responded in anguish.

She looks away with tears in her eyes expressing,

"Ishan, I understand that I could be happier with you or if not love, least you will respect me forever, I know, but you have to accept that we both are unstable now, you are in no position to take care of me or my child, I could have left if only I could have had the privilege to rely on anything, me or you. I'm sorry. Ishan. I can't.."

Arushi takes Ishan by the hand while sobbing in anguish. He stands still, locking his fingers tightly with hers and suffering the moment with her, as his tears were making her sadder. Arushi gets closer to Ishan and runs her hand on his face to wipe the tear droplets sliding down his cheek. She looks at him while both of them are feeling a slight form of affection, but neither of them can leave their helpless circumstances. She tries to control her sadness and expresses,

"Don't forget to see my little world..."

"Always, in your pains and in your gains. I'll come!" Ishan replies with a little artificial smile, Ishan was feeling angry, inept, and compelled to see his first love in a situation in which a man should never see his lady, but her permission was his only key.

He understood her side of situation and knew that any rush could be harmful to her baby. In a matter of seconds, a loud voice calling Arushi becomes audible, and Ishan helps her zip the back. He opens the window door and jumps out of the window. He shut the door slowly as he stood behind the window to eavesdrop. The room was still dark, looking back at her was hard. Arushi hid her tears behind a sad smile. Zeeshan steps into the room from the other side and switches on the light with an angry expression. He shuts the door with a big thud without realizing Ishan was around. Zeeshan slams the wall, next to the door and asks something to Arushi. Arushi remains still, and Zeeshan smacks her head hard on the wall. Ishan stands right behind the room, fixed with shock, unable to move, he starts shivering as her words cross his mind, he feels it over his ego and yet keeps yearning for her. Ishan stumbles and slowly walks out from the corridor as Arushi and Zeeshan leave the room. He enters an event hall where he finds Arushi's cousin brother Anish with Zeeshan's brother Ali, the music and laughter cover the hall, Ishan's mind and ears are still traumatized, he tries to snap himself back to senses as he approaches Anish and Ali's seat.

Ishan smirked playfully and asked, "So, Anish, how hard did you all try to get your sister married? I bet you have some amusing serving stories."

"Brother, she fought everything, even herself. You know, I didn't have the spine to properly support her. Ishan, I feel horrible. None of us truly fought for her. I was simply watching. And now, just seeing her bright smile makes me stronger." Anish responded in a somber tone.

Ishan's smile fades as Anish's words settle in. He looks to the stage and notices that Arushi arrives with Zeeshan, her beauty radiating across the room.

"She's bearing a lot, isn't she? I guess my prayers weren't enough to save you, sorry Aru.." Ishan whispers to himself.

Anish turned to Ishan with a mix of hurt and curiosity, "By the way, why do you care now? After all this time? You know, she missed you. You were her only close friend back then, but you never cared to ask about her or reach her here."

"I know, I feel like a coward, Anish." Ishan's voice trembled as he looked down at his cold-sweaty hands.

"I was not there for her. I did not fight for her. I don't feel like I'm cut out for standing. But seeing her from this far away makes me feel guilty. I feel like I've turned my back on my karma."

Ali jumped into the conversation by placing a hand on Ishan's shoulder; his tone was steady yet empathic. "Perhaps you were both cowards in your own ways. But what matters is whether we can improve now. Ishan, she's strong. But even the strong deserve friends who will support them."

Ishan nods, his gaze fixed on Arushi, guilt and resolve blending in his features, thinking, "Maybe it's time I stop watching her from the shadows and leave her memories as it is!"

In a few hours, Ishan leaves the place without letting Arushi know as he is scared to confront her wounds again. Arushi looks out for him until Zeeshan's family takes her home. That's when Ishan feels so less of a man, to not be able to protect the person he loved and yearned for years. Today, his love was in the hands of a monster which he always kept himself away from. While returning home, Ishan was listening to the radio when a random journalist mentioned that he heard about one of the Rigveda's eternal wisdom phrases "*Sam gacchadhvam sam vadadhvam sam vo manamsi janatam*," which encourages one to *walk together, converse together, and combine our thoughts in understanding.*" This insightful phrase was now stuck in his mind, for a while emphasising on the importance of what togetherness is? What is mutual support as the building blocks of a harmonious life? He was just missing a lot about facing life, in front of his cowardness and holding onto unreal expectations. While Arushi quietly fought her battles alone, her choice appeared like an exemplified timeless reality that required a communal strength, and a togetherness to solve. Ishan's inaction in times of such moral responsibility is just as serious as the wrong itself. He realized that acting courageously, even in the face of uncertainty, not only fulfills one's Dharma but also honors the sacred links that unite us all, which he failed as a human. We thought that the positive part about this was that, he's still learning.

However, after self-reflecting for a while, he realized that his perspective on love and relationships had been corrupted by his selfish aspirations rather than genuine connection. Instead of grabbing Arushi's hand and walking alongside her hardships, he hesitated, allowing his fear to guide his actions. Instead of sharing his heart and having honest conversations, he had remained silent, thinking she would not understand the things he had never spoken.

Instead of fully comprehending her grief and dreams, he had been preoccupied with his own. Nothing could have been wrong if only he confessed to her that he liked her or handed her that one letter which he kept locked for years. Well, now he thinks a part of Rigveda's knowledge can serve as a mirror to him, reflecting the contrast between what he aspired to and what he had done. He then vowed to his heart that he would learn to abandon his timidity, and expectations and embrace the spirit of strolling together, chatting together, and combining their ideas in mutual understanding. It was not too late, he realized, to start living by these everlasting words—to create the foundation of life not only with Arushi but also with himself, as a better, and braver man. Ishan felt lost, he was yet curious about self-discovery, the science of living beings, and the connection with spirituality. He recognized there's a thick difference between culture and religion. He was thinking about all the possibilities he could add on, as he reached his house lane and approached his house, he found an old man who appeared to be a middle-aged pandit, writing a quote on a shop's brick wall with a white paint, which said -

यतो धर्मस्ततो जयः

(Translates: Where there is (dharma) adherence to right action, there lies victory!)

When the pandit was done, he entered the shop. After standing for a moment and considering his situation, Ishan followed the pandit to the store but when he stepped inside the store, nobody was there. He then went back to the wall, where the quote was still there. He waited for a while glaring at the wall, trying to read the quote. As another pandit was passing by the wall. Ishan appeared confused to him, the pandit gently asked him if he was okay. Ishan observed him for a few seconds as he was dressed peculiarly with a bald head and a string of white thread crossed his bare upper body, tied at a waist end. Ishan greeted the Pandit ji by folding his both hands and questioned, "Pandit ji, why is this written in Sanskrit? We usually don't normalize Sanskrit a lot right?"

The pandit turned towards the wall as he read the quote and replied, "Prabhu, it is just not a language but also plays a part towards your dharma, your generation may not value it cause a lot of you youngsters are falling deeply into *maya-chakravyuh* and don't even know or feel about your dharma, that's why none might expects from you to learn but remember Sanskrit, everything is a *milawat*. Sanskrit is still the ancient heartbeat of Indian culture, carrying wisdom and spiritual energy for thousands of years. It holds a deep connection to our roots, used in mantras and scriptures that continue to inspire and guide the preachers till date."

Ishan felt a heaviness of shame, a challenge in heart and a hint of curiosity since he was losing his cultural and religious grip without even realising it; with time, many young people have forgotten how life and spirituality are intertwined irrespective of who you pray/submit to. Both of them runs separately and requires you dedication, discipline and time to understand. But why would a teenage or youngster need such devotion or spirituality? Isn't it too early or hard to maintain? Whatsoever, a lot more questions clouded his heart. He requested the pandit ji to share his wisdom and asked, "Pandit ji, but why do you call me Prabhu, I am not that great?"

The pandit smiled and replied, "I know who you are, you will know this very soon, but you look curious, so here's a trailer verse for you, you should understand this before anything.."

उपद्रष्टानुमन्ता च भर्ता भोक्ता महेश्वरः
परमात्मेति चाप्युक्तो देहेऽस्मिन्पुरुष: पर:

(Bhagavad Gita: Chapter 13.23, upadraṣhṭānumantā cha bhartā bhoktā maheśhvaraḥ paramātmeti chāpy ukto the 'smin puruṣhaḥ paraḥ)

As the pandit further explained, "Assume two birds are situated in the nest (that is your heart) of the tree (your body) of the living form. There are two souls: the individual soul (called jīvātmā) and the Supreme Soul (a.k.a Paramātmā). The jīvātmā has its back to the Paramātmā and is busy eating the fruits of the tree (effects of karmas received while staying in the body). When we see a delicious fruit, our mind feels a sense of joy, but when a bitter fruit is served, the mind reacts resistant to it. Similarly, the supreme soul is a friend of the individual soul, but he does not interfere, he's instead sitting and watching everything. If the individual soul can only turn around and face the supreme, all its miseries will end. And here the biggest note is, when I am speaking to you, I am denoting the 'Prabhu' call to this individual soul, respect one other, as I find god's greatness and acknowledge his divine existence in all forms. If you want to know more about this philosophy, learn to find it out yourself."

Ishan felt a breath of positivity was chiming around him, as bid their goodbyes, he strolled down the path near his house filled with curiosity, about every term the pandit ji uttered. Initially, he fell into deep thought about what could be so strong of a philosophy that billions of people across the world submit to it. He wondered about the ancient lifestyles and then decided to start exploring more by learning Sanskrit first. Indeed Ishan was distracted a little from what happened to Arushi but he was still processing a lot in his mind and this emptiness was the perfect time-match when he found himself with no guide, lost like birds in the storm and spending days without knowing the reason of his existence. Ultimately he grew to be more comfortable with spirituality and a lot of other college friends distanced themselves from him with the passing of time...

As Vidur paused to sip some coffee that Vani had ordered, Ayush interrupts with a sly expression .. "Guys, did you know Vidur and Ishan had a heated conversation when Ishan reached home after her wedding. It was just not Ishan listening to some preacher, how can you believe this? Cu'mmon.. I guess Ishan's reality check was a better direction. Everyone smiled stiffly as Vidur looked at Ayush

with side-eyes and Vani asked Ayush to talk more about it..
Ayush elaborates-

"So the day Ishan arrived home, we knew how devastated his situation was, even his mother could feel that he was sad and Vidur knew Ishan very well from his childhood. So he went to check on him. Ishan was sitting like an isolated statue under a yellow dim light. Vidur entered and tossed his bag onto the couch with a huff, his face clouded with a little frustration as his friend did not appear all alright. For a while, Vidur sat silently beside Ishan, staring at the wall in front of them, Vidur initiated, "You're back early."

"Yeah." Ishan muttered.

"So, What happened?" Vidur stretched.

Nothing.

Ishan and Vidur felt an uneasy vibe and yet communicated. That childhood friend who turns out to be an avenger when they stay with you- for you, realizing that you need them. Indeed, Vidur was..

"You're a terrible liar. Talk to me." Vidur initiated again.

"I said nothing! Why do you always have to dig? Just—leave me alone, Vidur.

Vidur rests his arm behind Ishan's shoulder to ease his outburst. "Not yet. Not happening. What's this really about? Is it... Arushi? Or wanna gym a bit?"

Ishan freezes to think.

"You're still thinking about her, aren't you?"

"Of course, I am! She's not happy." Ishan bursts in tears.

"And why does that matter so much to you? Afterall now?" Vidur interrupts.

Because I loved her!

(Silence gulps both of them)

Vidur absorbs the confession he does and asks, "Okay. So you love her? What are you doing about it? She's married, you crazy!"

"What am I supposed to do? She's dealing with everything, she's not supposed to, and I feel like, I'm just...sick to think about all this! I know." Ishan expresses.

"Why do you think you are "Sick"? Why did you feel you're not enough for her?" Vidur extends his questions.

Ishan expresses. "I didn't say that—I'm like.."

"Yes, you did. Why do you think she wouldn't want you around?" Vidur interrupts.

Ishan feels stuck and whispers. "Because I'm scared."

Vidur: "Of what?"

Ishan's voice cracks into raw vulnerability, "Of letting her go, not being good enough strong to fix anything. And of her gonna wake up one day, look back, and realize I'm just... a mistake."

Vidur lets the silence stretch. "Did you see what just happened? You figured out what this is really about. It's not her. It's you, man. Stop thinking you're not enough. That's your insecurity talking, not her."

Ishan exhales sharply, "Maybe you're right. I felt this coming, still, I travelled so far to satisfy my ego or whatever, then I couldn't afford the reality. I was uneasy to find the truth about her, insecure like a boy, and escaped from reality and even after all this happened, I feel like she chose Zeeshan but ...the truth is I left her. I don't know what do I do now?"

Vidur pats Ishan's back, "I'm always right. See, you should leave them be and focus on your life. And keep me around, you douche!"

"But what if something wrong happens to her? I'm just so scared and unstable.." Ishan sobbed.

They both realized that the truth could be way different than what they were thinking or looking at, Vidur shared a faint expression as the tension in the room softened..

As Alia and Vani look at Vidur with a floating bubble of respect, Ayush halts just there, and Vidur continues to express again...

I think it was a mis-connection between feelings but eventually, Ishan decided to move on cause there was nothing he could help or do. He appeared to be trying hard but nothing made any sense cause in the end Arushi had closed the gates of her heart for Ishan. Ishan tried living like a normal book geek, yet every time a dude used to text him or tried to talk to him about real-world issues he used to be distracted, look back, or pretend to be extra intellectual, and some days he used to roast them like real bad. We used to mock this but this guy was growing serious. Ishan used to be more of a conservative-rooted person but after this, he often used to drink and make music, all this was turning weird. When a person is accepting, calm, or soft – they are innocent / kind(yes), but it takes a lot to understand that a storm has already left them in ruins. The acceptance and calmness are the ruins that the storm had left in their heart.

I remember one such incident, It was with Raj, Raj was one of our college classmates who used to share a seat with Ishan in first-year batch days, had come to a reunion party at my house and he was talking to Ishan about his achievements as he worked at an FMCG-based company and Ishan was yet to get a job. Raj blurted with a cheers to Ishaan, "I have finally crashed into something golden, you guys don't even know about this job world. It's just that my work is really stressful but I get to party with girls in the evening, I love it, dude."

Ishan smiled awkwardly as the two were not conversing anymore, Raj was trying to weirdly influence them, "How are things going with your girl, dude?

"Yeah, fine. It's time for you to marry too, next stage of job-life, haha." Ishan stretched.

"I'm still young dude, I need to get a car, get some chicks rolling in other countries, and keep earning this spirit," by now Ishan was a listener and speaker zone now, Raj kept going, "I love girls with thick figures like the 4 large figures plus 6 large figures..damn that's so trendy. It matches my standards", Ishan felt more awkward yet asked, "What are six figures?"

"Earnings bro, they maintain themselves, they earn, take care of you and all that fantasy sh#it is great, damn. You don't have to pay for their nails and bikinis but they will still do all the show for you- just pretend you are dating them." Raj explained.

Now this was getting into a really bad vibe, Ishan no longer wanted to be there so he tried to excuse himself but Raj kept on following him and added to his words, after a certain time, when everyone was almost drunk and busy, making out at corners but this dude took it in a way serious of disrespect for women,

Ishan turned around and screamed at Raj, "Ae Bhe##c###, Idhar aa," Raj was shocked and a little drunk, as Raj approached Ishan who was holding a mixture of tequila and Whisky round up in a glass with 40% Pink Gin topped with green chilies - what junk! As Raj gulped it with his ego-walk. Ishan bombed a whole different show, "So, what were you saying, you cheap-fu##r, women with 4 figures? 6 figures? Have you ever seen any woman getting abused, facing her life, her periods? The f##k, if you do this then wait for what you get in return! Did your mother ever teach you all this? Such disrespect and how do you call yourself a man? Do you know what the definition of being a man is? You're way less than that. You dumb taint!"

Ishan gripped his collar as Raj passed out and punched him really badly at the end. We were fortunate to stop him there and then that night in between all of this mess, Ishan said a few lines that still strike me, *'Vidur, yeh daaru, hookup and temporary solutions wale ladke na kabhi hum sache-innocents ko nahi chorengey, sabki image kya hum sabko eksath kharab karengey aur jis kisine rok diya na, usko akela kardengey.' (Vidur. These guys who are alcoholic, practice hookups, and look for temporary bonds will spoil the innocent-truthful guys and our image will be at stake together, whoever stops them, will make sure he is alone in the end.)*

I realized he was indeed not drunk at all but now he was way too egoistic about his knowledge, and righteousness, yet trying to be a kinder person in society but his act of anger was indeed a wrong way that we couldn't even support. We cannot hurt and explain to everyone who smokes or drinks on the road, cause they know things are going to twist and come back for them- be it health or family wellness, they know there is that one worst day of life waiting for them to start changing. Ishan wanted to do all the change at once, forcefully. However, the part he was right about was to stand up against the normalization of disrespectful comments against women, whatever it was.

I realized how different Ishan had become then and how he felt every little thing about life more deeply. We were very casual and non-concerned about life until this incident turned everything up, we felt we had grown up responsible now- that's what a manly-ness may start with. Anyways, after all this drama we picked up Raj while he slept unconsciously and took off his formal clothes, leaving him in his polka-dotted pink-black pajamas, and dropped him outside his office gate, he was still passed out. When he woke up, his colleagues found his reality as we also pasted a paper on his chest with the text ' I have _ body count, don't marry me.' We had fun doing that but we spied on him so that he didn't lose his job. he did get suspended and with time I guess he got better indeed.

That's how Ishan was back then!

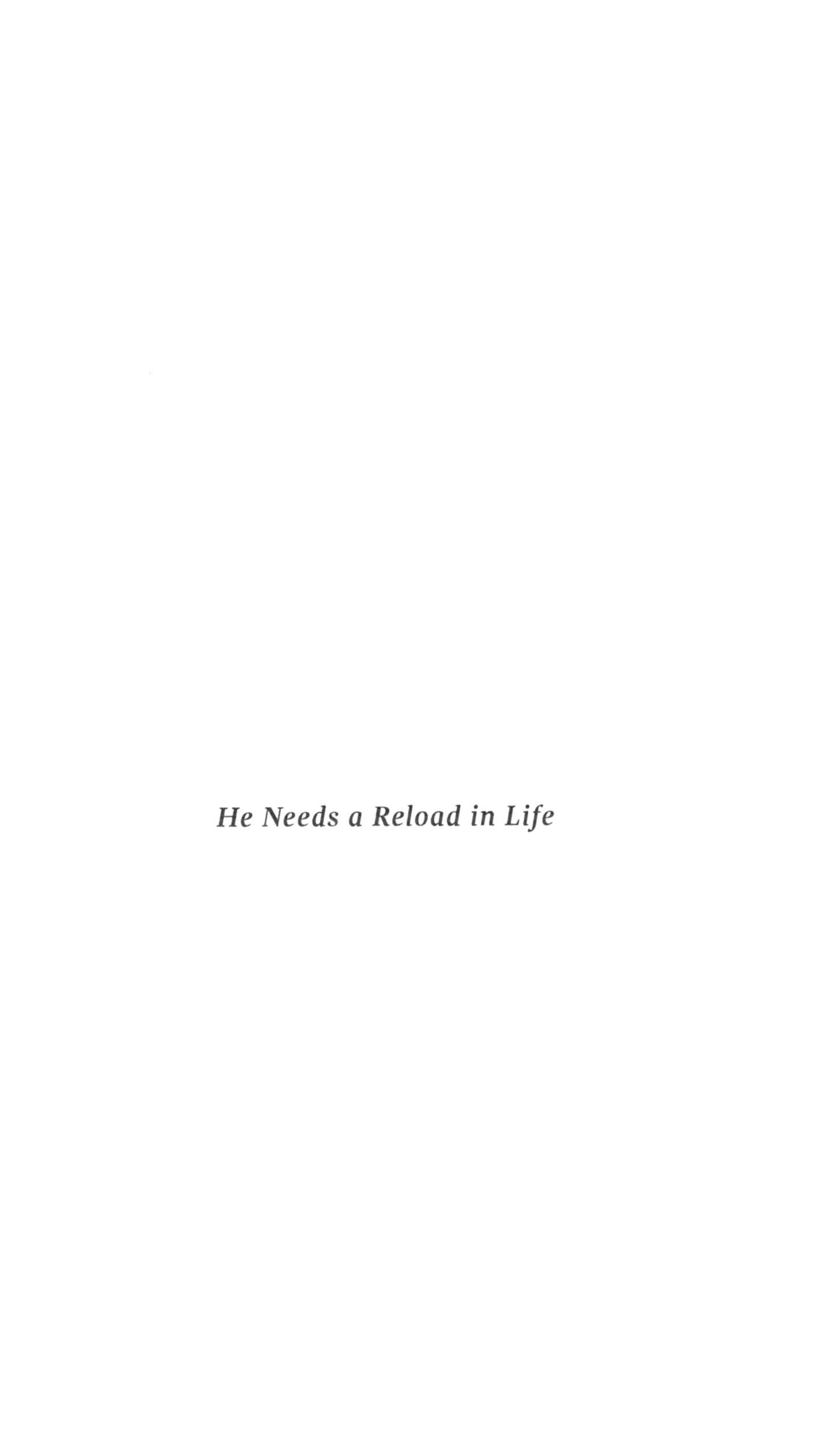

He Needs a Reload in Life

CHAPTER THREE

Dear Heart,

I'd do anything for you if even it means to

knit sweaters, write poems, make coffee,explore a new culture,

swim,surf,climb, travel across the world,

take you to the northern lights,seven seas,sunsets or plant saplings?

But I do not trust her,

I should not own her and I never want her to lead me again,

(Heart) Her Who?

My Ego...

Then why don't you learn to love it? Accept it?

Ego will leave me broken,

Broken from every bond I cherished, broken from my principles, my life's lead,

It will summon the lust, anxiety, anger, carelessness and selfishness,

All are sins that can drag an end to my delicate story with a full stop called 'Loneliness'.

Then what?

I will learn to live with grounds of detachment and pain.

I shall forget about Society!

Live with myself.

But you make the society too..

What appears sweet, could be bitter!

Days passed, and Ishan found himself in a weird situation in which his heart denied any romantic impulses. He grew to be less expressive, more rational, more caring, and investing in his intellect towards the right place, but his heart continuously reminded him that he was a coward. Ishan quietly closed himself off from the rest of civilization, asking himself, "Why am I me?" Why do others follow a defined pattern, whether it is intellectual, bad, or situational? What is my highest potential? He decided to continue being curious, and because he knew the pandit he saw earlier at the shop that day might have some answers, he kept looking for him until one day he found him in a local temple nearby. He begged the pandit to give him some advice on how to absorb the spiritual knowledge and life values to grow. It was not an easy thing to absorb the spiritual knowledge and reflect on it, Ishan was on such a path where he had to lead his mind and body through purity. He had studied physics, learned about biological processes, experimented with things using chemistry, and even learned scientific about utilizing theories yet he felt unsatisfied and lacked guidance. The Pandit ji suggested that he should get acquainted with the Valmiki Ramayana, and Mahabharata followed by Bhagwad Gita, eventually his curiosity would get him to the principles of living, and philosophies found in the Puranas. As Ishan became a little agitated about reading, asking, "Isn't that all about God?"

Ishan wanted to know why everything was happening, including life, nature, love, and grief. He did try to read a little by little, yet he was unable to absorb properly or balance the knowledge to its real purpose. The pandit smiled, looking into his eyes and simply walked away. Ishan started collecting the books and he felt relieved, grew eager to read about the Puranas, and made notes on the life values stated in the Bhagwad Gita – bit by bit. He was learning about reaching enlightenment through books, scriptures, weekly satsangas (associating with the wife) and started leading himself towards Sanatana dharma through his knowledge, and actions, without any force but purely a flow of interest. He realized why his grandparents always spoke highly of their dharma. As he improvised, he sat equally for all religions and felt absorbed in spiritual energy that led to understanding. Yet at times, when he looked in mirrors, it was as if Arjuna had forcibly beheld Draupadi's vastraharan, and his thoughts were surrounded by powerlessness and fury. Then he became accustomed to what 'karma' and 'dharma' are, it is not something very deep and religious, religion is just a part of life but to lead a life one must understand Karma and Dharma.

Karma directs your mind toward your abilities and capacities, prompting you to ask yourself, *What can you do to stop something bad from happening? Why do abstract things happen in life, the way they do? Or what can you do now about the situation you are in?* It is a subtle part of your consciousness, action-oriented, and leads you away from excuses, cowardice, or victimisation. You know your karma if you are taking responsibility for what your life has led you through, you are not making excuses for karma or victimising yourself in front of others. However, Ishan lamented not knowing this sooner while he was with Arushi. The same is true with dharma, which is an expression of righteousness that has nothing to do with religion but does suggest that you should always act morally. For example, as a student, you shall adhere to your dharma in order to study and so on. Think for yourself and absorb knowledge from successful individuals worldwide.

Ishan started to expand his focus towards bhakti (which basically comprises emotional investment and this technically is a method to preach the highest supernatural power or creator or what one can call Paramatma, but, but, but by humanising them first, i.e: the writings of the Rig Veda and the Valmiki Ramayana, conveys a clear message to perceive brahmans or gods in a humanized form first, enjoy the connection and then build a strong emotional bond through preaching) and karma (which is another way out to negotiate, fight and settle with the negative habits as you do not expect but only perform your duties as a human/animal in this).

He even focused on performing and learning daily yoga postures as he began to feel the weight of one's obligations and responsibilities.

Ishan realized that it was more crucial to concentrate on one's current life development and purity of one's soul than on the future and past.

He learned a lot about older scriptures when he came across the question that among all these gods and demigods, who do we pray to? Then he learned about the existence of multiverse, a supreme form known as Lord Vishnu/Narayana and his earthly formations, he became enamoured that the ultimate truth and the supreme power of everything, that is known as "the god " which is denoted to Lord Vishnu in the Shrimad Bhagwad Gita followed by local mythical/ popular stories about temples, he who also existed in the form of several demigods known as his avatars and while Ishan dug deeper he kept growing curious. He realized how every imbalance is balanced by nature which is directed by some kind of supreme power. Some preach Shiva, and some preach Hari-Hara (a name derived from Vishnu and Shiva's union), every devotee has their belief of supreme which is one of the existing parts in the multiverse, every devotee/ believer holds the liberty to preach and believe the god but there are indeed set of rules to guide the human form in the right manner of preaching/ expressing their love towards the supreme power. Ishan eventually grasped that sanatana dharma believes in 4 major ways to reach the Paramatma -Karma (Action/Deed), Bhakti (Emotional Devotion), Dhyana (Reflection), and Gyana (Knowledge). Bro was almost close to scoring himself with the cloak of a Mimansa believer. Yet, good that he did not!

He felt more satisfied with his curiosity as every day while going around the streets with city lights, started his mornings by practicing yoga asanas, and controlled his anger or excitement through knowledge. I just know these little things that he used to share with me so often, he could have explained it better to you all. But eventually, Ishan was pleased with his basic existence after college, looking for work, trying to get somewhere, and praying for

Arushi with a distinct minute and a heavy heart every day. Ishan knew where he was headed, he grew to be a better listener and he was correct except for the part where he couldn't forget what happened to Arushi. This left a subtle trauma in his mind, and he kept thinking about how he left her behind, he recollected when he read about Lord Rama, who crossed over a sea for his wife Sita. He couldn't erase his feelings for Arushi right away nor he had ever thought of making any excuse to cover the incident. However, he had always felt guilty about Arushi's situation. However, there was something he shared very dearly with Arushi that helped them grow, it was their love for planting saplings. Ishan recalled how they used to plant little saplings every month at random roadsides or parks, after their weekly classes. He used to appreciate her dedication, they grew closer due to this and she always felt happy throughout the day after this. With time he missed Arushi more and, he often visited the park where they had planted one last sapling. At least it kept him going.

He was so self-absorbed and busy with learning that I used to feel bad or maybe lonely I guess, indeed I was immature- a true friend who has been through your hard times had promised to be your friend or knows about your acts should support you irrespective of anything (that something great, Karna, had always depicted), in a way, I am his brother from another mother. I can still recall when we had a college party and I was pissed cause he was my only friend whom my parents trust so blindly and this parrot sleeps at 10, like what in the Venus..could have I done to persuade him for a midnight bash? Still, the two hopeful brain cells of mine called him on that weekend -party day at 7 PM, Incoming call from Vidur,

"Hey, Ishan! Do you want to sneak out tonight? Just for one night? Let's go for a drive please?" Vidur initiated.

"Uh, no, Vidur, I sleep in a few hours."
Ishan reacted with a soft tone.

"Kid, let's go, we might get something fun to do?"
"Vidur, no ..I need to wake up early for my routine and family is leaving for a vacation near Auroville town, they need some social isolation vibes!" Ishan objected.

"Ishan, just for one day – lets go!" He pleaded.

"You enjoy buddy..bye!" Ishan's tone resisted.

"Why do you keep going into all these readings and all? Isn't it too difficult, too lengthy and even if everyone has a religion but free will is also a choice right? Lets go buddy, come one!" Vidur begs.

"That's why you are invested, I am! It's not lengthy and it is a part of my choices. Why don't you understand that my life, my body, and all these walls I built, I choose to better live a life that was traditionally followed where people survived this long with real commitments, that's more of a man in me who seeks.." Ishan adds.

"Are you sure that this all you are doing is not an escape room, you're not choosing spirituality to run away from your pain, you think so? I think you need to party.." Vidur questioned.

"Everyone wants to run away from something but I chose to surrender, surrender to a supreme power and learn what I my body can do.." Ishan elaborated a little.

"Okay okay.. I got it, just go sleep, Useless!" Vidur reacted in a frustrated tone.

"Vidur see..I am sorry! I cannot be a friend who matches your vibe but I am trying to be someone better, who can at least be your help" Ishan apologised.

"You are a pussy! You have no damn idea whenever you needed me, I was there but when I ask you that I need just one friend to accompany-not to feel lonely there..you have your priorities, right?" Vidur bursts in anger.

"Vidur, I have never asked you to help, when you had this much issue with me!" Ishan replied furiously too.

"Ahh! Vidur sorry...hey? listen, dude?"

----Call disconnects---

Ishan: Stay home please, I am coming!

I felt like a sword just hit my heart, the only thing I never want to hear from the person with who I had shared my loyal efforts, my brother-like friend just bashed thunder over me. I had no replies. I felt like sinking, he had no damn idea that I have my plate too. I could be a little near his ego, but I was indeed a human a heart that was real. The same night Ishan arrived at my home, begged for sorries with my favorite drink, and we talked for a while until he made me feel at ease again. We skipped the party bash and went on a scooter trip in the middle of the night. He went back home by 3 but his words had left a wound in my heart that made me feel, I could never see him the same- never put in the same effort for him, again. The noise in my heart echoed a question, Are we supposed to grow up, just to mind our big world, manage it, balance the complications, and share just a part of it with friends? I am still looking for answers but maybe Ishan already has his part of answers. Yet, I have my life, my pace of learning, and my set of choices..so we just went on with casual texts and hi hellos, until one regular morning, Ishan gets a call from one of his friends:

"Hey, what's up? Want to come on a trip with us?"

"I'd rather stay home," Ishan laughs.

"Come on, this could be the last time we all go for a trip, wake up! You have to be there—no more convincing after this. See you, at 6 p.m. at the train station."

Ishan has been yearning for a change in his life, even though he has never travelled much with companions. I can tell you the greatest part, and the fact is that Ayush and I were eager to experience a new destination and had a limited budget when we saw the movie Yeh Jawani hai Deewani in cinemas. Arup, a Nagamese friend of ours, accompanied us there and he suggested we make travel arrangements for a different state. Ishan decided to put it out and accompany us on our journey. After a few days of decision rounds, we called Ishan around 6 p.m., on the same weekend. We gathered at the station and conducted a few last-minute checks. Our dude is not on a perfect plot, we were all freaking scared as it was our first time and Ishan didn't even know where they were headed! After everyone assembled, they insisted on having chai and samosas. Ishan approaches Ayush and asks him about the destination. Ayush smiles and replies 'Nagaland'. We all were perfectly scared now! Yet we had paid for the tickets so no looking back. The man in each of us was surfing about survival tips. They continued to discuss it after Ishan became nervous and Ayush persuaded him to stay and have fun because we had planned the itinerary together and the other two boys who had been keen to join us were now afraid.

Ayush bragged, "Everyone, remember,

Rule number 1 of Boys Trip – No Looking Back

Rule number 2- Follow number 1 and Survive till Home!"
Soon the announcement comes out at 8 p.m., and a train bound for

Dimapur arrives at Guwahati station. Passengers begin to board the train as Ishan, who is still nervous, feels better enough to proceed. Ishan got on the train with his other friends. That was not the end; as soon as the train arrived in Guwahati, Ishan and Ayush assisted others in disembarking and they took an old bus to Touphema; the journey took about 3 hours, and Ishan enjoyed spending time with people without regretting his decision. YET! The Touphema Tourist Village is one of Nagaland's ancient historical villages and a stunning recreation of a traditional Angami Naga village. Ishan was going to stay in a cottage with friends, enjoy bonfires, and spend time in the village with friends. When they arrived in Touphema, Ayush checked into his lodging, and a local boy named Chang, who was friends with Arup, assisted them in settling down. The cottage where they were staying was stunning; everything was made of bamboo, mud, straws, and wood, including meals, accessories, neighboring cottages, and utensils, everything had a part of bamboo. Ishan was captivated and chose to chat with Chang further about it. While speaking with Chang, they passed through a village lane and Ishan was approached by an elderly person who was selling rice wine in small cups. It tasted strange to him, but he appreciated the kindness and paid him some money. Chang smiled and told him about some stories from the Dzükou Valley, which was unfamiliar to him, and Ishan became intrigued to explore the valley.

The next morning, Ishan made plans to get a map and invited his pals to join him. However, everyone refused to go on the trek, it was tiring indeed. They insisted on exploring the villages and speaking to people nearby. Ishan was used to traveling alone but didn't entertain speaking to people much, so he started to make his way to the Dzükou Valley. Ishan arrived near a relaxing water stream, where the sound of river flow covered his ears, and his heart felt calm. He screamed his lungs out "Heyyyyyy" and surprisingly on the cliff a voice echoed, "Heyyy..". This was indeed weird, in a remote valley's corner, you hear your echoing voice come back with a reply. Ishan was astonished and he tried to get down to find who it was, as he was stepping down across a water stream, Ishan found someone sitting near the stream with a backpack, a self-built tent, and a grill. It smelt good, indeed food it was, Ishan felt hungry and climbed down to get closer. A girl was sitting beside the water stream with a small tent of her own, pitched finely with a small grill stand burning with coal in it. The smell of burning wood and cooked spices amalgamated finely, was spreading all around.

By the time Ishan got down, the girl had noticed him and when he reached the tent with a curious look on his face, she turned back with a smile as if she was expecting him and then she invited him to sit. Ishan found her beautiful and kept looking at her while she was preparing something, the moment was so soothing that both of them knew there was a sensitive vibe that attracted them to each other's aura yet they chose to carry on with their roles. In a minute, the girl brings him a water bottle. Ishan kept looking at her with a very calm look as if he was adoring the sight of her presence. She looks back at him with a sweet smile and offers him the bottle again. Ishan grows curious about her. He takes a sip of water from the bottle and introduces himself as Ishan. The girl responds "I'm Nysa" Ishan expresses gratitude by returning the water bottle and Nysa offers him to have a meal with her. He expressed he was open to whatever she cooked and simply wanted to experience the food in the valley. Nysa smiles and replies yes, as she approaches the grill and hands Ishan a wooden chopping board with some veggies; he understands what to do and begins cutting the vegetables swiftly to help her; while Nysa looks at him to keep up, she asks Ishan if he wants to know what's cooking on the grill. Ishan was more curious now, so Nysa brought some spices with her and elaborated.

"This is what I call the spice blend.
It is a strongly ingrained culinary heritage, and we are roasting it all by using a combination of available spices such as coriander, turmeric, black pepper, and cardamom.

It will immediately release the oils, which will be the flavor; it is very beneficial for digestion."

She starts elaborating more as she starts cooking and Ishan helps her along. Ishan keeps sneaking glances at Nysa and she makes him feel comfortable. As their curry and rice are prepared, Nysa takes out a long bamboo vessel with a small cloth cover. The vessel was not very hot but appeared interesting to Ishan. Ishan kept starting and Nysa smiled. She elaborates as she serves a gooey-creamy-looking fish dish with some visible coriander in it, here is *Ghalo*, it is a dish where the fish is cooked inside bamboo. I had to clean a fresh fish, marinate it with a blend of local spices, then cut this bamboo tube to length and pack the fish inside, sealing it with banana leaves to trap in the juices and aromas. Once the bamboo chairs, the fish inside will be perfectly cooked and easy to remove. This method preserves nutrients while adding a smoky flavor, making it a nourishing and memorable camping meal. Ishan enjoyed every bite of the meal as she explained the taste and enjoyed the meal together, Nysa interrupted while chewing slowly, "Thank god you are not like those vegetarians, you couldn't have survived here without that..." Ishan smirks and interrupts "I am"

Nysa looks at him with shock and asks, "Why didn't you tell me?"

Ishan stated that he was happy to see her and, as a formality, he did not want her to be disturbed because she was so dedicated to her recipes and details; as a guest, that was a small gesture he could make to show acceptance. Nysa regretfully questioned as she started to serve,

"I hope I am not interfering with your beliefs, I do understand if you have any religious restrictions or so on, and want to leave the meat, we can try something else, what do you think?"

Ishan calmly looked at her and explained, "It would be disrespectful and dumb if I did say that.
Have you ever heard about the Vedic era?"

Nysa nods with a yes!

Ishan continues, "So believe me when I say that meat-eating used to include a variety of other foods, some of which were cultivated specifically on our continent. Many regions of Bharat have preserved their culture to this day, and if you're interested in learning more, you should read through *Chandogya Upanishad, Anushana Parva, Sri Ramayanam's Saragas* and Nal Maharaja's *Pakdarpana* where meat-eating was a part as a survival, ritualistic offering but not always a compulsion but a complete choice of ones. This makes me a rational and a not-so-dumb person to accept your offered food."

Nysa is surprised to learn about it, "but what about the staunch vegetarians and brahmanas, I heard of?"

Ishan stated, "I believe it was the difference of eras; they followed a societal manner that is very different from what we do now, as we evolved and our lifelines/age decreased, we became more specific with our interests; this is just my opinion but also books, I respect their pure choice, but there is a lot I need to know about the life of brahmins, Vaishnavas who were sattvic."

"Are you always spiritual like this? How do you remember all this? It appears that you have absorbed it well into your personality, yet that is older than old-school culture! You may advertise an entire package to me, and whatever I want to believe is mine, hehe!" Nysa giggles.

"Um, sure, I'm just a bookworm! I think...so...sorry, I may be boring at times.
But what do you consider believing in?"
Ishan questions with curiosity.

"I think I am more of a Charavaka person!" Nysa looks at the stars and responds while relaxing.
"What is that? Sounds like Something deep but unknown!" Ishan grows curious.

"So, this is all close to the belief of atheism, it is known as 'Lokāyata' in ancient Indian schools. So, I look up to materialism and we tend to live in a movie of our own life. I do not believe in gods or supernatural beings, only in the present world or scientific realities. I appreciate everything and am familiar with numerous religions, but this is what my heart chooses to believe. Life is only one movie, and it finishes just like Zindagi Na Milegi Dobara!" Nysa explains with a sarcastic expression.

Ishan adds, "Sounds interesting!"

"What would you desire to be if you were born in the Vedic era or some part of Akhanda Bharat (undivided Bharata)?"

Ishan says, "I'd have liked to be the son of a knowledgeable writer who could teach me things for free and come from a simple happy family. Away from politics, how about you?"

Nysa exclaims, "Oh, I'd love to know how politics worked, the fights, the Kingsmen, and the attractive humans around; I'd be a princess. Oh wait...to be precise I would love to be queen Tara who was also depicted in Ramayana."

"Tara?" Ishan raised his eyebrows with interest.
"Why her specifically?"

Nysa's imagination glowed in her eyes. "While Sita and Draupadi are frequently discussed, Tara always stood out unique to me. She was more than just the queen of Vanaras and Sugriva's wife. She knew how to negotiate, and was an expert in the shastras, we haven't heard of the woman's life in the Vanara clan but only her with powers, and she offered advice that even Lord Rama took seriously. Vali's knowledge came from her pain while she was dying. She was evidence that knowledge transcends species and titles, which was an amazing inspiration to me. Her intelligence, her erudition, and her capacity to transform information into wisdom were her greatest assets, not her position as queen of the Vanaras. I want to be the kind of queen or princess that rules not only by position but also by intelligence."

"I didn't know you knew so much. I'm a fan now!" Ishan expressed.

"I did not, my mom is a good poet, she likes to talk about Ramayana and Mahabharat, I learned it in detail ever since I was a child. But the amazing part is, my dad's a Muslim and my first love interest was a Christian. I have lived and learned through diversity a bit more than you, I guess." Nysa spitted.

"Woah! Indeed, your life appears to be full of colors, much like observing dreams. I don't give much thought to other's religious choices, but it sounds odd to me now that you're growing up in a world where there are conflicting truths and opinions. It must have been difficult for you to establish your values and principles, but I think you're enough and have come a long way. Proud girl!"

They both giggled looking at each other and he felt good listening to her, speaking with her as time passed, they kept on jumping to topics, wandering around the woods until the sunset happened and they climbed up to an edge. The view was majestic and his breath felt free as he found her beside him, standing like she knew where she was and he knew where he was. Two people who have found their places, known their phases, and know what they are doing but are yet struggling somewhere in the run of life. He felt good as she was like him and Nysa kept on talking more about things that were insignificant but were interesting to her. Ishan wanted to know Nysa a bit more, and they spent the night in the jungle. As topics changed, time passed, and it was dark, Nysa settled back into her tent comfortably and smirked as she looked at Ishan asking, "Where are you going to sleep after dinner?" she appeared unconcerned.

Ishan shrugged, his gaze confidently without caring,"outside your tent," he said. "I'm not going back to this gloomy night, and you planned on living here alone? The entire night - no chance. Aren't you scared?

She laughed gently, her voice tinged with feigned defiance. "I'm not afraid." You?"

"More scared than you, to be honest. You know a few skills, I acknowledge. "But Nysa, there are a lot of possibilities to die early, why camp in a dark valley?" he confessed, his tone light but honest.

Nysa removed an old monk bottle from her backpack and held it up with a sneaky look. She followed it up with a swipe of her phone, exposing a playlist ready to go. Ishan couldn't help but smile at her easy assurance. To Ishan, Nysa appeared like a mood-lightener human who can magically comfort anyone with their ambiverts, while her self-dedication to stay and enjoy her own company from the start was quite a strong or gut-twisting move that usually normal people do not wish to take. The chilly night air surrounded them as she wrenched open the bottle top confidently without offering him a sip. He settled down next to her, Ishan observed her for a time before breaking the stillness. "Sorry for clinging to you."

Nysa lifted her eyebrow and took a little sip before responding. "I know guys like you. I have judged you already."

"Like me, but not me?" he responded with a half-smile.

"Why do girls like you, think you know a few wrong people and then dump that judgment onto good people too?"

"That's exactly what playboys say," she said, her tone tinted with contempt.

Ishan leaned back slightly, his expression unflinching. "Playboys don't care about your abilities, knowledge, or soulfulness. I did. As a bonus, I also believe in laws of attraction."

She gazed at him with a gentle interest, replacing her customary sharpness. "You sound like you've rehearsed that line," she remarked, her tone softer but still guarded.

Ishan smiled softly and shook his head. "This is not a line. Only the truth. Even Sir Newton stated about action and reaction!"

He peeked in the bottle that she held, then looked back at her. "Do you ever let anyone in, or is everyone just another story to you?" Her fingers tightened slightly over the bottle, and her walls became evident.

"Depends, on how much you can take...So, what happens when you let them in, Ishan? They notice the parts of you that they like, take what they need, and then leave. Or worse, they hurt you because you are who you are."

He groaned, leaning backward to the ground. "I'm here, aren't I?" He spoke simply.

"Sitting outside your tent in the middle of nowhere, when I could be somewhere else.
Nysa, I am not asking you to let me in.

I might be just a stranger and see that's good, all I'm asking you is to stop pushing me away.
I can feel this within you."

Her gaze fell to the bottle, and her thumb drew an unintentional line around its edges. "You're too hopeful for someone who seems so tired and even if we are strangers, you do look safe but I have my reasons. I know what I am doing and you should know that I will not listen. So, there is no point."

Ishan chuckled, self-aware. " Okay, I thought I could be a good pillow, but you wish! And you're too cynical for someone who seems so alive."

Nysa curved her lips into a genuine smile for the first time that night. She passed him the bottle without saying anything, as he sat beside firewood and shared dinner with Nysa as they decided to watch the sunrise together and shared more empathetic conversations where Ishan and Nysa chose not to disclose their identities yet. Somewhere both of them felt an insecurity about growing closer but eventually there were thousands of little things they talked about without knowing each other. Nysa listened to him like a very patient woman and comforted him as he fumbled to express, While Ishan was setting the firewood, he questioned Nysa, "Don't you have any such sadist stories? Sorry, I am being dramatic right now."

Nysa giggled, "I have never found much interest in romance as I travelled a lot throughout my childhood, kept changing houses and cities, left people, met people but never had a chance to confess any guy/You look luckier than me! My life is still so strange that I am honest to everyone I love or respect. It's either situations or our bonding, something crashes and I grow apart from them."

Ishan felt bad about her, "Well, I'm sure you will find someone! Stop oversharing like this...What do you think of me though?"

She expressed "Um, you sound empty, after hearing your side is like a "silent orchestrator", you are rare like those of rare elements on earth."

Ishan countered, "Is it? Do you mean something uniquely boring - like Astatine? Or Francium?"

Nysa competed, "If you want an analogy then, I'd say you are a Zinc!"

"Why zinc? Sounds weird." Ishan asked with curiosity.

"Zinc is one of the most stable elements in our body, we need just 1.5g to 2.5g of it, right? So, your body cannot produce zinc on its own (yet). It supports immunological response, protein synthesis, growth, and DNA synthesis. Like you, it is stable on its own..but when it forms bonds with other molecules, it produces some of the most vital bodily functions. Perhaps, I believe you and Arushi, could have been each other's savior. It doesn't have to change, just like in a metaphorical relationship, but it does help other components or compounds become their "best selves. "Interestingly, Zinc never truly "dies/ends"; instead, it simply changes forms and re-enters the environment, where it may eventually re-enter the food chain just like your soul, you may have left your love but you will find it again maybe in this or next life until then, you're changing your form by working on yourself, that's completely normal. I'm sorry that I had to bring Arushi but it's just what I thought of." Nysa paused to affirm.

"It's fine, it was partly my fault, so it's fine." Ishan reacted calmly.

"Okay, so. More elements are rare like zinc for example magnesium, but even though you have competition, you don't stop doing your work, right? So is zinc, uncommon, rare yet an important part of processes." Nysa elaborates.

"Well, that's something very new, but the way you think is uncommon, like it could have been anything but because you highlighted Zinc into an analogy with a soul's activity, so beautifully, I cannot help but agree." Ishan praised.

"I know right, I also think that it's just not you there are a lot of people around us, we see their bodies but not their souls or their soul functions. I just think, how many more zinc-soul alike could be there" Nysa expressed as she thought deeper.

Ishan was pleased by her intelligence to use such an analogy, he thought that someone had a unique perspective on his life and encouraged her creativity. He became more interested in her; she was, in fact, creative, attractive, inquisitive, intelligent, and might be a formidable rival to him. As Ishan shared more, she kept asking him about his experiences, lying under the stars beside each other. Nysa played her playlist keeping the drink aside, the songs began to play softly in the background, filling the solitude with music as the two sat under the big night sky, navigating a connection that was both challenging, they were indeed cool yet formal but quite understanding to each other.

The following morning, Ishan was sleeping close to the tent under a warm fleece shawl. Nysa's head was resting on his palm, she was comfortably resting next to him, and the sun's rays were gently caressing his icy scarlet cheeks. He felt his one hand was frozen. He thanked God for allowing him to witness this lovely morning while blinking his eyes. He continued to stare at her while she was fast asleep, her cheeks had turned a little pink, her creased brow was frowning, and her pink lips were parched from the cold. Ishan tried to wake her up loudly while he was appreciating her frowns and later helped Nysa pack her tent after she got up. He insisted that she should meet his friends on the way back, but she decided to take an alternative route because of her family's preparations. When Ishan bids Nysa his final goodbye, she holds him back with her gentle hands and murmurs, "Don't miss me, geek!" He responds, "Well, I should, I am a slow guy but I will work on that for you." and feels completely at ease.

As they ascend back, Nysa and Ishan exchange phone numbers, and she leaves. Our guy's failure to obtain her address was the most catastrophic thing he did. Like how can a normal dude do this? He spent the whole night in the tent, talking and joking and he did not want to see her again. Is it possible? Asking for a number is a gentle and decent enough act, at least she will know he might want to see her again. All we wanted was for him to meet her! We teased Ishan a lot while returning as he stayed the night out with Nysa, irrespective of the group trip and bro code.

When Ishan and we all got back from the outing. Ishan was visualizing his monotonous life in front of the computer, where he woke up, applied for jobs, helped around the house, and slept without much relevant productivity. However, when he returned, he found himself stacked with a heap of rejections. He applied for several more job openings from various portals, it was about to be 500 applications now, yet he hadn't heard anything positive. It is hard, jobseekers are growing and so is unemployment but not everything pays you, despite his intellect and sharp skills, he was still a seeker. When you reach a certain age and are surrounded by individuals who are also growing up, but who surpass you in excellence, demonstrating their hard work to parents and society, you begin to doubt yourself! It's challenging. Not only does society's frame matter, but a stable mindset is also crucial; nobody knows when to quit, but one may always make the decision. After days of trying, one day, Ishan decides to visit his college lecturer, Mr. Bakshi, who has always helped and advised him with his assignments! Mr. Bakshi, a lecturer at Ishan's college, had always attempted to teach him the best but at times he also had supported Ishan with strong networks. This time, Ishan knew it might work if he remained consistent, so he designed a cover letter, and the following Monday, he contacted Mr. Bakshi and requested that he meet up. As Mr. Bakshi professes his desire to be overseas and hears Ishan on the phone, he quickly understands the problem, seeks some time, and hangs up on Ishan.

"I can help you beta (son), but do you really want to be in this industry with the rat race, I believe you can be better if you wish to dedicate?" Mr.Bakshi texts Ishan.

This made Ishan feel bad for himself yet the professor assured him to grab the connection for him. In a matter of a few days, Ishan received an application answer from Wyom, a start-up that worked on an animated series script and cartoon making. Ishan accepts the offer and calls Mr. Bakshi, who assures him that he contacted Wyom on Ishan's behalf, but Ishan expresses that it might not be the perfect role for him. Mr. Bakshi then advises Ishan to focus on his current achievement of getting accepted, to think about the salary he'd make out of it and then he urges him to follow his dream of working on his motivation. Ishan had always wanted to visit Arizona University for a research apprenticeship program which he used to find very interesting. He was quite temperamental when it came to his career, his standards, his working style, and everything else that reflected professionalism except his will to get things done.

His First Proper Date

CHAPTER FOUR

Dear Heart,
Do you ever just want to run from life,
cause you have wrapped your childhood talents tightly into islands of
ignorance?
..And leave everything as it is, while it stays as it is?
But how can you stop things from changing, isn't that a runaway,
a give up in life?
Yes, but in reality we still keep lying to each human that we are fine,
Running away looks better than those lies.
But are we really fine?
No, behind every one it's fine, I wanted to say..
I need a distraction, I need someone to care,
I need attention, I want affirmations,
And lots of Love!
But do you really know all this time what was best in you?
What?
Your Patience, your kindness, appreciation for others and
the braveness to do the right thing for you.
But does all this even matter?
For the right people.
Yes.

As a child, Ishan aspired to work in an isolated setting where he could incorporate his favourite activities and give them a traditional twist to remain attached to his Indian roots but as he grew up, he realised the roots exist within and one needs to grow with the generations. So, with no other options left, Ishan starts to work for Wyom and develops his knowledge. Once while he was still applying for Wyom, Mr.Bakshi asked him, "Did you know why you got hired so smoothly? Just not my entire efforts but there's something interesting.""What sir?" He questioned.

"You were the only critic for their company and all other candidates were appreciating like perfection was served. You know what I mean right, believe in the difference you bring." Mr.Bakshi explained.

With this motivation, Ishan predicted that Wyom might hold one more test or assessment for him, but due to Mr.Bakshi's word of mouth, they didn't really...they just wanted him to learn and adapt. Days passed by, and Ishan's regular hectic, concentrated life and work balance never afforded him enough spare time to think about himself, Nysa, or his hobbies; instead, he isolated himself with his regrets over Arushi. Ishan swiftly becomes a valuable employee at Wyom, simply living his normal life to save money for another journey to Nagaland. One evening, the HR team sends Ishan an email inviting him to an after-party celebrating Wyom's 13th anniversary. He accepts and goes to the party because his coworkers support him and he understands that he must maintain his position at work. Ishan introduced himself to a number of his investors and colleagues during the event, which took place in a spacious, spectacular auditorium.

After a while, he began drinking wine by himself. It was a robotic corporate life followed by a people obsessed with materialistic desires but that's the order of the world, lead or follow! You gotta grow a little before you grind. Ishan was less interested in working 9 to 5 but he was forcing himself as it was the cost of being independent and how he hated financially relying on his parents. With all the monotonous thoughts in his mind, Ishan suddenly noticed a girl in a red shimmering dress and a crimson robe approaching her. She pulls a chair opposite to Ishan and settles gently. After a while of staring at him, the girl clears her throat to get Ishan's attention. Ishan was zoning out until she moved closer to him and pushed his wine glass swiftly with her long nails, as the glasses chimed.

"Hi, I am Grace..Grace Bharti..um.. from the HR team!" She introduces herself.

"Hi, oh..sorry..Ishan here. Ishan Raiyani." He snaps back.

"Yeah, I know, I mean..I have noticed you..and invited you here."

"Um..You are the daughter of Mr.Bharti, right? THE FOUNDER?"

"Yeah, but call me Grace, I don't want his part of attention. Soon to-be-self-made."

"OH..Sorry then..my bad..but nice to meet you..Grace!"

"Thanks, so here is the thing, I have been waiting to ask you out on a date but couldn't find you anywhere on social media."

"Yeah, I just use WhatsApp and sometimes discord or gaming apps. But why me?"

"I just have been noticing you ..or maybe stalking..sorry, but I find you really cute. Can we go on a date, just once and then you can decide whatever, just give me a chance!"

Ishan slowly nods a yes, "Okay, I have a hurry tonight but I will see you..see..you..umm..wherever! And he leaves."

In a few minutes, a text from an unknown number pops on his phone "See you tomorrow at 8 PM, Delight's Café"

Ishan replies with a thumbs-up, leaves the wine glass and takes a cab back home.

THE NEXT DAY...

So now, ladies or gentlemen, what should Ishan wear on his first date? How ought he to proceed? I'll tell you, this guy had a perfect colleague and' friend named Aden. Aden was a very fashionable guy, he held beautiful facial features and encouraged makeup, he even helped Ishan to set his fashion taste. Aden was a bit bothered about his gender but the office members always celebrated little changes he tried like black finger rings or Hawaiian tees with big boots, he knew fashion in and out for men! But away from all this Ishan chose to wear a casual polo shirt that was sap green and mud brown trousers that appeared very average. It was his first proper date, he had never been to one, but he wasn't ready to accept the fact that it's a date. Rude brat! Anyways, Ishan left the office at 7.30 PM and successfully got late while looking for flowers. Ishan knew flowers were a typical notion as Aden had fitted some tips in his brain and every female deserves one, so he intended to acquire a bouquet. When did the flower dealer ask him which colour? He was astounded; he had never delved this deep before, but he knew exactly how he felt; he chose yellow roses, wrapped in a bouquet with chardonnay. Fratelli Vitae Chardonnay was probably an average idea, you never know! What if she wasn't a drinker? I hope he also knew yellow roses stood for friendship...but that's okay!

Ishan arrives at 8.30 p.m. and finds Grace already waiting; he feels bad, and as he approaches her and grabs the seat in front of her. He notices her extra-done makeup, highlighting the shade of rose pink, her golden sparkling dress was shoulderless, as he could see a big black mole on her chest just beneath her collar bone that was dusted with little sparks making her efforts to look good, very obvious to him. Her dress was bordered with a matte black stitch.

Her outfit gleamed with a golden necklace that held a pink jewel and a bracelet that matched it as she rested her hands on the light green table cover. She had her nails done in a lovely shade of blackish-gold. She wore a rich crimson lipstick that made her lips look oddly swollen. Ishan felt drastic as he sat closer to Grace on the other side of the table.

He felt anxious as if he was cheating on someone, as if he is doing the worst to Arushi by moving on with something temporary or something he didn't know about, and he had prepared this hunch that if by chance Grace asked him for a relationship, he will be honest. Ishan takes out the flower and wine and approaches her seat; Grace expresses gratitude and smiles as she accepts the flowers. Grace puts a little box on the table and drags it towards him; it wasn't a ring, nor did she cuff him to marriage; it was only a pen drive. While Ishan opens it, he asks, "What's this?"

"That's a pen drive innit...with a distinct application downloaded here plus some extra storage hard-drive, and I have a good game collection, try it. I've noticed you playing games on the office PC, so I hope you'll like it!"

"Haha, Is that a gift for me? But how do you know I like games?"

"Maybe I have noticed you purposefully, playing it more than enough times!"

As they both giggle and discuss the food to order. Grace asks Ishan what he thinks about her and Ishan responds, "Please don't mind me, Grace, but I believe we both understand that we come from different worlds. I'm not ready to face anything romantic because I can't be the man you deserve or need, and the saddest part about all this..I will never be able to man-up for you."

"Why Ishan?" Grace asks softly..

"See, I already couldn't defend someone I cared about...so let's call this off after this; you're a wonderful coworker to me. Sorry, Grace..."Grace rolls her eyes.

"So, Margarita? Or Cheese Burst?"

"Ishan? Are you listening?" Ishan glances at her with a nervous expression, and she grins at him.

This facial expression was cool, but it was one of those assured faces when the other person looks at you and understands they have you. Ishan smiles along with her. Grace explains.
   "Okay, Ishan, but I think I know what's going to happen."

Ishan laughs and undoubtedly responds. "So, what's your opinion?"

Grace reflects, "If a man wants to know, why not...so I believe we both know what's going to happen; we'll go back and chat to our colleagues and friends about this date, about ourselves, and we'll have different experiences to share and rate. However, we will unconsciously strive to meet again, identify flaws, or trigger traumas every time, which may result in physical contact...all other methods to feel less rejected or regretted."

"Wait...no one knows about it?" Ishan interrupts with concern.

"Like I haven't told anyone I'm coming to see you? Grace did you?" Grace is stunned and becomes reserved. Ishan smiles and responds, "That's fine, you were right anyway, we'll try to fill the void in our lives that I don't need right now, but I know I'm creating it because you expect it from me, and I'm a good guy, so I'll let you take over here. My ego would rest here, but I know I'm making it because you're a woman and have the right to express yourself."

Grace smiles. "I hope you stalk me from time to time, share stories, and speak more about it."

Ishan adds, "No, Grace, the resemblance between us is that we are both yearning for love and settling for less or whatever we can get...you do not deserve this; you are an amazing woman."

Grace feels sad that Ishan does not even feel a little to give her a chance but she knows that eventually she will get over so she offers him a friendship.

"Lines don't work on me, we can be friends, I hope...but this was enough, Ishan; I know how you feel now, and there's no need to go any farther with dates. But can I ask you something? ...Am I not enough?"

Ishan stops speaking as he thinks for a while and adds, "Grace! You're more than enough a man could ever pray. But let's just be colleagues, I am worried that we may get attached or may feel more than reality..!"

"But you know how happy I am right? Willing to grow ...is the bare minimum one should have. I can be a better version for you,Ishan."

"I understand you, but you know that this will go nowhere," Ishan replied with sadness.

Now, this was terrible, but Grace had a smart brain, so they reached this agreement and spent more time eating as she proposed, "Okay, so this-us-thing will stop here but we will go somewhere indeed."

Ishan was scared now but eventually, they got over it and Grace introduced Ishan to a downtown live music area called *Sammelan*, a very dim gathering café-ish area where people loved to gather for live music, live shows, and comedy. Everyone enjoyed sharing an open mic there, talking about different cultures, and genders, and sweet romantic notes which highlighted every evening's charm. This place was a total gem when the open mic was not even a public trend, the talents followed the dim corners where people gathered, not judgments, appreciations mattered, and not professions! Where Broken Hearts won the limelight with their expressive creativities, away from the world of competition, just strangers and performers who play 9-5 average employee roles but become the limelight in the evening.

They entered a darkly lit hall room that appeared to embrace both the broken and the optimistic version of a hidden humans-zone, now that was something close to aliens-land. Fairy lights formed a constellation across the navy blue ceiling, putting golden halos over scattered tables and mismatched seats. The walls were a canvas for abstract art, with each brush revealing a story of defiance and unfulfilled hopes. Draped in a variety of textiles, and creative designs and illuminated by a single lighting, the lights turned on slowly and appeared to invite the audience to reveal their innermost secrets. Ishan took a seat and observed the dim room closely. The audience was a potpourri of dreamers: teenage poets nervously rehearsing their lines, older musicians clutching guitars, and office professionals releasing the weight of their day jobs for a moment of liberation. Performers entered the stage one by one, a woman read a poem about love lost and found, her voice shaking with passion. A man in his 60s played a mournful piece on his guitar with his eyes closed as if reminiscing the youth he once invested in music before life required something more "practical."

Grace leaned closer to Ishan as they changed their seats, the crowd was rising, and she whispered, "Most of these people are artists at heart. But life, you know? It traps people in expectations, social standards, offices, and routines. They come here to breathe, feel their real selves, and remind themselves of their capabilities through our validations at times." Ishan slightly rested his hands around Grace's waist, protecting her from the crowd as he smiled at her gently, acknowledging her words.

The concept struck Ishan deeply and he was shocked but still happy that this world exists. So many talents have darkened, buried beneath spreadsheets and schedules, 9 to 5 PM pressures, never allowed to shine or be appreciated enough. He felt he should tell Aden about it. *Sammelan* was more than simply a venue; it was a poignant reminder of what the world could have been if passion had been allowed to flourish, so sometimes rejected dates or first-time dates with strangers are not that bad, it might lead you to know something that you might need but didn't know you did, until you know it from others lens. It's just not a date, in genuine terms, just keeping your ego, extra-boosted experience and flexes apart will only help you see what the world has to offer to you. Or what other people around the world can offer you. Ishan felt a sense of sadness as the audience applauded another sincere performance. He saw the brilliance of these strangers, their tales, their talents, and wept for a world that demanded their lights to be turned off. This wasn't simply a café; it was a shelter for all of them indeed. Every drunk person there had a story of their own and Ishan never encouraged drinking or smoking but a part of him blended with the crowd as he felt a sense of similarity in their stories, he dived into the crowd with Grace and stood for a while as he realised, that cigarettes glowed like brief beacons in the dark, and the clinking of glasses felt both joyous and tragic. He looked at them closely: a young man still clutching his guitar, breathing deeply as if the smoke could cover the empty gaps left by his tune; a woman with tear-streaked cheeks sipping wine, her laughter brittle and almost remorseful. They had shared their secrets on that small platform, only to find refuge in things that softened the rough edges of their fragility and incomplete life goals. Ishan's thoughts fleeted that nobody asked these people why they smoked or drank, why they decided to seek solace in behaviors that harmed their fragile selves. Instead, they were frequently treated with judgment, with calls to forget smoking, stop drinking, and use medicines- which is okay! But wouldn't a strong reason or conversation might suit better?

How to be better, when we all have some hidden addictions, desires, coping mechanisms or overlooked fears, aren't they harmful too? No one ventured to ask these personal questions anymore, "What are you hiding? What are you running away from?"

Perhaps telling someone to stop was simpler than sitting by them, sharing their stillness, and listening to the burden they carried. Ishan realised that the world was full of onlookers who were quick to criticize but hesitant to empathize, who can brag about achievements and marketize their failures but will face their lows under their shadows. These raw and brilliant performers were attempting to fix something unseen, unmet hopes, unrequited love, and silent wars within them. Their art represented the truth, but their habits served as a shield. At that moment, Ishan made a secret pledge to himself - if he ever witnessed someone withdrawing into the swirl of smoke or sympathising with the numbness through alcohol, he would always try to ask them the why's and who's and then listen about their side of life experience. With this, Ishan and Grace spent a very stressless evening with some more people around, promoting their genders, friendships and eventually, they bid farewell to one another as the place closed. I guess the yellow roses were appropriate now! He just failed the date with intuition. While walking his way back home, Ishan realized that he had stopped thinking about romance as he just looked back, thought about Arushi, felt the pain of nightmares he went through those nights, and the fact that he could love someone, yet his mind suddenly reminded him of Nysa at that point. He was taken aback by the moment when he and Nysa spoke over different opinions and things in life throughout the night, without getting bored, that was a peaceful time for him. He got home, scrabbled all over his room, and raced back to Ayush's. Ishan looked for the bag they shared for the trip, they kept searching Ayush's room until they located it. Ishan was overjoyed to find Nysa's number on a small crinkled paper, he tightly hugged Ayush, hurried back home and texted Nysa with an extremely nervous feeling.

(Typing...)

Ishan: Hello!

Ishan here. The Dzukou trekker who shared THE dinner with you.
I hope you remember me, because I remember you like it was yesterday.
He keeps glancing at his phone, and in a few seconds, a notification chimes,
Nysa: It's Nysa.
Hello, Ishan. Oh, You're the Zinc guy!
I do remember you 'as if it was yesterday.
Haha, nice to hear from you after 6 months and 11 hours.
Ishan: Um, I apologize for not being able to text you back because ..I was so busy with my job hunt and stuff.
I zone off a lot, and I'm sorry for not checking on you.

Typing..

Nysa: Anyway, what's going on now? It's 12. a.m. now.
Ishan: I just wanted to know where you reside
Just because we have exchanged a lot of information
..but not this.
I have been thinking about you a lot, lately..
Just curious! You can say no, if you're ...not okay..with sharing..
Haha.
Nysa: I'm originally from Siliguri, West Bengal, state
but I run a small NGO called 'Sikshah' in Guwahati.
NO! NO! No...this can't be true.

(After 3 minutes)

A call from Ishan's number, which she had saved as Ishan with a green heart, appears on Nysa's screen and she responds with a puzzled emoji.

Nysa, on the other hand, was too self-assured or at ease to talk to someone who had not paid attention to her and was now very eager to talk, so she turned off the phone and went to bed to sleep. Ishan waited for her response as he scanned idly through his phone, his thumb paused mid-swipe when Nysa's name showed on the screen. Her profile image shone softly against the dim light in his room. He had never seen such a candid shot before. She was seated on a windowsill, half-turned to the camera and laughing. The golden hour sunlight filtered in, accentuating the curve of her grin and the slight dimple on her left cheek. Her hair was somewhat tangled as if the wind had played with it. He searched for her on Instagram, luckily it was a public profile. Ishan's chest constricted. Something about the picture—its simplicity, tenderness, and calm intimacy—made him hurt. His fingers lingered over the screen, ready to press, like, or comment, but he paused. Instead, he looked, allowing the moment to unfold. "She looks happy," he murmured to himself, though the words were heavy. Was she genuinely happy? He wondered if someone else was responsible for that radiance. The thought gnawed at him, a combination of missing her and hopeless emotions. He zoomed in slightly, his heart falling as he saw a small shadow of something—possibly a ring on her hand. Was it just his imagination? He couldn't know, and the uncertainty was excruciating. He closed his eyes and sat back in his chair. His mind flashed back to their time together, her laughing, the way she'd roll her eyes at his jokes, and the times she'd talk about her dreams as if they were just within grasp.

He opened his eyes and gazed at the television again. Her photograph was a fixed frame of a life that he felt was slipping through his fingers. "I hope you're okay, Nysa," he said quietly, shutting his phone and tossing it aside as if that would silence the pain in his heart. Ishan made two more attempts to call her to tell her how excited he was to live in the same city, but the abrupt and unresponsive silence didn't bode well for him. What can be worse and creepier than this? 22-year-old Ishan getting ghosted by a girl whom he felt a spark with. It's often true since every story has two sides, one where feelings sprout with hope and the other where hesitation creates barriers. Nysa believed Ishan's sudden desire to connect was too early, selfish, and weird, whilst Ishan saw her silence as a harsh end to what he thought was a give-up.

He decided to reach out, sending a simple message,

Ishan: Hey! Heard you're in the city. Would love to catch up.

For days, his messages were met with silence. He tried again, sharing a picture of an old memory they both cherished, but there was still no reply. As a week stretched on with no response, Ishan began to accept that perhaps this was the closure he hadn't realized he needed so he started following his routine as a work-life person bound with responsibilities and growth. Until, one night, his phone buzzed unexpectedly. It was Nysa. He picked up the call and her voice was slightly slurred, catching his attention off guard.

"You... you're so persistent, so formal, aren't you? she said with a soft laugh, though her tone carried an edge."

Confused but intrigued, Ishan responded, "I wasn't trying to bother you, Nysa. Just thought it'd be nice to catch up. But you sound drunk, are you?"

She cut him off with a sigh. "You're nice, Ishan. Too nice. But you don't get it. Guys like you... you're distractions.

You look at a girl and think you can fix her, or—what do you even want from me, after so long?"

"Nysa, what are you even talking about? Are you home? You're drunk, Nysa, I can hear it, please go to sleep. We will talk later!"

"What do you even know about me?" She screamed.

Ishan was taken aback but didn't interrupt. There was something raw and vulnerable in her voice.

"Nysa, I just wanted to talk, to reconnect—" he began, but she cut him off again.

"Reconnect? With *me*? I'm a mess, Ishan." Her words spilled out in a torrent as if she had been holding them in for far too long.

She spoke for 40-50 minutes about the struggles of being independent, how fighting for respect in a world that dismissed her was tougher, how she traveled so much that one stuck by her side, her bills, and work while balancing exhaustion and ambition while she was in her college days. Her voice broke as she recounted the loneliness of building a life on her own terms. By now Ishan was lying on his bed and listening to her, staring at the wall and thinking; *when did my ears subscribe to this?*

Nysa continued..

"And Love? I thought I'd found it once. There was this guy... I liked him so much. But you know what he did? Ghosted me. After he got what he wanted, he cheated on me with an older girl. And I was stupid enough to think that I mattered. Purity has died, innocence too, and his fate, whatever will be waiting for him. I pity his upbringing was not made appropriate to love or respect a woman enough!"

Her words were deeper now. It hit Ishan like a nostalgic punch to the gut. He felt bad that Nysa had gone through a lot and now that she was expressing herself, maybe he was a comfort to her. He recalled how he made efforts for Arushi but he has almost found his closure now. He wanted to comfort Nysa, just to tell her she did matter to him, but he stayed silent, sensing she needed to let it out.

"I'm scared, Ishan," she admitted softly.

"Scared to love. Scared to lose. And here you are, acting like I'm some... project or something. Why? Why are you even here? Why did you chase me? Messaged me so much?"

Towards the end, her voice grew quiet, her anger melting into exhaustion. Ishan waited, listening to her breathing even out as she drifted to sleep.

"I know you're drunk, I'm not here to fix you, Nysa," he whispered gently.

"Just to know you. But I won't get in your way." She hung up. His emotions swirling in—sadness for her pain, anger at those who had hurt her, and a deep reluctance to be another complication in her already difficult life.

The next morning, Nysa woke up groggy, piecing together the events of the night before. When she saw the call logs, embarrassment and regret washed over her. She called Ishan, but he didn't answer.

The Next Day..
(Typing...)
Hey, Sorry for yest..
(deleted)
Hey, Ishan I'm sorry for my behav..

(deleted)

Hey, I think I owe you an apology... Can we meet?

Yeah, sure! Where and When?

I can come near your office, send me the address.

I'll wait for you around 6ish pm, okay?

Okay. (Address attachment)

Ishan waited for her near the Wyom's office as they finally met. Nysa's cheeks appeared flushed pink, her lips were dried yet beautiful and her dark brown hair highlighted a sticky texture with a straight glazy vibe. She was dressed in a long-fitting brown dress with glittering silver earrings and a choker neckband. Her clothing had a collar, making her look both professional and attractive. Ishan admired her even more as she approached, and he appreciated how she was comfortable in her trainers, strolling like a model rather than straining her heels. He pondered why CEO ladies constantly wear heels to enhance their beauty, but Nysa's simplicity changed his perception that there are women who prioritise comfort over appearance or first impressions. It was one's free choice after all! Nysa diverted the topic with a little embarrassment, "Hey, I'm sorry for unloading on you like that," she said.

"I was... not in my best state too," Ishan added as he smiled at her, his eyes were kind but distant.

"You don't need to apologize, Nysa. I get it. Life's hard, and you've been through a lot. But I think... Maybe I shouldn't complicate things for you right now."

His words stung her, though she couldn't explain why. "So, you're giving up here, like on us? Should I head back" she asked, her voice barely above a whisper. Ishan sighed deeply.

"Ah..no..no, It's not that. I just don't want to be another distraction in your life, Nysa. You deserve to find your peace without someone who loves pulling you in a direction you like. Even if that someone is me. Feel free to let your thoughts flow." Ishan assured.

Though she tried to convince him otherwise, Ishan held his ground as they walked from his office. That day, he felt like he cared for her deeply, but he didn't want to risk making her life harder or losing himself somewhere in the process of winning her. They parted ways that day, not as strangers, but as two people who had met at the wrong time, leaving behind a story laden with both compassion and sadness. Nysa and Ishan understood it wasn't meant to be for them, and Ishan remained her ordinary friend. They met on occasion to discuss job difficulties and sample other events, and cuisines, but it was never anything spectacular because their steps and attempts were completely out of control, their past flashed like a warning, and they did their best to maintain their friendship.

After 2 years..

One usual Sunday Ishan wakes up and receives a text from Nysa asking him to meet her at her NGO office, with a short address attached to it although Ishan knew it but had never been there. She expressed that she wanted to give him an invitation to a wedding. Ishan felt unrest and tension rushing through his heart, he was unaware of such feeling and desperately asked her more about the wedding, presuming it was her. She confirmed it was her wedding and she had just a few months left from now. Ishan was astonished as he also felt that she somehow needed him, while he also wanted to be involved, he texted further

Ishan: Can I ask you something?

Nysa: Yes?

Ishan: Wait for me..Okay? I'm coming..

When Ishan enters her office. He looks good in lemongrass perfume and a cream-colored shirt topped with a denim combination that complements his light brown skin tone. He was both excited and worried about meeting Nysa after a long time, especially because they were both 24 years old. It was a hormonal roller coaster. As he enters the locality, he finds a small public school in the name of Siksha where there are a few old buildings and one of them was marked as the Office with a paper banner. He approaches the office and finds Nysa speaking on a call. When she notices him, Nysa hugs him, but Ishan appears anxious and remains still. Soon they shared hi-hello and the conversation grew on about life, while they spent an hour, in a subtle moment, Ishan just launched his question, the question he was dying to ask her, "Nysa..Are you happy?"

Ishan was able to read Nysa's face and ask her a question as she glanced away, her eyes watering. Ishan observed her expression as she took time to reply and he realised that she was not happy with her upcoming marriage. He did not know much about the person she was marrying, nor was he so curious. All focus was on Nysa if she would be happy. When Ishan and Nysa spent time in Nagaland, Ishan realized he was a less expressive but deeply emotional human until he met her. He knew that there was a spark and a small tension between them, which rose within their friendship, as they hung out irrespective of their busy lives. He was not sure if this was right but he knew that Nysa felt something too, and she might love him back if they spent some time together, with this in mind, he requested Nysa, "Okay, Nysa..can I just have a month with you or maybe...maybe just a few outings with you, let's do a few outings at least? I promise not to bother you after that, but please give me your precious time for a month, it's important to me. I want to take you to some places, spend time and just talk a bit with this very average guy. I haven't paid you back for the journey time, and I don't want to lose you just now."

"But Ishan you do know we felt a little tension between us when we hung out for the first time in Nagaland! I'm about to commit my life to someone and this can spoil everything, just let's be honest- you have lost it!" Nysa replied.

"No, Nysa..I guess I have just started. I just need a yes from you, I know where to stop and you know about me too. I would not let your respect fall- not even a little. But what I would definitely make sure of this - either you love me back or we live in this social setup peacefully, without each other. And ...I know with your expression that you are not happy with this social set-up so give me a chance. Maybe we can find something that we never knew or felt or experiences. Who knows, huh?"

"Ishan, no, this is wrong.." Nysa pauses with this, and Ishan looks at her with a frown.

"Okay then just tell me why 'you'? Out of everyone and not even my fiancé but why you?" She corrects.

"I know Nysa, but in my entire life, none has ever accepted me as a Zinc! Haha," Ishan giggles.

Looking at Nysa frowning, he continues, "Nysa, to be honest, none has ever stayed this long in my mind, just sparking like a challenge that my heart would love to fight for. You do know all of this and you still like this average guy to be your friend, I know there's something more to friendship as it might sound absurd but I have a gut feeling that I want to be with you, just you, take care of you for the longest I can and if 'we' workout out then I'm just another soul who wants to cherish you with all my best. Your Zinc.." Ishan expressed everything in a rush as his face grew red.

Nysa looks at Ishan with her numb eyes and smiles softly nodding a yes. Ishan gets excited and softly hugs her from the back. How sweet! They only plan to act as couples but can't be couples; not sure what these two were planning, but Ishan was a very average person and Nysa knew it, she encouraged his simplicity and his way of living.

Vidur stops as he thinks about something and fumbles to say it first. Everyone stares at him as he looks at the cup and sips his cold coffee. Everyone was expecting him to say something first, but he kept searching for something in his bag. Meanwhile, Ayush smiles mischievously, reminding Vidur of an incident: "Do you remember that time when Ishan caught Aden slow dancing in the archive room?"

Ishan's face flushed, though he tried to maintain a nonchalant expression but was shocked to witness it.

"How can I forget that?" Vidur muttered, his tone tinged with both disbelief and amusement.

Ayush chuckled. "The surveillance footage—oh man. Ishan dragged me into that mess like it was a secret ops mission. I had to find it and delete it so fast."

Ayush exhaled sharply, eyes gleaming with memory. "It was either delete it or watch Aden's entire reputation crumble- slow dancing on the Calling's songs with James. And we knew know how things were back then in India."

The memory unfurled in Ayush's mind as vividly as the day it happened. Ishan and Aden both huddled in front of the security monitors, eyes wide as Aden swayed in sync with his boyfriend to an old English tune of the Calling—Wherever You Will Go. Something poetic yet haunting that neither Ayush nor Ishan could name. Aden's face had been serene, flown at the moment, completely unaware of the security camera above. But what was even stranger was how Ishan had learned about it. Aden's phone contained a stray message that had revealed a tonne of secrets. In their conservative social environment, it had been both plausible and startling to accept. Ishan's heart was still free of judgment. Ayush's eyes glinted with false fright as he laughed softly. However, Aden's apologies were legendary. What was it he said? Is there a way the song is entering his mind?

Vidur gave a nod. "He just... fell for it when they were alone in the office. However, at least Aden was honest with Ishan...

Ayush added, "Ishan responded that justification is not necessary for love. It's a decision, and it need not follow any rules except commitment, which we didn't establish for ourselves. And gender? That is a personal matter. However, people had different ideas back then. It was against the law.

After allowing the impact of that sentence to sink in between them, Ayush smiled wryly to break the stillness. "Good thing we made the CCTV footage disappear like pros, huh?"

As the tension subsided, Alia asked, what happened to them then?

"Nobody found out, we saved Aden's secret!!" Ayush and Vidur giggled.

Vidur retrieves a journal from his bag and gently opens it. He removes the journal that resembles a black book. It had a stone-shaped glitter bindi on it with a haldi (turmeric) inscribed thumbprint with the name - 'NYSA', he places the journal on the table, and Alia snatches it up. She opens the 40-page journal and begins reading it aloud as Vidur tries to stop her with facial expressions, but she sits far away from him while Ayush restrains Vidur. Although Vidur believes it is improper to read it, he allowed them to do so because everyone was interested at the time. Alia was curious and concerned about Nysa as a friend, she knew about the journal and tried opening it. As the journal started with some empty pages, Alia eventually jumped to the initial page titled "Who," and began reading.

88

Pages From Her Journal

CHAPTER FIVE

Dear Heart,
Can you love someone so strongly that the other heart whom you had let inside
knows about your true scars,
Yet you let them scatter the truth you held so dearly?
Love holds a power and with great power, comes..?
great responsibilities...
So if you let anyone in,
the 'anyone / any soul' must respect the space they stay in,
But people grow apart ..
That is why,
People change..
That is why,
You have to love,
You have to know your soul before you choose to fall for another,
And learn to acknowledge how much space they can offer you..
But how will I know it is enough?
Stay true to yourself.
And, what if they are not?
Then remember, your end is you.
Is that all I should do?
No force or attempts to change have changed anyone,
until one's soul commands to!
The first page of the journal was titled 'Who.'

Hi, my name is Nysa. You probably know me if you're here or else, please leave the journal alone.

(Next Page)

So, I'm writing because I need to let it out. This is about how crazy it was for me to fall in love for the first time. I fell in love with Ishan Raiyani. From a little trek in Nagaland that got us into sparks to an unusual encounter of each other's nakedness in Udaipur, we drifted and balanced but the very start was our city, Guwahati, where I properly met him as a friend, he is a true man, and my human book who made my darkest day bearable by standing ahead of me, he withstood to every stream I faced, mountains, and jungles. I might have been unable to support him at times. Yet, we grew together through the storms of life and he stayed beside me. I had once mocked Ishan with a very rare analogy of my own, where I mentioned he appeared like Zinc to me, yes, I know right? You must be thinking why of all the chemical elements - Zinc! The reason was vague but philosophical. But it's my way of looking at it, before meeting Ishan, I briefly dated a person who taught me how precious a human can be bound with selfishness, thanks to my parent's work conditions, I have traveled a lot throughout my small life and realised none stays till the end and more than that, there's no end- we create one!

Let me turn this into a more metaphorical image so that you can understand what I meant by mingling expressions of love, zinc chemistry of zinc, and connection. Ishan taught me how every sensation in our body, every moment of consciousness, is like a gift from our remarkably temporary bodies where our souls are trapped for life's span over span. That night in Nagaland, under the starlit skies, I felt acutely connected to the thought of how our physical forms or bodies enable us to experience life's journey, be it vision, be it speech, or heartbeat. So big story short - Ishan came into my life with a subtle impact, much like zinc, which is not abundant in our bodies but plays an indispensable role in countless biological processes. When I look at the world, the genders who talk about love in this harsh growing generation, their souls appear to be like zinc- not abundant in bodies but play an indispensable role in the process similar to them in society by creating stories/memories and so did this appear to me! Ishan's interactions with those around him sparked transformative reactions including mine. Though he was stable in his core identity, he demonstrated an admirable passion for growth – much like zinc's theoretical "yearning" to achieve noble gas stability. Who doesn't want to be the best version of themselves? When Ishan met individuals around him, his friends and lovers, he discovered a better version of himself just by being his unique-average self. Him showing up in my life was seemingly random as the distribution of trace elements in nature proved essential to my own chemistry. But later when we connected more often, I could picture, I wasn't wrong, we weathered life's storms together, our bond strengthening like a molecular structure tested by heat and pressure. What began as a whimsical comparison deepened into a profound truth: sometimes the rare elements create the most beautiful compounds, and the most unexpected connections yield life's most precious reactions. Zinc is not the rarest but indeed an uncommon element for the human body, followed by more unique, better elements around it (i.e. magnesium) but this doesn't stop zinc from performing its role. Although our body does not generate zinc in particular, it's like the life or journey of a soul, that blends into vital processes and forms relationships with other elements to preserve some important processes in our body. I suppose it was a random analogy but he remembered this, random as our meeting was, but love is supposed to happen! I might not have many expectations from life but with him, I have witnessed my expectations becoming reality.

Well, I didn't feel amorous when I first met him in Nagaland, but I was drawn to his vibe, his simple appearance, his influential thoughts, and most importantly the way he treated people (especially me!). We exchanged a few texts, but nothing seemed to be working out. He was enjoying the rain for a short time and when the rain stopped, I noticed him preparing some food to feed the people near the backyard of temples. Since we were communicating well in terms, I used to stalk him without him realizing it. I cherished looking at him as he distributed the *prasada* to poor people who would sit begging near the temples and one day when I was missing him a little. I got drunk after work, stressed out a lot, and called Ishan by mistake, yet that was my first move towards him. After this, he felt that our presence in the same temple in the entire city was something daiva (divine) but somewhere it was true (except for the timing that I matched).

Most probably, we were the only people in the temple frontside, as I had successfully diverted the priest to check the backyard, while Ishan continued to walk toward me. He smiled at me and I felt a wave of emotions that flooded my thoughts. I was wearing a rose-colored silhouette dupatta that matched the color of my lipstick, paired with a yellow kurta. The wind led the dupatta over my head to drop down, and I began to approach him while holding an umbrella. Ishan moved closer to me and my eyes met his eyes. I angled an umbrella in his direction. He cleared his throat as I continued to look into his eyes, and he noticed my gentle dimple. He kept noticing small details about my dress, my face and it felt so lovely that I kept returning to this memory of us. We stared at each other for a few seconds until he ran back to the temple backyard, where there was a small garden with jasmine shrubs around, he plucked a few of them and slowly adjusted them in a circular pattern on my little hair bun. Indeed unexpected but it was him! Well, I knew what he was doing at the temple but he had no clue, he smiled and asked, 'Marry me, Nysa?' as he held my hand over the umbrella handle and didn't let it go while I continued to look at him.

"Why" I asked with a confused expression.

"Cause I just prayed. And the highlight is: I prayed to see you today and here you are, so beautiful, so divine, right here with me. Marry me and I'd be free, free to pray for you every morning we spend together.So?" Ishan expressed that his expression appeared a little romantic. After a few seconds of exchanging some silent looks..

"Did you fall for it?" Ishan laughed at me as my expression turned from curious to annoyed.

In a matter of a few seconds, raindrops touched his white kurta, and his dishevelled hair, and the drips rolled by his chin. I was staring at his lips that were getting wet with the rolling drops on them as he twice spelled 'Marry me?' while I was preoccupied with all these distracting thoughts of us, he continued to flirt with me. Though my senses were busy thinking about him at that point, but I quickly grasped what he meant, and I subconsciously blushed, asking, "You think it's funny? Definitely not ...yet!" I cried with a little dismal expression. He crossed his fingers behind his back as if he wanted to lock the moment and his confidence drove my intentions.

We wandered from the temple gates to the market into an old cafe, exchanging tea cups while he shared with me, how he distributes the *prasada* to the people sitting around the temple and some of them even came out from their houses to wave him 'hello' as we walked across some familiar lanes, talking for hours till the late evening. I adore how quietly we made an effort to be each other's company with pure friendship, understanding, and no interference in one another's lives. This was one of those days when we did not want to be a part of each other's lives romantically, he still kept up with some pickups from time to time but I was always the coldest one. We stayed the same counting days as he was the man who lived rent-free in my heart. I could call him and talk whatever but he would always respect, support, and balance both our opinions carefully. I have started loving him a little more now. I remember once we were travelling on a train from Mirza to Kamakhya Junction, as I had some reports to collect for my office, Ishan insisted on coming along as it was a weekend and we were talking about his likes and dislikes, my biggest question was, "Why are you not hyped about cars and sports, etc? Usually, boys love and die for that?" He chuckled and replied in a sadistic tone, "I did not have much time to look for hobbies, to look for what I like, and when I finally looked at them, I was older, it felt like there are more precious things in life, two of which are feelings and people you love. So, I would rather invest in their happiness. Cars and sports are great but that entertainment is not my thing!"

"What about you? How were you, as a child?" He grew curious.

"I was..."

Before I could respond, I felt a man try to purposefully brush his leg with my leg; I was sitting and he was standing close to me; I tilted my leg towards Ishan. Ishan was noticing the situation secretly and realised the man was doing it on purpose; he called up the man to stand to the other side; the man shifted for a few minutes as I looked towards Ishan; he blinked to assure me and cupped his hands on my bare knees, making me feel safer. Ishan was so sensitive that he was checking on me minute after minute, so I continued to talk my mind out, without being defensive. It does feel good to have someone take care of you as their own responsibility. I was sure of one thing Ishan does not choose to escape situations, usually when children grow up they are scared to face their fears or insecurities be it love or loss. Ishan on the other side had never found a way out so he went through and this also dragged him into responsibilities. His words and actions made me feel like he was a child who didn't receive happiness, was never understood, and sought love from his own until he made peace to just give and not to expect, which may explain why he is so pure and clear about his life. I wondered if my lack of faith or empathy would worry him. Even during Arushi's wedding, he defended her, but he eventually gave up and fled. It gives me a bad feeling. What if he did it again? But sometimes, when I see instances like these, I believe he won't.

Yet, I was not sure of his side of feelings but my respect for him was way above any rights or wrongs, any guilt, anything temporary in the generation or any oblivion above materialism. I just knew I was in the process of loving him and that's why I guess I started to explore what this prema (love) andthepossibility of you can lead one to. I bet it is better than the reality of investing in anyone else. It's serious when I say that, my heart is a space where my love is limited to memories and this person had given me a reason to give love and not just to wait for receiving. I might have received love before but this time my satisfaction and devotion remain firm as I am growing into love with him. The fun part - when I and Ishan met after the Nagaland trip for the first time, I was there in his mind or heart somewhere which is why all of this 'us' came into existence but to share love equally, it is important to be careful and aware of what the side feels if only the world was so simple but I trust him because he lives with a faith- a faith for god and life. Loving him was not my choice but my feelings led, and it gave me a prayojana (purpose). I always wanted to express this to Ishan as he might have felt it too. I knew he would read this thoroughly one day.

So, Mr.Ishan, remember this, I have always seen people around me falling into a deep sense of hurting with an intangible situation when they fall in love, when they think it's their individual game but actually love is a life-ground for two - partnership is survival, people work their feelings through communication but the biggest turnover is when adjustment might become a compromise.

As everyone loved hearing about them...

(The next page in the journal opened with a title, 'Dear Arushi' and everyone was in shock.

Alia continues reading...)

..There is a phrase in Japanese *Koi no yokan*..which expresses the first sight of love and it's understood with the term premonition of love by the people. I, however, believe if a person considers himself/herself a *jogi* (contemplative saint) for love, the person has known a part of *prema* (love) then. Ishan and I had never known that we could be each other's pillows, rocks, and seas. That day, his 'Marry me, Nysa?' turned my memories to this time, back, when Arushi's memories hurt him and brought him to a monochrome dark world. He used to mention that he didn't want to heal because losing her to someone else was such a painful thing for him but that pain remained her last memory to him. I could never stand up to defend him on this, but when I heard him seeking to take me up and love me from where I am, I was left with no thoughts but his well-being. This pain that he is still healing from had brought us closer in these few days, yet we sought more, forgetting the fact that we had just a few more months before my arranged wedding would crash everything. I may live far away from him, but with my closet-like life, I could still read his unspoken words, I knew when he tripped cause of overthinking while we walked together, when he ordered too much spicy food just to cry comfortably together, and when he cautiously clutches my hands while walking across the road or conversing without letting go until we finish a topic. I just know all this...I also know that something is going on; something is disturbing his peace.

Oh, wait..wait..there's a line he used to always drag whenever we had little fights, it was, *Nysa...you know I cannot be always there for you, I cannot be always observing, I will give my 100, my best whenever and with whatever I can but at some point when it might become 60 or 20, please stay! Put your trust in me, 'cause I need you then.. until it's 100 again and I promise to heavens...that 100 will always be yours.*

When I asked him - *what's with the number thing?*

His reply was - *It's an estimate of my efforts towards you, full is 100, and rest so you know..*

This was indeed childish but it worked on me. Cause I know! Sometimes you are not ready for life to be this simple, especially with a person who does what he says. I knew he was fighting against a lot. And sometimes you just want to make a special space for yourself in the heart of someone you love, it is indeed natural. Yet, I just wonder if 'just staying' is possible when the person you fall in love with demands change, tries to introduce changes to you and you take it as the way they want to be loved. It becomes a complication indeed. Not everyone is clear about what they want but when you invest efforts for your love unconditionally, you may dissolve but you grow/ solve real-life problems. What was more comforting was that he had never hidden what we had, like just two souls exploring this connection and accompanying each other without the pressure of tags, nothing physical, what he felt, and how I felt his vulnerable side.

Dear Late Arushi

CHAPTER SIX

Dear Heart?

I had a good time with her, I think I know everything about her,

Did you?

Yes..

So, have you seen her naked?

Her smooth skin, the curves on her body, her makeup, and her non-makeup appearance..

..And what about her soul, her shivering in the cold, her encountering the truth of existence?

her unraveling dreams thread by thread,

Sometimes her silence did appear bothersome to me!

What about the masks she wears for the world, and the raw fears,old scars of battles she fought silently

Hopes she shelters, her heartbreaks behind a smile that says she's fine?

Have you seen her laugh? Her naked smile while she doesnt fake feelings?

Her unpolished visions and her beliefs about life?

How does she make herself confident, happy or self-sufficient? What she likes to do and what leaves her

feeling angry, empty? The darkness in her stories, and the beauty of her brokenness.

I'm a human, I feel that too..

So you should know, cause you said you love her!

So, tell me again, Have you truly seen her naked?

No...

I recall hearing about the nature of detachment and loss when I learned about Imam Ali, according to Imam Ali, "The key to eternal rest is detachment from this world." Detachment is primarily about realising that holding on to fleeting things just makes our pain worse, not about rejecting love or ties. He highlighted how the soul is put to the test by separation, which drives us to consider the real meaning of our relationships. Imam Ali taught one should welcome the hard time of separation with endurance and faith since every setback is an opportunity to learn something new and become closer to the eternal (a.k.a. Akhirah). We frequently find clarity or closure in separation but for Ishan - it's all thanks to Arushi, the first woman in Ishan's life who he loved romantically, she had made him a man enough to face life where situations are tougher. To me, Arushi appeared to be the person whom Ishan liked, and eventually, she grew into his memories, with her abusive marriage and her choice of staying in that marriage, she overlooked the fact that she was dear to Ishan.

He held a strong emotional corner of his heart, self-sabotaging and blaming himself for everything that happened due to her choices, irrespective of knowing everything. Ishan was devastated and sad about her, at times, with this, he got himself into guilt trips and had always found his way out through practicing positivity, spirituality, and dharma. Ishan even witnessed her being abused during her wedding, and this broke his heart as a good human being, as a lover, and as a person who respected her. He kept holding onto her memories until she left. This made me realize some humans fail to look after themselves throughout their lives or forget to care about themselves, but they eventually get attached to feelings that lead them to another person. I could tell he was attached, but I could do no magic to cure him, it was my helpless boundary with a shield of care.

After Ishan attended her wedding and returned, after three months to it, he received a box with a funeral invitation and a short letter for him. Ishan was never ready for it; he opened the short note as it read,

Hey Ishu,
I hope you're doing okay! If not, let me first teach you how to make a filter coffee that can make you feel better,
- Ground the coffee with a cascade of water and a gentle steam, use a brass filter, embrace the smell that flows, and close your eyes as you feel the melody of flavors around you, with a little warmth like your love. Swirl it in the milk, and allow the sweetness to mold, time will teach you how sweet you need your coffee to be. As you will also adjust to the fact to hug different cups, as your peace will grow the coffee!
Anyway, that was my favorite.
This short note is just a last message from me as I shall start my married life now.
I might not be able to travel to you or see your future baby, you would have loved them in one of their favorite aunt's arms, but here's everything I want to say to you.
If you ever have a daughter, make sure she learns what respect feels like, and she should never withhold her feelings or regret the wrong choices she made cause you're THAT spikey spooky dad.
If you have a son, make sure he learns how to respect each and' every soul that stands in front of him, irrespective of his ego or manhood. Don't be sad about our incompleteness, just be happy and be strong enough to give love when you fall into it.
Your Dear Aru

He drew out those sets of papers and a journal that was inside the box as he bawled like a crazy lover who just lost his world. He removes that old journal and dusts off the dirt, which had a vintage cover page with the words 'Fate' written on it. He hugged the journal as he stood in the rain for a while he sobbed and burst into tears alone. He was sent to a dark world with Arushi's memories, and his demons attacked him, saying, the only words I heard were, "The pages smell like you, how can I let you go like this..you do..don't..deserve...this, I know...I knew..it."

Even though he couldn't comprehend a word she wrote in the journal, he kept turning through the pages with Arabic notes, his heart devastated and eyes welling up. I felt terrible since the letters were for him, and he couldn't comprehend what she expressed. What if she was looking for help? Why doesn't he look that up on Google? I had a lot of mixed feelings a lot of questions, but all I could do was watch because it was his place, his zone, and he deserved all the time to determine what to do with the letters. Hours passed while he stood crying, her memories filling his head and her aroma weakening him. If only she was still alive, he felt so guilty, and the thought of her death broke his heart. But the bravest element I noticed in him was that he was so dedicated to his commitment, careful about his feelings, made me feel heard, and sometimes his efforts were extravagant.

To respect her even after she's no more, oh! This man was in my heart. I wanted to be his part of thick and thin while he wanted to be someone else, maybe that's the essence of selfless love. But I have my story, the untold parts of my life where the vulnerable part of my soul calls every sense off and plays a victim card. It's my fault if I put myself to be a victim, I know, and that's what Arushi should have also realised by now. I was hoping he could attend her funeral but as the letter arrived so late, he missed it...he missed his last chance to be courageous. I tried my best to mention Arushi as little as I could yet he was the bravest man for me. I wondered what if we dated but then I looked back at myself and felt like I had comparably very less to offer him. And it's not just me, it's also about him loving me back and dealing with his scars, he's just a boy in his 20s, how can he erase his scars and act mature every time? I could be overthinking this but I never want him to kill his inner child. Sometimes the world appears as if it is drifting apart just because someone special to you is no more. I have seen people struggling to accept and eventually, when they do, they build their escape rooms. Ishan did too. After all this hard time, he grew to be a great human, indeed a lot formal a beautiful soul who was sensitive, observing, and understanding. I was a viewer throughout who supported his change and we grew closer without any tags. I know what I am signing up for when we started growing closer, and every bond has its terms and conditions where there's just not the accept button but also a button called adapt, which is rare, but it is true. I sat beside him in the corner of his room where a paper lamp was lit with a very sober vibe as my sweaty fingers and cold palms gripped his shirt softly, he was sobbing there like a still person and bawling as he held Arushi's letter.

Maybe the great poet Kabir Das Ji wrote correctly, *The river that flows in you also flows in me,* which means that what we perceive in others, we also see in ourselves.

But that's what I and Ishan perceive in each other the best; this is not visible to anyone else. Soon after this wave of sadness, Ishan took some time to process his emotions and accept the truth about Arushi; as he felt helpless and guilty, I kept him company. He was a priority to me now. I knew how important he was to me, how important his innocent soul was, and the darkness of sorrows and traumas that wouldn't let him sleep, always awaited a pampering soul to feed its voidness. He had stopped eating properly at times and resisted leaving the house, which prompted me to see him more frequently. I supported him the best with whatever I could, while his parents understood me and encouraged my efforts to help him. That's how I just happened to grow closer to his parents, too.

With this, I recall Ishan expressing to me one evening about his meeting with a Pandit ji whom he admires a lot and how he met him from time to time. Pandit ji's advice had helped him to find direction from time to time even after Arushi passed away, he held tight to the values and learning. It was not easy, not everyone could stay stable at such times, especially when he was very attached, he was not complete, and he was not a great scholar but indeed he was able to give his best after such huge guilt had stomped his heart. One evening, Ishan finished the sunset aarti, and while walking back, he observed the familiar figure of Pandit Ji walking by a nearby tea shop. He ran to him and welcomed the Pandit ji with folded hands along with a made-up smile, the pandit ji recognized him as he could tell Ishan was unhappy.

They exchanged pleasantries, Ishan hesitated before expressing his sadness. "Pandit Ji," he called softly as they walked slowly towards the local market.

"What do you do when you lose someone you love ..forever? When all you have are their memories, and you know you'll never see them again?" Ishan finished.

Pandit Ji's eyes smiled, he felt Ishan needed his wisdom and softened.

"Prabhu, the pain of separation is universal. From what I have known and learned, I can tell you that the Bhagavad Gita's verse 14 (ch;2) taught that the soul is neither born nor dies. It never ceases to exist, those you love have their essence transcending time and form. To be clearer, the universe is formed of matter, which is made up of energy that has always existed, and it is the source of the Universe. Thus, the energy responsible for the physical cosmos was always present. As a result, we can conclude that energy is neither created nor destroyed. This is a fact, and time cannot change it. It is the universal truth. Substitute the term "Energy" with "Soul." I am sharing this with you wisdom so that you can realize to ease up that, she must be in a better place now, you have to believe in souls-existence within, it's true, and learning more about this will help you reason and heal.

"But Pandit ji, that's what Bhagavad Gita says, but what about other religious beliefs? How am I supposed to believe in different scripts, texts, and stories? Being a sanatani, I believe in my religion, but I am still confused about the right direction. Please guide me more with your best." Ishan reflected.

"Prabhu, I see that you are struggling with one of the most important questions in life. I would like to share some wisdom with you, not to lead you down a certain path but to help light your path. Whether you are in a large library, imagine that each shelf contains a variety of books of wisdom, some ancient, some modern, some discussing divine presence, and others celebrating the beauty of nature alone. Just as you wouldn't choose a lifelong passion by having someone else choose it for you, your spiritual or philosophical path should come from your investigation and sincere questioning. Start with your encounters and end your life with this personal belief, flaunting your belief wrongly, fakely or too unaware souls is certainly a path towards confusion.

Do you wonder at the physics that produces such beauty, or do you sense a divine presence when you watch a sunset? Does helping someone in need feel more like expressing our developed empathy or like carrying out a sacred duty? Do you find comfort in prayer, meditation, scientific knowledge, or maybe a mix of these when you're facing life's obstacles? Talk to people of different faiths and philosophical backgrounds, question everything, but do so with respect for both your doubts and those of others. See how each experience aligns with your inner truth. Keep in mind that spirituality and reason aren't mutually exclusive, nor is it a fight between which is the best religion, it's about balancing and co-existing with people who cherish their religion as a positive directive towards their personal lives or souls. Be it the oldest religion or atheism, everything is fair when balanced well." Pandit Ji elaborated.

"Pandit ji, how can I naturally understand and accept all this without bias or any judgments?" Ishan desperately questioned.

"Prabhu, I leave this up to your conscience to find the truth your inner self holds, but my hint towards this question would be that many find their faith reinforced by scientific understanding, while others find profound meaning and philosophies in a purely naturalistic worldview. Some find truth in ancient traditions from Vedic eras, others in modern interpretations and art forms, and still others in forging their unique life path. The most fulfilling belief system is one that enables you to live morally, discover meaning in life, and establish strong bonds with both people and yourself while retaining the humility to continue learning and developing. You don't need to rush this journey; your understanding will develop as you grow, learn, and experience life. Your understanding will evolve as you grow, learn, and experience life." Pandit ji entangled Ishan with a responsibility to find the inner truth as he continued to question his sorrow as he glanced down, his voice grew softer.

"Pandit ji, I still do not understand how humans can continue to live with the guilt or sorrow of their loved one's absence?"

Pandit Ji patted him on his shoulder with a smile. "Prabhu, you live by honoring your loved ones in your deeds. If you have done nothing wrong to them, they or their soul shall know that your presence was a gift. Not just Sanatana but also I can help you mark that Buddha once taught that we should let go of attachment but not love. Keep the memories without clinging to the hurt, as just like the soul, love transforms and does not cease to exist. Even once, the Dalai Lama repeated that love and compassion are necessities, not luxuries. Humanity cannot survive without them. So, the love you shared is still with you. It does not evaporate, but it becomes your strength and guide." Pandit Ji elaborated his wisdom as they reached the local market.

Ishan nodded and greeted the elder by joining his folded hands; his heart felt heavy but content. As they parted ways, he remembered the Pandit's comments. He looked to the horizon, feeling better than before, experiencing the bittersweet truth that love in us never fully disappears, urging us forward even in the face of irreparable loss.

While all this was going on, I was planning something up, something fun to divert him from; I do not know if my decision was correct! So, I asked him, "Do you want to come with me for a trip?' He said 'No."

I felt he might want to enjoy some time outside..(I was dumb, I know, but sometimes you can read through the person you like cause you are focused on them and have dealt with them at times, so I thought I was doing the right thing for him). I looked over a few itineraries, bookings, and places and planned a secret trip to Goa. Everything was on the way to be booked for the next week, it was half my salary, phew! But his priceless smile was all I cared about. I went to him the next day with the itinerary. He was fixing a weird box that was full of dust, he heard about my plan and screamed at me with a tense tone, "Nysa, why haven't you asked me before? Do you even realize where I am now?"

"I just want you to change your environment, Ishan. Look at yourself; it's been days now! You don't even look at me anymore, work/sleep. Is this your life?" I replied with a louder voice.

"Why are my feelings and consent so granted to you?" He asked me with a slightly angry expression.

"It's just my way to help you. You had so many days by yourself, I understand. She's not coming back, life's moving, and you know everything - the reality of life - soul, but your feelings are pulling you back.

When will you fight over it? We all, your parents, friends, me - we are waiting for you, Ishan!" I explained.

"Have I asked you for any of this, Nysa? You're just doing this for your satisfaction, and even you know, at the end of the day, I have to deal with everything. If anything goes wrong on the trip while I'm like this, I have to be the responsible cause...cause I cannot lose you there. I am Sorry...Sorry, Nysa, can you please just leave? I'm not going with you."

And he cried to leave him alone...I felt discouraged and left while trying to gulp my sadness and stop my tears while I walked back on my way home. I kept overthinking if I had done something wrong or if he was just talking to me through his grief. This introspection made me feel the same way I did when I used to be upset about my dad's absence when he used to leave me alone as a kid. With all these thoughts in my mind, I did not notice that Ishan had started chasing me by this time.

Healing Is a Process!

CHAPTER SEVEN

Dear Heart,
They say healing is a process mapped between one's mental and
physical flow
Yes, cause time bends, expands,
and transforms pain into something normal...
But why do we still feel the after-pain when it's about the heart?
Why do we not forget the pains that you go through?
Maybe I don't want you to forget the lesson you learned,
Then why did you cherish the last goodbyes
and not the regular presence of a person?
Even after knowing that the moments are fleeting.

The city hum filled the evening air as I ran down a dim street, after a few steps towards the street, I realised, Ishan might be feeling sorry and could be following me. I held my ego high and scarcely noticed anyone until a strange male voice cut my attention, a very new but harsh and demanding voice.

"You think you can just walk away?" he snarled, reaching out to grab me, I walked faster, and he chased me with a wind speed. It wasn't Ishan.

My fear paralyzed me for a minute, and I mustered up some courage to prepare a fist as I turned to hit his face, but his grip was untimed, he locked both of my hands on my chest and pushed me to a wall. His grip tightened, and I was struggling, all I could see was a man with a mask but a wicked man behind the mask. Before I could shout, another shadow flashed like lightning. I felt my ankles were bruised, but I struggled to escape. Ishan came running towards us, his calm countenance concealing the tempest that raged within.

"Let her go, leave her alone," he shouted while running, his voice full of authority.

"So, who are you? "Her guardian?" The man sneered and gave a dry laugh.

A hit to the wrist released the man's grip, and a sweeping kick knocked him to the ground, Ishan looked at me as if I was all right. When the stranger stood up, snarling, Ishan threw one more blow, a solid but controlled punch to the chest—that left him gasping for air. The man attacked again with a small knife as he was trying to get onto his feet, Ishan moved fluidly and dodged the knife effortlessly. He sidestepped the attack, his stance solid, his body coiled like a spring as they pushed each other very hard. I recalled how he was once talking about his months of yogic practice and the basic knowledge of body postures that he had learned through his uncle. I could see he had honed his precision about fighting, but how unlikely he used it as he believed in ahimsa. He kept checking upon me and assured me to stand still aside, I was worried about him getting hurt but I was sure that he would beat the s#it out of him. At one such moment, he deliberately made me feel protected, how the core importance of my existence is that someone has cared to follow me home back, check on my safety, and is now protecting me by crossing his boundaries.

His final hit on the face of the man was unpredictable, but this made him realize that he was no match for the boy, so he ran for his life. I stood motionless, with my hands quivering as I grabbed my scarf and wiped the sweat on my face. Ishan came running towards me and his warm hands grabbed my face softly to check if I was okay. If I was hurt, he looked at my bruises and frowned in sadness looking into my eyes. As he was about to hug me, I felt his fast breathing and my face felt wet. I called him in a shaky voice "Ishan..." My words halted when I noticed his raw bleeding knuckles.

"You didn't have to fight, why are you even here? Should have left me alone.." I dragged him by hand to a corner of a street light and he hugged me softly, edging closer.

"You could have just called for help or called me, Nysa" Ishan turned towards me and we sat on the footpath nearby, his expression remained calm despite the anguish in his hands. He noticed my upset look and tried to convince me.

"I'm sorry, I was rude before! I know you understand, but I need some more time. I promise we will go somewhere fun!"

"Why are you here, take your time!" I rebelled.

"I couldn't just stand there and wait, Nysa. When I see a woman in distress, I will fight not for violence, or bragging but to defend what is right. And when I like someone, how can I let you walk home alone and fall into trouble like this?" He expressed continuing, "You're the most beautiful human I've ever met and I cannot lose you like this. Do you know who that was?' his eyes welled with tears as he kneeled and fixed my broken sandal.

My quivering fingers untangled my scarf and tore a thin strip out of it as I asked him, "But what about you?" I was putting the cloth strip around his knuckles to stop his blood loss. My touch was soft, even reverent, as I feared inflicting him additional suffering.

He maintained a steady stare at me. "I'll heal," he replied simply.

"What matters is that you're safe. I will find out who that was." Ishan turned to me, his expression was calm despite the anguish in his hands.

I was not angry anymore but sad that I was not the one, whom he chose to be his escape partner or to stay beside his hard times. I did write him a paper fold jar of '6 locations we could visit', then '13 places to soothe my mind', and so on, but his response was harsh earlier. I felt like I was putting him under pressure. After that, we decided to get some fresh air because I was still in shock from the incident, so Ishan and I sat on a park seat nearby, talking about everything and nothing. I was happy! Yes, happy and in love to find someone like Ishan who protects me with all his heart, unconditionally, thinks about me and believes in his actions so strongly. I'm happier to be a part of his world. But as I laughed at something he said, a startling wave of dizziness washed over me. Before I could comprehend what was going on, the world tilted and went black.

The next thing I knew, I was in a hospital bed, with the clinical odor of disinfection filling the room. Ishan subsequently told me that he grasped me just as I slumped off the bench, panic coursing through him as he phoned for aid. He brought me into the Apollo hospital nearby, his voice was shaking with anxiety, tears covered his face, hands quivering as he recounted everything to the attendants. He kept holding my hand tightly until my stretcher was carried inside the ER. All my little consciousness could hear was the siren of the ambulance and the voice of Ishan who contacted my mother right away, but she was miles away so sent him some money via her bank account to spend on my check-up, medicals, and insisted that he must stay with me, the transaction took some time but he felt bad while receiving the money yet it was a part of the family concern, he understood the thin line he was on, picturing he should have been stronger for me.

As my mother's voice cracked over the phone, begging him, "Please stay with her, Ishan.
Do not leave her side."

And he didn't leave.

He sat beside me, his hand firm and reassuring on mine, while the doctor announced the diagnosis - it was Crohn's disease, an inflammatory ailment damaging my intestines. The doctor outlined the hazards, which included the possibility of consequences, including cancer if left untreated. It was significant but treatable, necessitating close monitoring and a small operation to repair the existing damage.

"The healing process will take three to six months," stated the doctor, "but significant improvement could show within two weeks if everything goes well. She had anemia in her medical history which was seen frequently and irrespective of that she ate so less, this could be a higher cause of this."

Ishan was not alone in deciding what to do. He sought some guidance and financial help from his aunt, who was a woman with extensive healthcare experience. She walked him through the care I'd require, from food changes like a liquid diet to managing post-surgery discomfort and a good routine to help me heal. At times his family would call and ask about me and he confirmed I was healing which wasn't true mostly but this kept from distracting Ishan and he kept working from my hospital room chamber, staying up at night, some days he'd go to the office and return late at night but he'd prepare my porridge for me with an alarm clock to remind me of eating, before he leaves. He got himself a little mattress beneath my bed in the admitting room, he used to sleep, cook soups in a kettle for us and help me most of the day, stayed up the night, woke me up at times, and eventually he started following a well-made routine which was important for me to improve, he was my lead. I was kept on steroids and at times I'd lose my mood, become quiet and cry, and suffer at night, he used to carry me on his back to the bed, some mornings he'd wear his big blue reading glasses like an old teacher with a stopwatch hanging on his neck. It appeared funny and he carried a small notebook to write the progress I made every day and most of the time he'd make me dictate the routine.

He often started with, "So, what's for tomorrow?"

"Wake up, breakfast and brush," I reply.

"Brush first. Then, next?" Ishan looks up and smirks as the glass on his nose hangs subtly.

"Medicines!" I responded.

Good girl! After which..? He cross-checked ahead.

Resting. I paused.

Two days after my admission to the hospital, when doctors decided to use anesthesia for surgery, they notified Ishan, but he preferred to shield me from the gravity of the situation by assuring me that it was a minor process, "You'll be fine," he said softly, stroking a strand of hair off my face as I slipped in and out of awareness.

For three days, he was my silent protector. We also did some slow yoga asanas that he studied over and over for me. By now my mother called him frequently as she was traveling back to the town, her voice filled with fear and gratitude for Ishan's devotion. It seemed bizarre, this sudden outpouring of caring from everyone around me as if the universe had surrounded me in a cocoon of concern.

After the surgery, the doctor verified, "Steroid medications are the initial line of treatment. They can alleviate symptoms by lowering inflammation in the digestive system, typically within a few days or weeks. These are frequently taken as tablets once a day, but in some circumstances, we provide them as injections. The regimen may last a few months, but it should not be discontinued without medical care." Ishan listened closely and nodded, but fear flashed across his features. Then came the mention of surgery.

"When medications fail to provide relief, surgery may be required. The most common surgery is a resection. To remove the inflammatory part of the colon, we make small incisions in the abdomen and use keyhole surgery. The healthy portions are then sewn together. It is performed under general anesthesia, while the patient is asleep." The doctor paused to let the seriousness of the situation settle in.." While surgery can reduce symptoms and keep them from returning for a while," the doctor explained, "Crohn's is a chronic condition, so symptoms frequently return.

She will require a few months to fully recuperate from surgery, although she may only be in the hospital for a week."

Ishan asked me every question he could think of, noted everything in a notebook, making sure he knew precisely what I was going through or feeling then. Despite the weight of the knowledge, he remained calm and composed. When the doctor concluded, he made one thing clear, "This will require time, patience, and care, but with the right management can regain her quality of life."

Loaded with this information, Ishan braced himself for what lay ahead, silently vowing to stay by my side at every step. How can I forget this? How can I accept this man, he's everything that a true soul in love is. Soon, it had been a week following my little surgery, and while I had made some progress, I still felt the weight of Crohn's disease pressing down on me. Soon my mother arrived, and checked on everything, Ishan and my mother worked tirelessly to ensure my relaxation and recovery. A week passed by, I got discharged, and every evening after work, Ishan would come over with some of his handmade Ayurvedic concoctions. On some days, he produced a soothing tea, while on others, he applied a thick and earthy paste that he claimed would help relieve my agony. It helped me feel better for a while. Ishan was my anchor. No matter how exhausted he was, he never wavered. One day, we went out for a walk. After many weeks I was walking, we walked, and the pain grew excruciating. I was breathing heavily, my body was spasming, and my eyesight began to blur.

"Ishan... I—" I could barely get the words out before dizziness set in.

His face furrowed with concern as he hurriedly looked around for assistance.

"Stay with me, Nysaa. Just breathe, okay? You're fine; just breathe," he urged, his voice quivering with urgency. But my breaths came in tiny gasps, and my vision blacked as the world spun out of control. Ishan did not hesitate. He ran to the car, muttering encouraging words to keep me awake. His hands gripped the steering wheel tightly as he sped toward the hospital, his knuckles white.

"Stay with me, Nysaa. Please," he whispered, his voice broke. By the time we arrived at the hospital, he was frantic. He parked the car recklessly, jumped out, lifted me into his arms, and dashed down the hallways like a man crazy. His cries rang across the sterile halls, pleading with someone, anyone to help.

"Please help her! Please help her breathe; she's slipping."

My mother arrived shortly after a doctor was able to care for me, her face pale when she saw Ishan, his face smeared with weeping. He was barely holding it together, yearning for reassurance and holding out hope that I could make it through. Three hours later, I awoke with the harsh aroma of antiseptic burning my nostrils and the hospital room's immaculate whiteness overwhelming me. My eyes opened, and there he was, standing behind me, his eyes red and swollen, his hands trembling as they held mine. But at that moment, all I could feel was exhaustion. As it was only a trifle to him, I would have gladly left my soul with him, but when I consider how he had been losing people in his life, I wanted to be more than alive and present for him. A sadness had fallen deep inside my chest, I never wanted Ishan to go through all this, especially after his heartbreak. My voice was faint and harsh, barely came out, "I don't want the world to remember me... not anymore."

Ishan's face dropped, and his heart broke all over again as he heard the dreaded words, "Despite my failure, he secretly promised that he would never give up on me. Not now. Not ever"

The doctor's remarks provided bittersweet relief. It was encouraging, the doctor assured us, and I would soon be well because my condition was stabilizing. It wasn't a cure, though, as medications were still required to manage the sickness. The fact that I wasn't going to get much worse for the time being relieved everyone's burden. But, as much as I wanted to be appreciative, a gnawing fear persisted in the pit of my stomach. The reality that I would never fully be free of this condition, that it would haunt me for the rest of my life, did not go away with the doctor's optimism. The room was filled with relieved sighs, and my mother, even the caretaker, was busy talking to Ishan's mother, who had come to visit me. I could see them talking, their voices calm, but my focus was on Ishan, who sat next to me, his hand softly holding mine. I could tell he was waiting for the ideal moment to say something—something he had been thinking about for a long time. He leaned closer, his voice a gentle whisper.

"Nysaa, I want to be there for you regardless of what happens. Trust me right?"

I nodded yes, softly. He continued, "Even if you are pregnant, I will be there for you. I want to take care of you through everything."

His remarks struck me like a slap in the face. My heart raced, my head throbbed, and the wrath flowed through me like an unstoppable tide. How could he say that? How could he talk about pregnancy and taking care of me when I was in constant pain and felt like my body was betraying me? It felt like an insensitivity that I couldn't tolerate. Maybe it was the steroids interfering with my emotions, or maybe it was just everything piling up in my head, but I couldn't hold back. I screamed, frustrated, "How can you say that? Do you know how much pain I'm in? What if I don't survive this?"

"You heard what the doctor said, it's not treatable! And pregnancy? What the hell do you know about pregnancy? What do you think it will be like for me? What's with this 'I'll be there' nonsense? You brag about death as the end of a life, right? That is where I am at, right at the peak and you're giving me some futuristic hopes which are baseless. Do you want to watch me in pain every day? Just leave—I can't deal with this right now!"

I saw the hurt in his eyes, but I couldn't help myself. The words split out before I could think. I fuelled my wrath by not giving him the opportunity to explain himself. He opened his mouth to speak, but no words came. He attempted to say something, but I was too overwhelmed by my feelings to respond. The door suddenly opened, and our mothers hurried in, alarmed emotions on their faces. My mother noticed the tension and entered the room, she swiftly turned to Ishan with her voice hard yet gentle. "Ishan, maybe you should leave for now. This scenario is already stressful enough for her." I could feel the weight of her words, but it didn't calm the storm that was still roaring within me. I couldn't force myself to apologise as Ishan stood there with a wounded expression and tears in his eyes, I really wanted to. But not when I was still too confused about everything, too angry, and blaming myself for not knowing how to handle the situation. As two days went by, the intense sting of my outburst faded, but the shame of how I had treated Ishan stayed, nagging at me. I knew deep down that he hadn't been wrong. He had only wanted to be at my side, to support me, even when I couldn't see beyond the anguish. But in my desperate attempt to shove everything away, I had created walls too high to see the reality. I wasn't angry at him anymore! It was just that the pain and fear made everything seem out of control. And deep within me, the worry persisted, "What if I die sooner?"

It was a continual voice in my head, a fear too great to handle, and part of me wondered whether it would be best for everyone if I just kept my distance. I didn't want to hurt him anymore. I didn't want him to be burdened by me, the uncertainty of my health, and the growing realisation that this wasn't a struggle that could ever be entirely won. It was hard to accept. So, I maintained my distance. I spent my days in bed, resting and trying to block out the world by minimizing my screen time. I asked my mother not to let me see Ishan. It wasn't that I didn't want to see him; it was simply that I couldn't take the notion of him gazing at me with hope in his eyes, knowing that everything I felt could be a lie. Ishan respected my decision, but I could sense his absence throughout the home. I had one of his purses where we added some coins like a piggy bank to invest, his brown scarf (smelt like him), and the notebook of my improvements -ah! I missed him, indeed. Sometimes I'd wake up to find him sitting in the doorway before he left for his work, looking at my window with stillness in his eyes. He never entered the gate of my house; he would only stand there for a brief moment, some days his tapping footsteps were a gentle reminder that he was still there, waiting for me to welcome him again.

It had been about four weeks since my operation. The world felt as if it were standing still, as each day went with a whirl of pain, healing, and uncertainty. My engagement, which had previously been only a blip on the horizon, was now much closer. My parents had postponed it by two weeks to give me more time to heal and relax. But, even so, I couldn't shake the notion that nothing would ever be the same again. My marriage, which had been scheduled for the near future, was now postponed for another three months. Everyone was making adjustments around me, but I felt like a ticking time bomb. The future seemed precarious, and I wasn't sure if I would ever have the strength to face it, with or without Ishan by my side. I was there but maybe we cannot force ourselves into our life spaces where there was no commitment. I know somewhere I was wrong but I also knew that he needed a part of time and privacy. After I asked mom not to allow his visit for so many days, he kept waiting for me, sent me text messages, and sometimes called me for 15-20 times but I was in my own world. Out of the blue, one evening he rang my doorbell. I was surprised to see him as I opened the door and he was breathing heavily. My days of love drama melted with the warmth of looking at his desperate eyes. I welcomed him inside my garden and we sat for a while worrying about each other. Just looking at him then, feeling his presence and his desperation turned everything in my mind to a certain peaceful flow. We didn't fight over the past, no guilts but only craved to see each other and he stepped ahead. How his ego would have stopped him throughout or did he just forget to feel his ego, I wonder! He helped me with making some coffee and asked, "Do you want to try some oat biscuits with your black coffee? Or maybe some healthy chana chaat?"

I nodded with a no and looked at him with a sorry face, his face was about to question me again until I said "ice cream."

Ishan gave a weird reaction "I have heard of coffee liquor but instant black coffee and ice cream scoop? Is that a match?"

We giggled for a few seconds, "Yes, that's a match and you will feel it matching more once you try it. I have read somewhere that marshmallows are also a good-to-go, I haven't tried that though."

He kept resisting as I brought a scoop of vanilla ice cream to share. I apologized to him and informed him that I was doing all fine along with my responsible medicine chart. He felt assured and hugged me as he expressed that I was rude and his ego did hit him but my condition and our bond as a team to get over such a situation is the real deal about being with someone. I tried to escape from his hugs as we joked around and ran around the small garden like two little kids. I felt at ease that he understood my boundaries and me at a core. It felt like I was not dealing with a boy, even though I had never had a great experience in dating but the way he came to me after some time, made me feel better. The way he talked to me, worried about me, and the way I witnessed his affection, felt amazing. He realizes that it's very complicated to customize a human in your life but it's more complicated when you make it a challenge or a tug of war between us. After spending some time with ourselves, our weird scoop-coffee combination. Ishan mentioned that he found something. I questioned him with a suspicious look, and he responded, "How about we go on a trip to Rajasthan?"

I suggested 'Udaipur, how is Udaipur?' (He did not question why, but for me, I loved how Udaipur was called a city of lakes; despite being in a state where you could see desert, the city was famous for its historical buildings and touristy artifacts; I had already visited Jaipur once, so I wanted Udaipur, this new city, to be one of our romantic memories.

He agreed, 'Whatever you like madam!'

Now the question for us was 'When?' It wasn't very tricky to check our schedules and match my medication timings, after a few check-ons, Ishan booked the traveling immediately, we decided to leave in three weeks, and a lot of bookings, itinerary, and finance handling fell into our task carts. Ishan's expectations completely overshadowed my feeling of anxiety and I loved the way everything was going. He took responsibility for the bookings and itineraries. I guess he understood that I was also busy with my engagement preparations. By this time, my wedding was in 2 months and my engagement was just next week. My heart was worried about Ishan and my to-be-fiance never showed up at my house. Ishan clearly knew I was not interested in this marriage at all but he did not know it was just a business contract and he was also someone who is my closest friend now. I did not know what was right or wrong but I wanted to spend these little moments with him. I was hoping to tell him everything while we traveled but I was scared how he might take it. But anyway, he started booking as we created a little travel saving pot of ours and he continued sharing the details, making short lists after discussing likes and dislikes. I was blown away by the fact that he's handling so much. It was also making me at ease that his corner about Arushi was not pushing him into being someone else or depressed, he was living as is, as she wanted him to be. Lucky girl!

I was indeed falling for him but everything was so complex that I just wanted to halt and escape with him. Days passed by while we enjoyed a cup of tea and imagined our vacations, and Ishan used to work from home at times, so we spent time to and fro, texted, shared street foods, he used to bring some healthy homemade samosas and I used to get him palak chaat, and days passed with this as we grew closer emotionally. Soon, D-day was here, I was expecting Ishan to help me out with something but the fact that I hadn't told him that this marriage was not consensual but a contractual deal, kept making me feel for myself. I could not muster up to tell him this and Udaipur was perfect to wait for this. I don't know how he'd react. It was an engagement, and I was as involved as my mother. I asked Ishan to come over to our reserved location, and he assisted the event management team because some of my relatives mistook him for one of the management team members, they kept directing him, and he foolishly kept listening; the man had no idea what he was assisting with! I did interfere but he was enjoying the decorations set-up eventually.

I know it's too early but sometimes I felt we should have discussed our plans. He told me once he always wanted to do a research course at Arizona University but he was still grinding for it, keeping a balance of his work. I felt I might be a hurdle but it's weird that being friends, holding feelings for each other and we skip this major life commitment aspect as teenagers. I know we might have awkwardly redirected the conversation elsewhere at times but now there was no use of it. My free-spirited mind found itself navigating complex emotions while I was getting dressed in my yellow kurta with a pastel shade and a Prussian blue border where the little mirrors were stitched to reflect the sunlight on my face as I walked outside. Ishan becomes concerned when he notices me with a tense expression, trying to fit in, he realizes that I am suffering, but he hides it behind a fake smile. That evening, amidst the celebrations, I knew if any change was possible to skip my and Aryaman's bonding, then it was now or never.

I found a quiet moment to speak with Aryaman (oh! Aryaman was my fiance-to-be) as our families were mingling well. I did not know by what means or how I could convince him about this mess. He and my mom had done their deal already and I thought he could be a good human too, he would let me go and keep this secret. I hope this manifestation works. Soon, I took a moment, tried to get a hold of Aryaman, and expressed to him my uncertainty about their future, my feelings about Ishan, and how I have been caught up in all of this. After a while, he took his time, but Aryaman misinterpreted the situation. With an unpleasant sense of entitlement, he pulls me towards a big curtained window, to speak in discrete, he declares that he claims me as his and pictures that he'd fix everything after marriage. It was a foolish and strange expectation of him, but this dude will not deliver, I felt I knew. In no minute, his face draws closer, eyes intense with intentions to kiss my lips, the air grows thick with unspoken tension as he leans closer for the kiss – uninvited, assuming. But I know my heart's truth, my commitment to Ishan, and with gentle firmness, I step back, turning my face away. Sometimes our hormones might find it hard to control or fight, in such a situation but I had always portrayed a picture of Ishan and me, ahead of all these minor problems/ situations, a beautiful girl always knows about the consequences of being beautiful (haha) and with this, I also know about the sudden difficulties that we might encounter. Irrespective of all these dramas, I wonder, how his nature of love had never disappointed me, never ever, even not a little that I could think of someone else in his place. So hormones? What the hell, it would be straight cheating on him!

As I pushed Aryaman away, softly- not to offend his masculinity, or create a scene before he could get ahead of himself. He straightens in the ensuing pause, comprehension showing on his face. No force, no rage—just acceptance of my decision, while we adjusted back with awkwardness. My uneasiness turned to resolve, and I stood severely shaken. I continue to ask him to leave me out of this marriage but strangely he excuses himself from me. Unbeknownst to me, Ishan witnesses the scene from a distance. Feeling powerless, he begins to question his place in my life now. He tried to confront me, but my attention was pulled away by the overwhelming demands of the engagement. As Ishan saw me from afar, getting engaged that night, he wrestled with the reality of my commitment to Aryaman as he felt like a nobody and yet appeared sad not angry or jealous, he felt that we shared a bond away from all the mixed feelings that could push away the wrongs of the world but we never confessed commitment more firmly. How can I explain this situation that's just happening, Ishan doesn't know everything yet..how can I explain this guy- who protected me, shielded me like a shell, loved me like a fragile porcelain, and cared for me with all his heart...that I only love him. That evening he promised himself to be bolder and even as this doubt or heartache clouded our present, I saw him leaving my engagement in mid-celebration. I thought it would all be okay as we meet in Udaipur soon, I thought I would fix everything!

What Happens in Udaipur?

CHAPTER EIGHT

Dear Heart,
I want to started believing people who stay longer in my life,
Is that for a lover's hand or a friend's warm embrace?
Both,
while in chaos I want to hear "I've got your back."
Through storms that rage and nights that ache
I want to hear "I've got your back."
in a world where hearts might break,
where people may cheat on other and where people might ghost you,
I just want to hear"I've got your back."
And alas, dive into their warmth of love that makes me feel you're
never alone in the fight,
So, do you have anyone yet to confess about it?
I don't..
There's a difference between romantic and platonic,
you do know, right?
I know, feelings might differ but
'staying for someone' remains the same.

After two days, we went through a cold texting phase and I was expecting to see him in Udaipur. I had taken this for granted: I had not paid attention to many small details, such as the fact that we had not met since my engagement, and I assumed he was taking his time accepting reality, preparing things around, etc, etc..maybe I was not a good enough person he could picture being with. I had yet not given up after what Aryaman did. Instead, I kept telling my mom that I needed some time to sort my feelings. I had no hope and no energy but just wanted to make more memories with Ishan. The evening after my arrival, I sat on the edge of Sajjangarh's walls, the cold breeze carrying whispers of an unspoken incident that had never happened to me before in life. Udaipur had welcomed me, but despite my heartfelt desire to stay until the end, he did not. The station's ticking clock had mocked my hope as I waited, dressed in a peach-purple kurta which he liked and a set of cool silver bangles matched with light purple eye shades, holding a few pages full of our bucket list. But still, he didn't.. he didn't show up at all.

Dear Girls! Is that even acceptable?

So, I did what I never thought I could, I boarded the train alone, dropped the list into a trash can mid-journey, and allowed the world to fade. The Musafir Hostel became my haven, a cocoon of strangers and laughter in which I spent the night crying tears of trust.I tried calling him, there was no response (worst part indeed).The next day, I met a local - Vansh, who was staying in the same hostel as mine. We strolled around the old city and walked towards the Fateh Sagar lake, while he told me about Mira and Arjun, who were lovers from two different worlds of the same society as they met secretly in a valley, while they developed a love for each other. Arjun was forced away to marry, and Mira's heartbreak flooded the valley with tears, forming Fateh Sagar Lake. Her spirit still lingers, blessing lovers who vow by its waters, ensuring their promises stay where her love could not. I was mesmerized by the beauty of the lake. I stayed until the night, stargazing while Vansh returned to the hostel.

As the lakes mirrored my stillness, their calm waters absorbed my silent questions. After a while, I planned to return to the hostel and leave the place soon. The next morning, I got ready with a yellow glowing kurta and the same silver accessories that matched my matte maroon-shaded makeup. Vansh asked me to join him at the Udayay Vilas to enjoy some authentic Rajasthani cuisine- Dal

Bati and Churma, I said yes. We soon reached there with a warm welcome, until I discovered Vansh's family was one of the investors to the Udayay Vilas, indeed funny but as long as it was a free tour privilege, I didn't mind. He was a great company and friend to me, we were talking about different cultures around India and how we shared a food-exploring interest, and as the warm food was being served.

I heard a voice. It sounded familiar, the voice approached me in a clearer and louder manner,

"Nysaaa, Nysa"..calling me desperately twice, thrice and I turned back pushing my seat away.

It was Ishan.

Him with disheveled hair, sweat dripping down his chin, standing breathless, as he approached me with a half-torn train ticket in his hand, a rubbish backpack, with a bunch of marigolds, and those old trekking shoes. He spotted me sitting on a bench, laughing softly with Vansh. Hope he wasn't insecure this time, but lol why do I care? He should've never left me alone. His steps falter, jealousy flickering in his eyes, but he swallows it, composing himself, and kneels in front of everyone expressing,

"I'm sorry...Nysa..look at me! I missed the train. Missed everything. Missed you. I might have broken your trust, and broken our promises but just give me one more chance..you've become a part of my life, and I cannot afford to lose you. And especially not when I'm in love with you, 'cause you have been the only person who had always listened to me yet you never asked me to change, Nysa, I had a situation- just give me another chance, I can explain!"

I was surprised as the smile on me was subtly replaced by unreadable emotion, the person you love is scared to lose you and is confessing his feelings but wait, it was still not an *I love you*, what does he mean by I'm a part? Just a part? Not a priority! And what in the world was he doing when I tried to reach him out? He ghosted me for two damn days and now he's here. Not forgiving.. I'm going through the most now. Vansh tactfully steps away as Ishan comes closer, Ishan was looking forward to sharing hellos later but Vansh gestured towards me that he needed to go. Ishan stood up, stepped closer to me handing me the bunch of marigolds, holding my other hand gently, placing his hand over my palm, expressing,

"For you...I booked everything again and ran all the way here, ' cause it's now or never, I don't want to ruin all this (he looks at me with a little tension), but ..but I just want to confess I was wrong. I was wrong about everything, I was selfish and I was a coward. Please... forgive me. You can ask me whatever you want and I'm here, holding you ..holding you to never let you go and to live every little moment in the present with you. I'm sorry Nysa but I know now, I love you."

I know right, it took him a long time but that's everything I wanted and I was about to be wedded now. His voice trembled as he apologized, each word heavier than the last. I listened in silence, my eyes were carrying the weight of hurt and my heart followed the love.

"Let's talk about it later when we are alone. I'm not forgiving you yet, for the rest of the time we have here, let's stick together." I said softly as I sniffed the marigolds secretly.

He had no hope but he nodded. Any little chance felt like a relief to him, his heart was aching as he realized this was all we could have been. I asked what, and he had me wait about two minutes. As he returned, he was carrying two clay cups, but he placed them aside on the stairs, making me even more inquisitive. He bent down and forced me to sit on the stairs nearby; he knelt on his knees and took off my heels--which weren't much--they were only 3 inches, but he noticed how my toe was set into a triangular pattern while my ankles appeared all red where the lace was tied...he took off the heels and popped out a pair of chappals from his pocket, expressing "we have to walk indeed, I cannot stand this, you're hurting Nysa!" I questioned him, "We do wear it for fashion. You cannot change it, Ishan!"

As I slipped my feet into the chappals, he smiled at me with a mocking expression, "I did not blame you for anything; wear whatever you want--I know you're a better judge of your surroundings and I know how you feel; anything but do not feel hurt. You may make it a habit to hide your pain behind your outward appearance, but I don't care about anything other than you--you are naturally more than gorgeous, bold, and my favorite diva. So, wear as many heels as you want, but allow me to change them for you the moment you feel pain. Just one gesture, that's all I need. Okay?" Then he carried the two clay chai cups ahead, handing one of them to me. I blushed for real.

He offered me one of the cups and explained, "It's called *gulabi* chai (rose tea). I didn't have roses like every guy does, but you'll love it and it will improve your mood first, I hope. If you don't mind, I may lead ahead from here, ma'am." After tasting the chai I was stuck, "How did they make it? Oh, it smells so good?" I questioned with curiosity.

"So, just imagine you're making a normal milk chai, add some cardamon, rose petals dried and fresh along with a hint of ginger, let them all boil with the milk, then add the tea leaves, sift, and you're done. I knew this was going to happen, so I watched the process closely, haha." Ishan explained.
I smiled and agreed with him. As a lady stopped near us, seeking money, Ishan offered her some snacks, while leaving she blessed us with her prophetic lines, *"Beta, Jeevan mein Maya aegi toh bandhan*

bhi aega, but bhagwan pe bharosa karna, vo aengey to har bandhan tut jayega aur bas satya reh jaega " (which roughly translates: People, Maya will come to your life but believe in god, he will come and once he arrives every materialistic attachment will shred and the truth shall remain.)

We walked ahead as I and Ishan dropped the clay cups at a shop's corner, and we noticed a small restaurant within a house where a small family was watching television. We decided to wait there, and have some snacks as we reached there..we noticed how happy the family was. They were running this small restaurant where none arrived much due to less advertisement. Yet, they were happy like those in fictional stories. Ishan ordered some *vegetable pakoras* and *an omelette.* We sat there for a while and conversed a little with the family as they told us how tough living was, during winters and how they survived through thick and thin. Ishan's comforting expressions kept changing as the experience he heard of, mesmerized him and he was the most curious human in the room. I loved watching him speak as we dodged reality, spent quality time with each other again and I kept on hearing his side with a calm smile. This made me feel better and I wondered how every human dealt with the balance between materialism and truth. I remember he explained to me briefly why he got late and a to z's, so the thing was, He awoke to the regular sound of his alarm, feeling groggy but eager for our upcoming journey together. He changed into my favourite shirt and sat down to recite his morning prayers. As he sought strength for the day, the gentle chants helped him to pray and relax. When he was done, he went to his mother and asked for her blessings before heading out. I'm going with Nysa today, Maa. With hope, he enquired, "You like her, don't you?" His mum sighed heavily before answering, her features hardening a little.

"Ishan, beta Nysa is engaged, even though I know she has been with you this entire time. It's time for you to let her go.

Don't obsess over her, she is going to be someone else's life now. Her words stung, but Ishan stood his ground.

"Maa, I love her. She loves me too. We're going to make it work," he said firmly, his voice filled with a mixture of determination and vulnerability. His mother shook her head, her tone laced with worry.

"Ishan, I've seen you cling to broken dreams before. Don't make the same mistake you made with Arushi. You couldn't win her love, and it shattered you. I can't watch you go through that again. I have been through so much in my life still look at me- I am not happy where I am, and this is a kind of compromise, don't confuse Nysa, you know her parents have found her a match and as a parent, I know you are not ready, son! I worked this hard, supported you all these years, did you realise if I had been myself then what would you and your dad have faced?"

Her words felt like a slap, bringing back painful memories of a love that had once eluded him. His mother continued and he kept shut, after a few seconds, her voice shaped - soft but resolute. "I've already started looking for a girl for you. Someone who will help you move on, will financially support your future, and give you the happiness you deserve. We're (dad and mom) looking through horoscopes from different companies. You have to believe in us.."

"Just like when you left me with Amma (grandmom).." Ishan whispered in a sobby voice.

"Ishu, my son, we had our careers- we were young, big dreamers and your dad has been supporting our dreams. We did what we felt right!" His mother replied with humility.

"Exactly Mom, I am young.." He expressed how his heart sank, the weight of the conversation threatening to crush his resolve. He knew he had to fight for Nysa, but his mother's words lingered, planting seeds of doubt in his mind.

Ishan took a deep breath, his mother's words ringing in his ears like a relentless echo. He clenched his fists, trying to keep his composure. "Maa," his voice trembling with a mix of anger and desperation. "I promise you, I have checked hers and mine - it's perfect except for some dots..so when I come back from Udaipur, everything will be clear. I'll bring a solution, and I'll bring Nysa along. Just trust me for once." His mother, unmoved by his plea, crossed her arms and looked at him sternly.

"You're pursuing a dream that isn't yours, Ishan. Nysa has a fiancé. She is going to be a different person- someone's wife soon. Why are you unable to see that?" Despite her scathing remarks, he remained unflinching.

"Maa, I can see more than you realise -we have our understanding. I understand how she feels, and I understand how I feel." With a determined expression on his face, he insisted, "I'll put things right. Wait for the right time- it's just an odd situation."

With a sigh, his mother's voice became more softer for a while. "What if you are unable to? So what, Ishan? You'll return empty-handed once more. You're going to break yourself again."

"I will not fail," he declared resolutely.

His mother, however, wasn't persuaded. "All right," she answered, hardening her voice again. You travel to Udaipur and take care of everything you feel is necessary. Ishan stormed out of the house, with his mother's permission, his steps fuelled by despair and rage after the ultimatum hit a chord. He noticed the clock quickly and saw that he was running late. He checked the train timings, which had already left him behind yet he ran to the train station with disbelief and hope. The weight of his mother's words weighed heavily on his journey ahead as the realisation that he missed the train. He inquired at the station's ticket counter about the next train, only to know that it was a day later, he secured the damn ticket and planned to stay with Vidur in the meantime. With memories of my engagement weighing heavily on his mind, Ishan sat on the edge of the station's bench and gazed at the floor. Vidur drove to the station and parked his scooter in the station's parking lot as Ishan had informed him about everything. Ishan finally talked to his best buddy Vidur, while the pain in his chest was too huge to diminish, and his voice faltered.

"Vidur, I can't get over the expression in her eyes that day. Despite knowing it wasn't true, knowing how Nysa is and how we feel about each other is so pure..everything seemed to slip out of my grasp. She grinned, but not at me. I still feel foolish now for continuing to cling on."

Ishan felt Vidur's reassuring hand resting on his shoulder. "Ishan, you're not an idiot. Although there are no assurances when it comes to love, if it is genuine, it is worth fighting for. Haven't you always had faith in your relationship with Nysa? You just need to confess to her, that's her! Get the clarity, bro.." Ishan nodded, but he was unsure.

"However, what if I was too blind? Too preoccupied with my own convictions to see what's disappearing?"

"You should stop there," Vidur replied softly. Even spirituality, your non-emotional mentality can occasionally distort your judgement. You overlook what's outside—the intricacies, the signs—if you are too inwardly focused. Let go of your ego at first, whether it is spiritual or emotional. Listen and be present, really present. The way will become more apparent to you. I know you can make a way out of it and remember you both are humans before anything else so submit if it requires to, it will not make you less of a man,' With a glimmer of hope returning, Ishan looked up. "Do you believe that I can fix this?"

With a comforting smile, Vidur remarked, "I know you can."

As they were talking, Ishan's phone rang, it was Ayush's mother. Ayush's mother was on the other line, her voice weak and filled with worry.

"Ishan, do you know what happened to Ayush? He was involved in an accident. He's asleep, and they're giving him an IV drip in the hospital."

The words sent shivers down Ishan's spine. Without hesitation, Vidur grabbed his keys, his mind racing with concern for his friend. Ishan swiftly followed, and the two of them raced towards the hospital, tension thick in the air. When they got to the hospital, they were led to a sterile room where Ayush lay on a bed with an IV drip in his arm and a band-aid covering his forehead. His eyes were closed. He appeared so vulnerable in that moment, in stark contrast to the typically bright and raucous guy they knew. The doctor offered a reassuring nod. "He is stable. There are no significant injuries. "He will be discharged soon."

The relief washed over Ishan like a wave, but when they reached Ayush's bedside, they could see the deep conflict in his expression, even in his unconscious state. His mother, her face covered with tears, stood quietly in the corner, observing them with tiredness and concern.

As Ishan and Vidur stood nearby, Ayush stirred. When he finally opened his eyes, it was as if a tempest was boiling behind his serene appearance. He turned to his mother, his voice scarcely audible.

"Can you leave for a minute please? I need some privacy." She nodded softly, her face a painting of concern, and stepped out of the room, closing the door behind her.

When they were alone, Ayush's façade broke. His face distorted with passion, and he burst into tears, sobbing uncontrollably.

"I broke up, dude," he blurted out, his voice heavy with anguish.

Vidur did not take it well. His jaw tightened, and rage filled his gaze.

"What the hell? You didn't even break up, I heard everything from Nandini and your office colleague. Look at you do this? Did not even care to tell us!" He stepped forward, his fists clenched in rage.

"You can't just do something like this and hide it from everyone!" Ishan added. He acted fast, placing a firm hold on Vidur's arm to halt him.

"Calm down, we're not helping him like this," he said.

Vidur gazed at Ayush, his fury simmering beneath the surface, but he said nothing. Ishan gave Ayush a chance to gather himself, his heart was feeling sad for his friend. Ayush wiped away tears, his palms quivering.

"I don't know how to deal with it, man. I feel like I am addicted to this negative lifestyle now.. don't know how to escape. " Ayush admitted gently, his voice rough.

"It aches a lot. And I had no idea who to turn to."

Ishan nodded and pulled up a chair near him.

"You turn to us, Ayush," he whispered quietly.

"We are here for you. We'll speak it out, okay? But no more hiding or suppressing it. We are your friends. We have got you."

Vidur's voice rose over as he turned to Ishan, his words laced with sarcasm and anger.

"This dude wants to write," he spat out, his eyes narrowing.

"Yeah, he wants to be a damn scriptwriter. See you didn't know right?"

Ishan blinked, his face a mix of confusion and shock.

"What? A scriptwriter? Seriously?" He had known Ayush for years, and the idea of him wanting to pursue something like that was so far from the carefree, party-loving persona Ayush flashed.

"Yes," Vidur snapped back, his tone biting.

"He wants to become a scriptwriter. But guess what? His dad shut him down, told him it's not a 'real earning job.' So what does he do? He goes and becomes a damn waiter at a bar to prove a point. A waiter! And now he's overworking himself there, running around, doing everything from washing dishes to serving drinks, pretending to be some '5-star chef' at home. All he does is overwork, write, and—"

Vidur paused, his face darkening with disgust. "—fuck around with drinks and girls like it's all some big joke."

Ishan's eyes widened as the words hit harder than he expected.

"Wait, what? He's doing all of that?" he asked, still struggling to fully grasp what Vidur was saying.

"Yeah, that's the sad part. He thinks it's all fine, he walks around like he's some kind of hero, but what he's really doing is just proving he's running from reality. He's avoiding everything that matters, including himself," Vidur continued, pacing in frustration.

"He wants to talk about his future like it's all a joke, but when you start walking on a girl's dignity like that, what kind of person are you, huh? Would you like your future daughter to like a man like you? Fucking new-generation shit, all talk, no respect."

Ishan's face turned serious as he processed Vidur's words. He didn't know all the details, but the anger in Vidur's voice made it clear that this wasn't something minor. Ayush had been hurting, hiding behind a mask of indifference, and it was starting to show in ways that no one could ignore anymore.

"Vidur," Ishan said softly, a mix of concern and understanding in his voice, "I get it. But we can't break him like this. He needs to set some terms and conditions for his life, this is so embarrassing, coming from him. We must help him face his demons, not bury them deeper."

Vidur stopped, the frustration still evident in his posture, but Ishan's words made him pause.

"Yeah, I know but you think your spiritual ego will help him? It was better when these social media and trendy dating things were not settling in our society, look at him and look at you. Never not the same. Does he even realise what it means to approach, propose, and wait for a girl of your love? That's the real deal man." He muttered, his shoulders sagging with the weight of the conversation.

"But sometimes, it feels like he just doesn't want to help himself. None is good enough to help him, maybe Nandini."

Ishan's eyes softened as he looked at his friend, who was clearly battling his own demons.

"I know, I'm bringing any spirituality here but no one can help him unless he wants to be helped. But we're here, and we're not going anywhere. That's something we can control."

Vidur didn't respond immediately, but the tension in the room seemed to ease just a little. They both turned their attention back to Ayush, who was now sitting quietly, wiping the last of his tears away. For a moment, it was silent, heavy with the weight of everything that had been said. But in that silence, they all knew something important: it wasn't about fighting or running away anymore. It was about finding a way to face what was really going on, together.

Ayush sat up, wiping his eyes and trying to steady his breath. His shoulders slumped as he spoke, his voice thick with emotion. "That was the past, man," he said, his voice cracking. "It's over now. I'm cleaner now."

Ishan leaned forward, confused. "Who are you talking about? You hurt so many girls just for you're a less of a man , they won't / might not trust guys anymore. Destroying yourself, your body health and definitely your dreams." he asked, his eyebrows furrowed.

Vidur, with a weary sigh, stepped in. "While Ayush was fucking around, he met a girl," he said, his voice tinged with bitterness.

"Her name's Nandini. She was... different. Competitive, driven, and mature about everything he wasn't. She didn't try to change him, not really. She just wanted him to improve, stop at future goals and support her along, THAT WAS ALL. But he saw it as a challenge. He thought she was pushing him too hard, she's toxic and complex to deal with, so he bailed. And then she broke up with him. Plus he also needed money to get out of all of this. And now? Well, now he's regretting it."

Ayush's face twisted in pain as Vidur finished speaking. He could feel the weight of the words pressing on his chest.

"Look at him now," His voice laced with frustration.

"Ready to commit, champ?" Vidur mocked as Ayush's eyes welled with fresh tears, and he looked at his friends, his voice shaking as he spoke.

"Dude, it's true," he admitted quietly.

"But look at my side, Ishan. My dad and mom don't support my dreams. They think it's a joke. They want me to get a stable job, do something *real*, and every time I try to talk about my passion for writing, they shut me down, so I had to pretend.I needed money to publish or even get on a track, I had none to ask for. And then... and then there was her. Nandini... She loved me for who I am. Not for what I could be, not for what I should be. Just... me. And she was so easy to talk to. She was intellectual, futuristic, way ahead of me in so many ways. And I just felt this ego, man, like she was challenging me, trying to change me. But she wasn't. She just wanted me to grow and my immaturity couldn't see through her.I couldn't see that... I left her too because I thought she was too good for me... She was so beautiful, inside and out. And now I'm just a mess, dude. I'm a damn mess."

Ayush's voice broke as he leaned forward, his hands gripping the edge of the bed.

"Look at me now," he continued, his eyes hollow with self-loathing.

"I wear a shirt, put a pen in my pocket to maintain my class, ink spills in the pocket. I put bread in the toaster and burn it every time. I go through the motions like everything's fine. But it's not. I sleep with girls like it's nothing, just to fill a void, and I wear like five layers of emotions, just to hide how shitty I feel inside. I know I need money but I do the least for it. I'm a freaking wreck. She deserved better. She still does. And I don't know how to fix this."

His eyes were distant, and for a moment, his tears stopped. The anger had left, but the emptiness remained. "I need time to get over this," Ayush whispered, his voice small and fragile.

"Just... just get me some coke, bro. Please."

Vidur shook his head, frustration building again.

"You think drowning yourself in all this is going to fix anything? Victimising yourself won't either do any good. You could have asked us for finance, we have been together for so long, there's no need to be uncomfortable when you know we have always balanced our friendship so finely, even less and more, thick and thin, we have been through it all. You shared a 10 rupees chai with us both and you think we will not help you thrive when you need us the most? Look, we're still here for you.." he snapped, but Ishan placed a hand on his arm, stopping him subtly.

"Let him talk his heart out," Ishan said quietly, his gaze softening as he looked at Ayush.

"We're here for you, man. You don't have to do this alone. Now, tell us what you need?"

Ayush didn't respond immediately, his eyes clouded with confusion and sorrow. He realised how few friendships remain so permanent that you can be vulnerable in any way to them, financially, emotionally, or physically, they would always stay without any judgments or blames. True ones never look for small excuses to leave, instead they build some, to make you stay and cherish while you are alive. At that moment, he felt a sense of weight lift off his chest, as though, for the first time in weeks, he wasn't carrying it all alone. Ishan sat quietly for a minute, his eyes looking at Ayush with more than simply sorrow. He could see his friend's anguish, the weight of sorrow, and everything Ayush had been attempting to bear alone. But, deep down, Ishan understood that drowning his sorrows in booze or allowing his guilt to fester and devour him was not the solution.

"Listen, Ayush," Ishan eventually remarked, his voice calm but forceful.

"You are not as lost as you believe you are. We can become so preoccupied with what is going wrong in our lives that we forget to look inward, into our soul. We forget that the answers are always there, waiting for us. Make a positive and negative quality-based table in your mind, see what's more?"

Ayush was looking at Ishan, his expression still twisted with bewilderment.

"What do you mean?" I do not see how any of this can be resolved, there's nothing positive.

"I ruined everything." Ayush sobbed.

Ishan shook his head, a soft smile on his lips. "You did not ruin anything, Ayush. What you're going through now is part of your development. Life has a way of throwing obstacles at us when we least expect them, and it's easy to become lost in the suffering. But the key to moving forward is to recognize that nothing in life is permanent, not even suffering."

Ayush blinked, unsure where this was headed, but Ishan persisted, his tone firm and encouraging.

"The thing is, you're so focused on what you've lost and what you think you've failed at, what's negative, that is where you're missing the bigger picture," Ishan told me.

"Your dreams and enthusiasm are not gone. They're still there, deep within you, waiting for you to reignite them. Ayush, Nandini was never supposed to fulfill you. She was meant to show you a mirror and help you see your own potential. But you didn't have to rely on her to determine your worth. If you want to pursue her, be honest with her. You how we guys are, you have control over you, think when you have a daughter or sister and you treat her like every girl you treated in the past, that's so wrong. You have to slowly change yourself, and see that realization is the first step, you are here already!"

Ayush's face softened slightly, as though something was slowly starting to click, but he still seemed lost.

"But I messed up, man. I pushed her away. I wasn't ready to look at my lifestyle, I feel like an addict to this. How can I be a better person for her?"

Ishan nodded. "You were not prepared, but that does not mean it is too late. If there is one thing I've discovered, it's that time heals. And you can only recover if you stop avoiding yourself. You must accept where you are right now.

And that includes forgiving oneself for past faults because you cannot alter them. "All you can do is go forward."

Ayush exhaled, pointing towards the saline that was on its last drops, his head lowering into his palms. " Even the saline drips here are not with me, how can I expect her to. I don't know how to move on or ask her again?"

Ishan placed a hand on his friend's shoulder, a soothing gesture that screamed volumes. "You start small, set your terms and conditions that lead you towards something positive, not all this, you are way mature now, respect what or who you have in life. Take one step at a time, be grateful, and plan to reconnect with your passion and dreams. Don't let anyone, including your parents, convince you that you can't be who you want to be. Don't consider Nandini a loss, she can help you in this, to set your terms - limiting alcohol especially. Just think of it as a lesson or chase, if it's meant to be then there's a chance she might see your truth. You are learning how to grow and become a better version of yourself, it's okay. And if it is meant to be with her, it will happen. But first, you must be completely well. You need to be ready."

Vidur's frustration calmed as he reclined back on a chair as he sat, his voice continued with concern,

"You know, Ishan," he continued, "when someone gets caught up in certain habits or lifestyle—be it smoking, drinking, or anything else, the world is quick to point fingers.

They say, "Stop it." Fix yourself. But nearly no one asks, "Why did this start? What are you trying to get away from?"

Ishan and Ayush stared at him, fascinated.

"You think it's all escapism?" Ishan queried.

"It isn't just an escape, it's a coping strategy. Unresolved grief, unmet needs, or emotional gaps, all these are frequently the fundamental causes of addiction or habitual behavior. It is way deeper, not casual. I once read that Mr. Carl Jung observed and stated Until you make the unconscious conscious, it will keep directing your life!"

"Why so scientific dude?" Ayush added. Vidur gave him a death stare as Ishan continued to ask...

"So what you mean to say is people do not adopt these habits for no reason. They're attempting to soothe something deeper, something they may not even comprehend themselves. So we need to know 'What's hurting Ayush?' rather than, 'Why is he doing this?' "

Ayush hesitated and remained silent for a minute, allowing Ishan's words to sink in. "You're right," he finally said.

"Perhaps understanding, rather than judgment, is what the world needs more of. Someone who truly listens." Ishan grinned slightly.

Ayush gazed at each of them, how the hospital room had become a knowledge center with espresso shots of guilt filling inside him. His tears slowly stopped as the weight of their support settled. He felt better although something clashed his mind..

"And what if I'm not prepared? What if I can't get through all of this?" Ayush questioned.

Ishan smiled warmly, his voice full of kind wisdom. "Ayush, start it when you are ready, you will know. Trust yourself. Trust in the process. Life isn't about knowing all the answers right now. It's about learning and growing, which occasionally entails making a few mistakes. But that does not make you any less deserving of love, success, or peace." Ayush nodded slowly, the weight on his shoulders remaining yet slightly lighter than before. He felt as if, for the first time in a long time, he was being seen—not just as someone who had made a mistake, but as someone who could be forgiven. Despite his brokenness, there was a glimmer of relief in his eyes, he wasn't alone in this as they were to listen to him after everything happened.

"Thanks, Ishan, Thanks Vidur.." Ayush said quietly, but sincerely.

Ayush was so inspired that he called Nandini right away, Ishan was about to leave but Vidur stopped him.

"Hello.. Good Evening?" Ayush greeted in a shaky voice.

"Hey?" Nandini replied to his call.

"Nandini, actually I am at the hospital right now, I will share your address, can we have a chat, please?" Ayush requested.

"Oh, Is everything okay, Ayush? I'm really sorry to say but I'm with my boyfriend right now, I can visit you tomorrow if it's not urgent!" Nandini expressed.

Ayush was shocked by whatever this was, Ishan and Vidur started laughing at him as the girl he wanted to chase was already taken.

"I needed to hear that." Ishan nodded with a big laugh! I'm always there for you, man. Start with your anti-alcohol movement.. Haha!" Ayush rested on the bed, letting out a quiet sigh as if he witnessed an old World War 2 clip. Ishan sat near the edge of Ayush's bed, his journal open on his lap and his pen motionless. The vibe was dense with the smell of moist medicinal smell, but his mind was elsewhere. Ayush expressed that ahead, for weeks, his life had felt like an unravelling thread—work stress, failed relationships, and a growing estrangement from his sense of self. Everything he touched seemed to shatter, and Murphy's Law hung over him, 'Anything that can go wrong, will go wrong.' It felt like the universe was out to get him and he needed to set some terms, to accept what reality was, to revert from negativity to a better version of himself. But because of

Nandini, something did change - his gym motivation was upgraded to 2x now.

He mentioned how he met her through an unplanned encounter with an elderly bookseller. Ayush had stumbled into the dusty shop to avoid the rain, and so did Nandini. She gave him a philosophy book. "Choice," thinking he was the owner of a bookshop and he replied simply," The only real thing we own." Ayush expressed and Ishan scoffed with a sarcastic look. That evening, as he read the entire book in his dimly lit room, something snapped his heart and he kept thinking about how beautiful she looked with rosy cheeks blushing in cold that she kept biting momentarily, her moist curly hairs covering her mirror-worked earrings, disturbing the mole at the right side of her neck, her fair complexion and pulpy rose lips held another translucent mole on her upper lip, and her big dark green eyes looked at him with a different sensation. Ishan began to realise that Ayush had allowed his circumstances to define him, and had succumbed to the weight of his failures rather than setting his terms to live, learning from past mistakes. He felt, that we just don't believe in discipline but not having one is also not wrong, as long as you hold to your terms and conditions.

After he had expressed all this, He added, "You know Nysa, after loving Arushi and getting my heart broken on her wedding day, I did not think that I would ever need anyone. Like NEED! And then I met you, we became friends, we clicked well, and until a few weeks ago, I thought I couldn't fall in love or that I didn't need anyone longer because every time I see someone, it's the same painful story, and I'm not sure if I can take another heartbreak. I assumed for a brief second that someone would approach me using the phrase "love" without knowing it, and the inner child in me would be delighted to be loved and cherished, but what if their priorities shifted and my unconditional love and efforts were twisted? I would be abandoned again, but when I met you, I knew that all the contrasts I was thinking about, life may. But when I met you, I discovered that all of the opposites I was thinking about were true: life can be better, and I can still love someone unconditionally who will never criticize me for being myself."

I felt he was fighting through a lot, his Arizona dream, Arushi's memories, and then us, so I let my grudge go. We walked aside the river where I found a few children playing with pebbles (we learned that it's called *Kancha*), Ishan observed the same thing, and we both smiled; it transported us back to our childhood memories, and we sat by the riverbank, enjoying the game and beginning to share about our childhood experiences with the game as the sunset. Ishan wanted to stay there a little more to meditate. We adjusted our lowers, sat by the Fateh Sagar Lake bank, and meditated peacefully in our ways for half an hour. We returned to the hostel for some supper, but in the meanwhile Ishan suddenly received a call, and I suspected something had happened to him. He appeared troubled while speaking on the call, which concerned me. I felt he was present with me, but something had triggered him severely as he dropped the call in silence and tried to lock himself up in a room. For the time, I remained quiet as a lot was running through my mind, a lot of questions that I wanted him to answer, but he was my priority, and every concern was about him. After his call, I calmly asked him, "Hey, are you okay? Do you wanna talk?"

He nodded, biting his lips and scratching his hair. We headed to the roof of the hostel, where there was a restaurant. As we ordered something to eat, I asked him about what was going on.

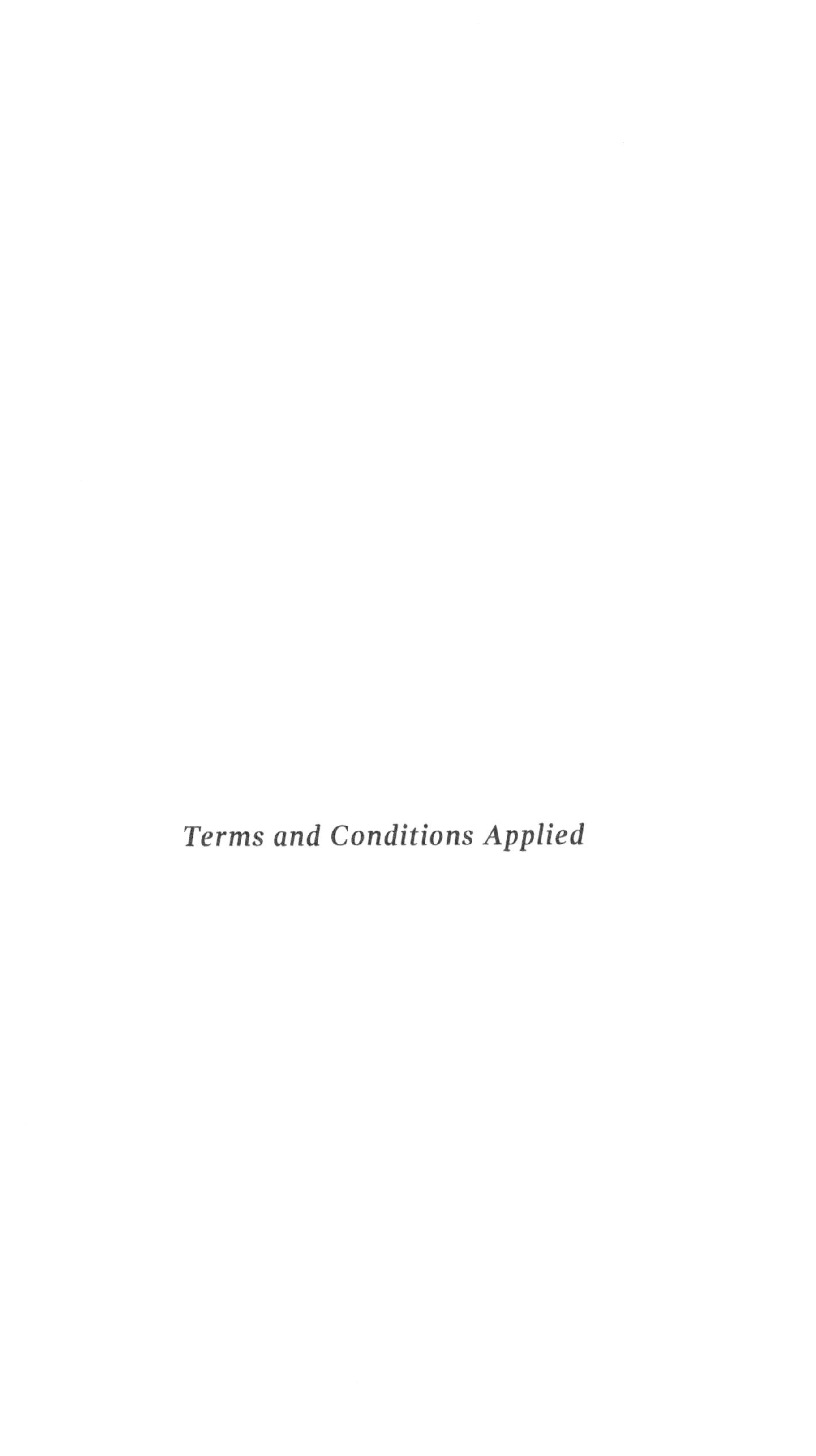

Terms and Conditions Applied

CHAPTER NINE

Dear Heart,
Did you know?
Life comes with small surprises, dreams, and hopes.
It comes with voids, nothingness, and possibilities too,
Yet being kind, being meaningful, and remaining positive till we hit zero
is crucial.
It's all a lie!
Wake, work, eat, and repeat—here's your fate's woven disguise.
Terms and conditions in life are well-printed lies.
Why would you say so? I still have hope..
Hope is good but expectation is not,
kill that mockingbird in you - that says you have to live without terms
and conditions..
What If I do not?
The paradoxes will gulp you in..

He expressed that the call was from his home, his parents wanted him to marry someone from their knowns and he was disturbed by this sudden pressure of expectations. Ishan was feeling distressed as he liked me very much and wanted us to grow together until we decide anything. We sat across the roof after our dinner, sharing a moment of silence. We both knew where everything was going, and where we should be, but yes, we liked each other. I was wondering about the possibilities. We walked to our hostel room as he went down to sleep. I spent some time under the stars outside writing my thoughts in my phone's notes. The same night I found him in the toilet sobbing alone, questioning himself 'why' as I slowly opened the door, walked towards him, knelt on my knees and held him close to my chest, feeling the pain his tears express. His face was red as a cherry punnet, his hands were sweating, and he wept, "It's..just..tt..aa..anxiety, I'm okay Nysa, I'll get some air, can you please leave me alone for some time...see Nysa, I'm sorry."

I hugged him tighter, I knew that maybe I was overestimating this love somewhere but it is what it is and slowly he stopped sobbing as he hugged me back for a few seconds. My heart said he needed me but then he tried to untangle my arms, slowly pushed me back towards the wall, cuffed my hands to the wall with his grip, and stood as close to me as I could feel his heavy breath over my lips. I looked at him, his teary eyes, his sweating hands, and his warm gaze dove straight into my eyes, expressing himself in a shaky voice, "I don't know what's going on Nysa...I love you, and I love you so much now, I don't know everything about you but I know you're the one for me and we can keep growing/sharing, I have no reason to hold you back because of my stupid feelings and this tension between us, should we stay apart? I just keep craving to see you day and night! It's hard to control myself, away from you. I cannot stay apart from you and I don't want to pressurise or terrify you, but this is just me and you. We need to find a way out of all this!"

As he slowly released my hands, which made me feel a bit strange I waited for a few seconds, expecting he'd talk more or hug me or anything..but my heart led and I left the room with a weird impression. I knew I would have lost my words if he were there in tears, right in front of me. He sat down on the floor, banging his back to the wall. I shut the door and sat on the other side of the door, saying, 'Ishan...I love you...but his shaky voice interrupted, "Not now, Nysa. I can't."

The silence between us grew heavy as if the door wasn't just wood but the weight of everything, we'd left unsaid. Our I love you(s) expressed how deeply we stood to affirm each other and only cared about the souls. We sat on each side of the bathroom door for a few more minutes, sharing a calm silence...I pressed my forehead against the cold surface of the door, my eyes were noticing the cracked paint lines on the wall in front of me.

I tried initiating again.."Ishan, you can't keep shutting me out like this.."

I muttered, my voice shaking from the exertion of fighting back tears. I knew his quiet wasn't resistance; it was his way of drowning, drawing himself into a whirlpool he didn't think anybody could enter, while my fingers trembled as they traced invisible lines on the wooden surface. I envisioned him sitting with his head in his hands, the weight of his thoughts pushing him to the floor. He was a fortress, erected not for strength but for defense, concealing a maze of worries and guilt that even he couldn't comprehend.

"It's not just about you, Nysa," He finally whispered through the door.

I replied, my voice soft but firm. "For now, I just need you to let me in, even if it's messy. I don't care about anything else right now, but your heart. I can see that you're hurting, come on.."

He explained further, "It's about me. I don't even know who I am anymore. I have never been this unstable, or over-concerned and I think we should set some terms and conditions between us, just for some time until we sort out our marriages. I know what I want, I know what I can do or should do but I'm a human too, I don't know where I am heading with all this."

My chest tightened as I realized his distance wasn't rejection; it was a layer of protection for him, and maybe even mine. "I don't need you to know everything, or solve it instead, I just want you to be with me, that's all on my terms, for whatever it takes, just promise me you will be okay, Ishan." I left as there was no reply from his side.

Ishan and I decided that we would return home and consider our options. I felt like a stranger or an intruder as I traveled back with him, just observing how the wind blew his hair back as he adjusted himself on the train seat, yet his protective side rested his hands on my waist while the angry young man was enjoying the window seat. I loved staring at him, as he was deeply into his thoughts. We did not speak much but somewhere, I knew that all he wanted was time to battle his thoughts, and his response to that has somehow buried my side of expressions. He didn't enquire much, and I was unable to share my thoughts with him. The silence stretched, thick with the complexity of two people trying to navigate a storm they didn't fully understand. I stayed there, anchored to the door, hoping he'd find a way to unlock his own. I was scared a little, to be honest, if we'd be able to fix things or not.

(As Nysa's journal was being read, suddenly Vidur got a call from Ishan and he spoke about his arrival. Ayush and Alia wanted to discuss the matter. Alia stops reading and smiles...Vani looks at Alia with a shocked face, Alia teases her ..

"You sure weren't an outcast, but we want to talk about the next' Vani smiles with reassurance and everyone sits back to hear the story ahead."

So, after they got back from Udaipur, we all gathered around an old café near the college called Primrose and shared a few steaming cups of chai as we sat untouched between them. Nysa fiddled with the engagement ring in her hand, its sparkle was a painful reminder of what lay ahead. Ishan stared out the window, his jaw clenched, as though searching for plans to neutralize finances. Vidur got up in between all these and suggested "Guys, let's try confessing to your families or family members?"

Nysa added, ' I cannot, no..no..no my parents do not live here and I share a very formal bond so..bad idea. It's a death trap.
We can try something else, maybe for Ishan.'

Ishan was not confident but everyone insisted and the next day he took us all to his house, what we noticed was way more draining, Ishan's mother was busy attending to guests and she was stuck with the preparations, her expectations belittled our hopes to convey her anything emotional. So we decided to start with profiling, Nysa and Ishan gathered information about their fiances,

"We're such a mess," she said finally, her voice barely above a whisper.

He turned to her, his eyes softening. "Yeah, a complete disaster. But... it's still us, isn't it?"

Her lips curved into a bittersweet smile. "It's still us." A moment passed before he leaned forward.

"Nysa, I don't know how we're supposed to just—pretend this doesn't exist.
But I can't ruin your life. Or mine. We have responsibilities now."

She sighed, her fingers tracing circles on the rim of her cup.

"We can't change what's ahead, Ishan. But maybe we can help each other get through it?"

He nodded, his gaze steady.

"A plan, then. We deal with this together. A way to... compartmentalize the feelings."

She laughed softly, through her eyes glistened.
"You make it sound so simple."

"It's not. But we owe it to ourselves to try."

They spent the next hour outlining an unspoken agreement which was about being honest as it got too hard, reminding each other of their chosen paths, and most importantly, being there if one faltered. It wasn't closure, but it was a start. We all considered many possibilities, such as kidnapping Nysa's fiancé, sitting at a round table of honest talks with Ishan's to-be-fiancé, crashing their weddings, saving the money lost and running away, or simply confessing to the families; each trick and tip had more consequences, with the bonus of disrespecting the parents' choices, and in Nysa's case, it was far worse. So, after a long time, we stepped out into the cool night, Nysa and Ishan's unspoken bond wrapped tightly around them, a fragile shield passed against the messy world waiting to tear them apart. Ishan had always been enchanted by Nysa's vibrant energy, her enigmatic smile, and the way she seemed to light up every room. Yet, something about her had always seemed just out of reach to him.) Alia looks out for a page with a date and continues the conversation by putting the journal closed, So, that day, curiosity got the better of him as he trailed her from the café where they had parted ways, staying just far enough behind to avoid being noticed. When Nysa turned the corner and disappeared into her building, he hesitated. Then, as if fate compelled him, he followed. But she caught him mid-step.

"Ishan? Are you... stalking me?" Her voice was incredulous, her face a mix of shock and confusion.

He stumbled over his words. "I just... I wanted to talk. To understand you better. Please, let me come in."

Reluctantly, she sighed. "Fine. But this better not become a habit.'

She looked at him nervously in the eyes as if she was hiding something from him."

He had never entered the backyard of her house as they used to hang out in the garden, Nysa led him through the huge backyard into her airy flat with modern decor. A few things appeared changed, he noticed the average beige Toyota Corolla in the parking lot of the backyard, he had never entered her house until then, it was just the hall and the garden talks. Everything appeared different from the backdoor, the art on the walls to the perfectly placed furniture in the hall room. Nysa busied herself in the kitchen, preparing some coffee, as he wandered in the hall, something caught his eye: a photograph perched on a corner table. In it, Nysa was arm-in-arm with a man, Ishan instantly recognized the guy (Vansh)she had spoken to warmly during their trip to Udaipur when he arrived. The realization stung.

"Who is this?" he asked as casually as he could manage.

She glanced over briefly. "Oh, that's... just someone I got to know a while ago, he's my mother's friend's son. Why do you ask?"

Ishan didn't respond immediately. Instead, he wandered further, his mind churning. Nysa pointed him down the hall as he asked to use the restroom. Inside, he splashed water on his face, trying to clear his thoughts and think clearly. Then, a glint caught his eye. Peeking into a half-open drawer, he found something he didn't expect: a sleek black Glock 19 gun with no bullets but an empty case along with it. His heart raced as his fingers hovered over it and he was curious, what must be the need to this extent? Why would Nysa, the carefree woman he thought he knew, keep a gun? Is this for real, he was more worried than scared. His hesitation weighed heavily on the room. The walls, books, and papers were strewn around the desk as he came out, the result of an agitated mind unable to concentrate. A cold cup of coffee lay abandoned near the edge, its dark surface rippling slightly when he shifted in his chair. Ishan cast a short glance at it before returning his gaze to the journal. The words that were not present felt louder than any that might have been. He hadn't meant to think of her tonight, hadn't meant to allow Nysa's memory to sneak in like a thief and take his attention. But it had been this way for real now, she was waiting for Ishan to come out of the washroom, and she stood in front of a painting—a wild splash of reds and yellows that he didn't like but the way she stared at it, as if she saw something no one else did, had stopped him in his tracks. He hadn't intended to speak to her, but the words came out, awkward and hesitant, yet enough to entice her into a conversation that lasted the entire evening. Nysaa hesitated, her hand instinctively scratching her nail ends. Ishan's gaze was sharp yet trembling, betraying the nervous energy he walked towards Nysa and softly stopped her from scratching, keeping her palm on his right hand and pressing his left hand over it. Her voice sounded curious but firm as she asked,

"Is everything okay?" Handing him the cold coffee cup.

Ishan's voice was steady, but his thoughts weren't. "Nysa, is there something you're not telling me?"

Her eyes flickered with something unreadable fear, perhaps, or a calculated calm.

"Why would you think that?"

Ishan took a sip of his coffee, already knowing tonight would reveal truths he wasn't ready to face.

(Alia stops for a while to breathe...a voice from behind her interrupts her 'Let me continue'...Everyone turns around and sees Ishan standing. He was drenched in rain as he entered the room, and everyone gasped and was stunned; he looked at Alia with a tense expression, as if he had lost something very important but couldn't talk about it out of embarrassment.)

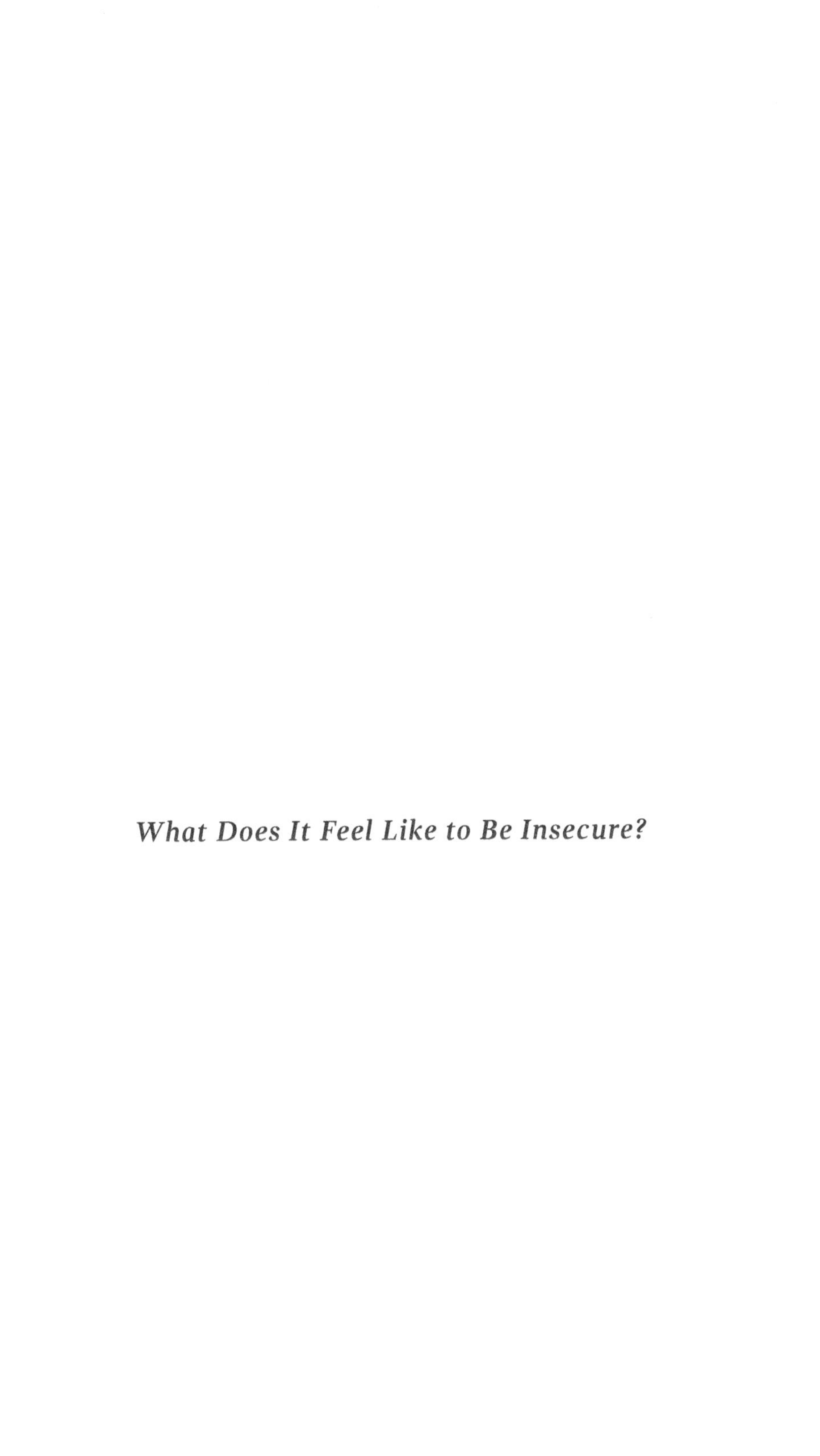

What Does It Feel Like to Be Insecure?

CHAPTER TEN

Dear Heart,
She brushed her hair on my warm bare arms, beneath my strong biceps,
a quiet fear called me into its darkside,
And what did you see?
A mirror,
Mirror of what?
A mirror where a man's demon hid behind her reflection,
The demon softly questioned,
Am I enough for her? or not?
She headed towards me, the demon gripped her with his doubts, a storm
of questions,
hideous judgments and built a wall around her, her smile vanished..
A wall of what?
Insecurity..
Insecurity to be touched,claimed or called by any other man's demon.
So what did she do?
She could not feel it at first but she felt it when I looked at it,
she kept beating the walls until a portion broke out and
I stepped in to protect her...

Ishan starts to continue calmly, So...this is all just for the sake of our friendship, I should not be sharing this but you guys have helped us a lot, so you deserve to know about this indeed. Nysa was not the type of person you fall for quickly; she was intricate, enigmatic, and both too much and too little at the same time. All this time, I was just thinking about my side and underestimating hers; it was something he never expected. She was a source of amusement in crowded places, as well as a quiet rebel in her worldview. But that night, I wasn't thinking about what made her impossible. I was reflecting on the events that made her fear unforgettable. She tilted her head when she was intrigued. Her eyes shone brightly, as if she saw the world not as it was, but as it could be. I placed my palms to her face and exhaled gently, a pathetic attempt to remove old rash memories.

"I can't do this," she whispered under his breath, even though no one was listening. I wasn't sure if I had planned to fall for her or attempt not to. In any case, the thought of her had settled into the peaceful corners of my consciousness, and I wasn't sure if I wanted it to leave. Nysaa hesitated, her hand instinctively scratching her nail ends. My gaze was sharp yet trembling, betraying the nervous energy I walked towards Nysa and softly stopped her from scratching, keeping her palm on my right hand and pressing my left hand over it.

My voice sounded curious but was firm as I asked, "Why do you have a gun, Nysaa?"

She exhaled, her breath shaky as if the words were barbed thorns she had to spit out and she was not lying to him as this could lead to any disagreements, misunderstandings, and whatnot, she didn't want to lose him. Her fingers intertwined tightly, and her lips parted, releasing a whisper that carried years of buried anguish as if none ever asked the desperate child in her knew how she is or how she coped out of fear. She felt relieved to share it with me but at the same time she was amazed, scared, trusting less.

'Nysa you know you can trust me, right? We have been together for a while and you have been with me at my worst breakdown, holding my hand, just like that - no questions, no judgements, I just want to be there for you and if you let me, we can talk about things and fix feelings..' I convinced her.

"It's my mother," she started, her voice cracking on the edges of the confession. "She's always been... everything to me. My rock, my shield, my strength. But our life hasn't been kind."

Nysaa glanced at Ishan, his concerned face blurring in her teary vision. She pressed on, "She wasn't always like this. My mom used to be bold, fearless, a force of nature. She worked for a task force, you know? Protecting others was her life, her mission. But then she met my dad, and everything changed."

Her words faltered, weighed down by the weight of memories she had long avoided. She bit her lip, struggling to form the sentence that had haunted her for years. "He cheated, Ishan. My father! The man I was supposed to look up to. And she found out after I was born, and she stayed, not because she forgave him but because of me. She wanted me to have a family, even if it was fractured and fake."

She cursed under her breath, fists clenching as the tide of resentment surged within her.

"He's the reason she started keeping a gun. Not for herself, but for me. Every time he was out—and he was always out—she felt like she had to protect me and one day when he was away I faced threats while he was away.... and since then my mother kept this gun to protect her. We kept changing houses, cities over years for her work, the gun never changed its place and dad never showed up after a while. We were alone.'

Nysa felt a feeling of assurance as I moved closer to her, as she expressed what happened ahead,

She expresses, "When I was eight years old, a memory seared itself into my soul, leaving a scar that will never fade no matter how many nights I spend trying to forget. It was a hot summer evening, with the air seeming thick and the shadows appearing to stretch a little longer. My mother had gone out to get groceries, leaving me at home with a promise to return soon. I was too young to comprehend how minutes could turn into eternity when anxiety permeated every second. A sharp, urgent knock echoed through the solitude of our little dwelling. Curious, I glanced through the peephole, hoping to see a neighbor or my mother come home early. Instead, I saw a man unkempt and unshaven, with eyes like hollow pits. I stepped away from the door, hoping he would go, and my little fingers shook. But the wood shattered under his weight, and the lock was no match for the power of desperation. He went inside, his presence heavy and oppressive. I was paralyzed; "Don't scream," he growled and pulled my skirt which got torn.

My instincts kicked in: fight or die, but an eight-year-old has few options. I staggered backward, colliding with furniture, the thump of my small frame ringing across the room. He lunged at me, his hands rough and calloused, grasping for something other than my innocence. His goals were plain, as was my powerlessness. My chest ached with suppressed sobs, too scared to weep aloud. I was on the verge of being completely consumed by the icy edge of sorrow. I'll always remember the fire in my mother's eyes when she was there. She hurried in, shocked that someone had broken in, and I was lying helpless. As soon as she looked at the man, her hands leaped to his waist, where a gun's steel gleam taunted our weakness. She fought hard to get it from him in a flash of willpower, scaring the man, and I slid nearer to her.

"Run, Nysaa!" she exclaimed, her voice.

I raced, my boots beating against the floor, my lungs burning as I dashed out the back door, and she was injured, I'm not sure how, but she was gripping the gun firmly. Even as I fled, the sounds of their conflict reached me: grunts and shouts, and shortly the cops arrived and detained that man. That night, I left behind more than just my home; I also left behind a piece of my childhood. Since then, the darkness has not been the same. It whispers, recalling nightmares that turn my nights into mazes of horror. And my mother...she retained the gun. A silent reminder of what may have been and what was not allowed to be. The firearm, cold and dead, became a talisman of protection in our home, but the saddest thing is that we are so detached from my father that he doesn't understand the gravity of the situation. But no amount of steel can protect me from the haunting memories or the darkness that once belonged to a face.

It wasn't about her anymore. Her freedom, her dreams, they didn't matter. She lived for me, and I saw what it did to her. The way she carried that weight, how it bent her, broke her. She was just like an average mother whose uniqueness is hidden, she spent her days stitching her child's dreams together cooking, learning, and nurturing, sacrificing her own life without a second thought. She becomes a silent hero, living only to see her child soar. Nysaa's voice dropped to a whisper as she stared at her trembling hands. "She wanted me to marry someone else, Ishan. She wanted me to be happy irrespective of my truths and acceptance, she doesn't see what I see. She went shopping for my wedding like she didn't have a care in the world. But how can I not care? How can I ignore the signs?"

She looked up at me,her voice trembling as if it might shatter under its own weight.

"You're spiritual, you're calm and you have a good family background, Ishan. I know I was marrying Aryaman out of my will, you must have seen this through me and this was all for mom's happiness. And my dad, he's the opposite to what you are. Every single day, I watch people like him chip away at people like you. I can't stop thinking... What if it's you next? What if you lose yourself, just like she did?"

I moved closer, my eyes softened by her pain.
But Nysaa took a step back, shaking her head.

"Don't say it's going to be fine, Ishan. You don't know that. I'm scared. Scared of becoming her. Scared of watching you become him. Scared of looking at this gun every day because it's the only thing that makes me feel like I am protected or I can fight back. Scared that after a time I won't be enough, just like she wasn't."

The silence that followed was deafening. The weight of her confession lingered in the air, raw and unfiltered. For a moment, I said nothing, my hand outstretched but hesitant. I didn't know if I could touch her brokenness without shattering it further.

Finally, I whispered,
"Nysaa... I'm here. I'm not him. And you're not her. We can be something different. Together."

I sat closer to her as I wiped her tears rolling down her cheeks which were making me weak but yet patient enough to communicate and I expressed, "You see, Nysa, we know each other less but they say you must know what values are guiding a man before you choose to step your life up with him. I want you to know that from my side," I continued with a voice rich in reverence, "the ancient Sanskrit texts and Puranic values have always held humanity at their core. Take the concept of *Purushottam* if I disclose to you—it doesn't just mean the 'ideal man'; it symbolizes respect for women. Every religion, in its truest essence, echoes this truth. In Hinduism, the *Shakti* is revered as the cosmic energy that empowers creation. Islam teaches about the elevated status of mothers with the saying, 'Paradise lies at the feet of your mother.' Christianity honours the Virgin Mary as a symbol of grace and compassion. Buddhism, too, extols the role of women like Queen Maya, who birthed the Enlightened One himself. So there is no way I would ever disrespect a woman in front of me and I can forever confess my sin for not standing up for Arushi. Still, today, I am more than ready and committed to fight for you, irrespective of everything and I hope Arushi would have encouraged us for this. But don't leave me here with my feelings, I love you.."

I paused, watching Nysa's face soften as my words touched her heart. I continued, "From ancient times, women have been the backbone of societies, not just as nurturers but as warriors, thinkers, and creators. But what truly binds these teachings across religions is the belief in *karma* that humanity, our actions, and our treatment of others, define us far more than any ritual or prayer. If we can't treat each other with dignity, if we can't honor the women who shape our world, then we've strayed from the path of any faith. Religion, at its core, isn't about division. It's about connection through respect, through action, through love towards each other."

My words lingered in the air, a timeless lesson rekindled in the quiet intimacy of their conversation. Nysa sobbed, "What do we do then? You're true, I was not that aware but definitely I don't know how would all this work for us?' We sat for a while with a disturbed mind as she took a heavy breath, "I think it was better if we were kids, our parents would have taken care of things without letting us know."

She agreed, I began to ask her about her objectives and the future she might envisage with me, and she emphasised how she had always enjoyed spending time with me, writing fiction and found it pleasant to travel while writing. I was the total opposite; I like learning but was more of a legal person; she was a wave of creativity who was also lovely and gorgeous. I suggested, "How about we set a meeting for our parents and tell them the truth, you just need to get your mom's permission?' Nysa hesitantly nodded yes and they called it a night with a warm hug."

(Ishan felt emotional as he patted Vidur to continue and rested his back on the chair to listen, until he dozed off. Vidur continued the rest of the incident and everyone stared at him with curiosity...)

The next day they planned a dinner along with their parents and would spill the truth. The next morning, Ishan rings the phone to Nysa and explains to his parents that Nysa and her mom will be arriving as guests, Nysa felt a bit resistant to it because she was scared that if anything happened wrong, her mother might get disrespected their house, it might be a slight trust issue to her so she gulped it in as Ishan didn't think much about it. Nysa's voice remained calm yet tired, crackling across the phone speaker.

"See you soon Ishan, hope it won't go wrong."

I assured her, "Don't worry Nysa, we are now adults. They will listen, even if they require time to comprehend it. We are gonna make it through the path of truth, I will be with you for whatever happens cause it's a team of us expressing what we want."

Nysa felt better and he sighed and glanced at the clock. The evening's plan hung over them, weighty and inescapable. Nysa replied this as she was getting ready, "You're correct. We will tell them together. Let them see that we considered this through."

She dressed up in a traditional chiffon saree with beautiful pearl earrings and a vermillion lip tint with a sunscreen only. Her skin glowed and shone like a white sand with a vermillion sunset on the beach. She called her mother and despite his reassurances, Nysa felt a nagging unease that wouldn't go away. Her stomach churned as she envisioned her mother's worried forehead and quiet but sharp queries. It wasn't their friendship that worried her, she knew they trusted her judgment, it was the abruptness of shattering the carefully managed expectations their parents had set.

That evening, the dinner went as planned: sluggish discussion, cautious grins, and a perceptible sense of tension. When the time came, Nysa clenched her fists tightly beneath the table as Ishan cleared his throat. "We need to tell you something," he said.

The confession unfurled like a meticulously choreographed play, with each word calculated and weighted. Their parents listened attentively, their expressions alternating between astonishment and thoughtfulness. Finally, after an awkward wait, Nysa's mother broke the silence,"You're both grown up. If this is what you have decided, we will not stand in your way. But both of you have to promise us that you will neutralise the current situation by confessing and apologising to your counterparts tomorrow, and we will manage after that, as your guardians. Deal?"

They nodded a yes, Nysa's comfort was immediate, and her restless anxiousness transformed into a peaceful appreciation. Ishan grabbed for her hand under the table, his fingers brushing against hers in subtle comfort.

When Karma Leads,

Dharma Changes

CHAPTER ELEVEN

Dear Heart,
I found her vulnerable today! Vulnerably entangled by the societal
strings, her health,
Yet untangling how we (men)function and falling back to prove her
strengths,
So what did you decide?
I'll fight for her, I want to give my everything just to be by her side,
How does these words even matter?
Im standing against the doubts that knocks her through endless night,
Being her guiding light where she needs me,
being her secret and loudest cheerleader where i can be,
No strings of fate,
no battles between you and me?
No, it's just pure I'm her, she's me...

Ishan and Nysa entered his room after their arranged dinner was a success, their vibe buzzed with excitement, giggles spilling through the door while their parents were still enjoying the dinner as they spent time beside the room's window, feeling the chilly winds that touched their skins. The next day Ishan decides to meet the parents of the girl (his so-predicted fiance) that his parents spoke to, it was Karol Baugh, Delhi and Nysa could not follow him as she was handling some important paperworks for her NGO. So, here's the cogedy (comedy + tragedy) of arranged marriages in India, if you guys don't know yet, this is where the real family court should be, it is the only practice or investment where ROI is so unclear, and could be scary too.This practice is technically *for the parents, from parents and to the parents*..they conduct "interviews" after applying their SEO skills through checking horoscopes and what not to find someone suitable for their adult children, cause they won't participate in this game of responsibility- which is valid! But this SEO is great until they forget the main / final step for the process- yes! CONSENT..how can you forget about your child's CONSENT! This practice is more intensive than job recruiters doing their biodata exchanges resembling investment portfolios, it's a centuries-old saga of expectations, awkward tea-samosa sessions, and sometimes it might turn into surprise love stories (could be abusive too! But the investment and process matters more than ROI). Sometimes it works, sometimes it's a mystery repeating itself—dramatically, of course! So, Nysa did know all this , she trusted his man indeed.. Ishan and Nysa had committed to each other and it's been just a few days, these adults in their twenties looked at life so maturely, that they were perfectly sure and ready to commit to each other.

Sounds amazing right? Ishan's family wanted to marry him off to a stable family but when Ishan learned about everything his mother heard about the Yadavs, he was sure that they might take time to understand his side but they might understand his feelings sooner or later. Parallely he was focusing on applying for an AI guided course at Arizona University. Ishan reached Delhi from Guwahati after a rushful journey by train. His office was already going on, so he decided to switch to flexible working as he travelled, like a work from home, for a few days until he persuaded the family. So the Yadavs had their one and only daughter-Simran who was supposed to marry Ishan and his mother told them Ishan was here to meet Simran. Ishan calls his mother as he reaches the Yadavs house and their homecare lady welcomes him. She allows him to stay in the guest room until the rest of the working family arrives. The house was big as a bungalow but the god of hell, they had their own farm-backyard with two tractors.

Ishan calls his mother.."Hello maa?"
"Hello beta, did you reach?"

"Maa, yes, but ...but you did not tell me you had such filthy rich friends, it's Delhi but they are already surpassing the Mughals I see. I'm surprised but anyways, give some time to Nysaa if she comes home, I'll be back soon after rejecting your crazy rich asians.."

"Beta, I know..it's not easy to say 'no' to them but make sure you eat and work well, things might go opposite but I know you can take care of everything, I trust you, just believe in yourself, I'm sure life is there to teach you."

"Yes, maa I know, okay so.."

"okay, so I'll hang up now, your dad needs some tea and I need some gossips, haha"

"sure madam, acha maa, listen," "What's wrong Ishan?"

"I love you, see you soon , and thanks for believing in me."

Soon the Yadav's family returns home, Ishan waits for them in the hall room, Simran and his father arrive and welcome Ishan to sit for a coffee with them. Ishan did not notice her mother but he felt an awkward vibe among them. Simran looks at Ishan and smiles, her father questions Ishan about his job and future as the coffee arrives. Ishan answers honestly, her father questions why he wants to marry Simran and why so early? Ishan hesitates and rep-lies, "Actually uncle ji, with all due respect, I have come here just to inform you that I cannot be marrying Simran, I love someone else and she's waiting for me back home."

As Mr.Yadav hears this he grows angry yet holding his anger with a tensed expression, he replies, "Is that what your parents have taught you? We, the Yadav's have never heard what 'No' is and especially when your family has committed, my daughters dignity is entangled with this, we were all set for preparations, how am I supposed to tell the relatives that the man we were excited to welcome in our family, rejected my daughter. Look at her, do you think she deserves this?"

Ishan feels guilty as he realises that he was talking (more likely negotiating himself) with a father who was emotionally driven for her daughter's well-being and future image, he carefully expressed further, "Uncle ji, the decision of marriage was made without my consent and I am here from my will and my family's side to take back our words and instead of this you can punish me, charge me or scold me however you want. If you think I am doing wrong to you and if you think being transparent before anything starts is wrong. I can assure you that you will never see me again and I will ask for forgiveness to whoever you have told about your daughter's wedding, her dignity is equally important as my consent. I hope you are a wise person and as an elder you will understand this."

Mr.Yadav thinks for a while and gets up from his place, "Okay, you may leave the day after, you have to say sorry to everyone who I'll take you along with, I'll ask Birju to help you.By the time, be our guest!" As Simran's dad walks away, Simran follows him and murmurs something.

The Next morning

Birju wakes Ishan up at 4AM and asks him to come with him to a room, Ishan enters the room, drooling in sleep and discovers that there is a very bright light, the room is decorated with a lot of clothes here n' there. A tailor appeared to wait for them, as Ishan was shocked that he brought a measuring tape along, as he appeared to be professional and did not even smile easily. Ishan kept questioning him but instead of any response, the guy gestured to Ishan to come closer.

Birju abruptly pushes Ishan towards the tailor. "Take it off," the tailor commanded.

Ishan was more shocked and he had just woken up from sleep, so he just decided to follow them until it sounded safe. Taking off clothes was safe? This man took off his shirt and he was just wearing his pyjamas, that steel rocking toned-body was enough to amaze Birju.

"Are you gay?" Ishan asks Birju.

Birju nods with wonder "what that could be?"

"Stop glaring at my abs, it's hard work man." Ishan commands rudely.

Ishan stood on the wooden platform, arms out like a reluctant scarecrow. The vibe was bromantically silent as he got to know from Birju, the tailor was known as Dev, he moved with precision and grace, his measuring tape dancing across Ishan's exposed shoulders.

"Hold still, macho" Dev grinned in frustration, his body's tingy-tacky odour covered in sweat was barely bearable because it was masking the scent of fresh fabric. Only his perfectly oil-setted hair and fitted waistcoat helped him stand out. Dev's fingers brushed against his neck.

"Be careful there," he muttered, uncomfortable with the close proximity.

"My apologies."
Dev's voice was controlled now, highly professional.

His hands subtly moved down to measure the inseam, he sniffed Ishan secretly and Ishan felt something slip into his right pants pocket – the movement was so subtle that it could have been mistaken for adjusting the fabric. Dev's eyes met his in the mirror, carrying an urgency that contradicted his calm demeanor, he directed Ishan, "The fitting room is through there if you'd like to check the drape of the fabric."

Ishan caught the deliberate glance toward the back of the shop.

"Right. Good idea." In the small fitting room, he pulled the carefully folded note from his pocket.

His hands trembled slightly as he read: "You're being watched. Run away as soon as you can!."

Ishan was scared now, yet Dev's way of approaching was weird, he felt insecure of himself at that point.As he walked back towards the wooden stage, Ishan started casually."

"looks fine..."

"But I recommend the darker shade," Dev said, tapping his fingers twice on the countertop.

"It's better suited for... evening events."

"Evening events.." Ishan repeated to confirm..

Dev squared his shoulders and maintained his professional demeanour. "Should we continue with the measurements?"

Before Ishan could say anything, the measuring tape was wrapped around his chest again, this time tighter, and each touch held the weight of sensitivity. Dev's odour was already killing Ishan and now he was acting really weird. The rest of the fitting was a dance of subtle signals and delicate movements, with both men conscious that their every motion may be noticed, but Birju was distracted by his phone. Ishan utilises this time to calmly think about the situation and wears the dhoti-kurta. Birju takes him to Simran's room as she opens the door, Simran appears to be fully ready as a bride- she appears beautiful and sober. Ishan looked at her and he understood the assignment. But our guy was THE backbencher here, he was not interested in doing the assignment instead escaping was important.

He steps back and pulls Birju to a corner, "Birju, I will pay you 80% more than what they pay you, just let me go." Ishan expresses tension.

"I'm her cousin's brother, you moron." Birju scoffs.

"Then tell me some way to escape, you know this is wrong." As Ishan and Birju negotiate, Nysa tries to call Ishan but he has to hang up. She felt anxious.

Simran was still getting a little more ready, Birju suggested, only if you give up in front of us all we will get on the stage as the ritual takes place and beat you, but we will let you off. This is a win-win to save you from all of this. Ishan realizes, he could be spitting the truth cause, a few punches from them will make Simran pity him and let him go. The relatives will think he's a fraud to be a husband and Simran's brothers are very caring about her future, violence is wrong but in this situation, it was a wise escape. Ishan agrees and asks Birju to plan accordingly. After a while, Simran comes out and expresses she knows everything about Ishan. Ishan was shocked but Simran assured them that everything was planned, it was her idea that Birju was following and just to comfort her dad, she was doing all this. Ishan agrees to play along. He chants god's name and meditates before he leaves for the marriage hall.

As he enters the marriage hall with Birju, he feels scared but he trusts god, everyone is looking at him. Simran arrived in a few minutes and she started to argue with Ishan, their slow play became serious and everyone became curious as the music stopped and they dragged Birju, Birju called the other brothers, the pandit fled and the other relatives became the audience, Simran's father was shocked about everything that was happening in that auspicious moment. Birju and his two brothers start Ishan with punches, and he defends himself by laying on the ground curling his arms around his head, and folding his knees to protect his stomach from the heavy kicks, Ishan does not fight back until everyone leaves the palace and the brothers eventually stop. Simran leaves a note in Ishan's room,

I'm helping you because I know what love and happiness is. I do not want this auspicious bond of marriage to be disheartened. I felt bad to be rejected so you deserve the pain! Sorry, and thanks.

Ishan was bleeding - his head was scratched from the back, his arms bled so badly, his side chest was blue with kick patches and his face was hurt too. He returns to the guest room, thanks god for keeping him alive, and notices Simran's note. In a while, as he takes off his clothes and treats his body, he finds 45 missed calls from Nysa. She was indeed worried. He calls Nysa and updates her about everything except the part where he was thrashed at the wedding and then he also speaks to his mother, bro repeats the same story. But the solution was nowhere, he decided he would sneak out of the house that night. As Birju called him to have dinner, Ishan wore decent nightwear and climbed down the stairs.

He found Simran's father upset about everything, as Ishan entered the room. Her father handed him a guestlist of 6 families with addresses and shared, "These are the people who did not attend or left the wedding because of you. If you care about Simran's dignity, we might find a match for her among these families, go, seek forgiveness, and ask them to give their son's hand to us. We will let you go anytime you want, this list is upon your conscience."

Ishan felt bad as he wondered how a father could possibly feel after all this and he asked Birju to help him out, after three days of wandering like a hooligan, knocking on strangers' doors, asking for forgiveness and healing from the wounds, the guilt, Ishan managed to persuade a family for Simran's marriage, Birju approved the same and they finally stopped. While Ishan was ready to leave, he bid everyone goodbye with his pranama (a gesture).

Birju asked him a last question, "Why did you do all this for her? You didn't even look at her or like her, just cause of your parents you went through all this"

Ishan smiled, "Brother, it was my choice, parents and their kids share the responsibility proportionally when they grow up, I wish you could see them, they are kind. Come to Guwahati anytime -be our guest, I shall be your guide. Also, this was because of my love, I love someone and I have committed, Simran is like my sister, I understand what Mr.Yadav must have felt, and as a brother like you I was fortunate to find someone with potential for her."

Birju was amazed at this response and smiled firmly.

"Why are you even working from home? That's materialistic, right? You should go take Sanyasa. I love your wisdom and innocence." Birju mocked as he was helping Ishan to drop off his luggage.

"Brother, I wish I could..I think that's why one should learn about spirituality, it never bans you from working, that's a part of your life and karma, what one should not include is greed here. And above everything do you know what's common between you and a pandit?" Ishan calmly questioned with a funky smile.

"What?" Birju asked with shock.

"Both of your bodies will be cremated. We do not realise what life is and how it works, hence, we think we can play around the world. The human who knows the ultimate truth of life, can be anything and working anywhere but is definitely spiritual and knows about the boundaries of life including the fact that every bodily and material pleasure ends or stops at death in this world." Ishan responds.

Birju feels a little ashamed about mocking Ishan, the guy who was innocent and that he helped his sister, protecting her dignity over his boundaries. Birju realised Ishan was highly driven by his values and cared less about the world's attention on him. As they bid goodbyes, Ishan boarded the train back to Guwahati, he called Nysa, she was indeed curious yet missed him. After a day, when he reached the station, he found Nysa, waiting for him. Nysa found Ishan with those terrible wounds and a stitch on his arm. She felt sad, so she approached him and hugged him with tears, as Ishan expressed he was okay and everything was eventually getting sorted out. Nysa breathed calmly on his tight arms, they talked about how Ishan got hurt, spilled all the tea to his queen and headed home. Nysa felt assured that he was alright, she made sure his wounds were properly checked upon, even helped him setting up his medicine alarms, applied ointments on his wounds and she even covered them with foundation at times, as his mother was still not aware of this extent of drama. She would have definitely been worried for him. While all this was still ongoing, Ishan asked Nysa "How's things with Aryaman?"

Nysa expresses that Aryaman is very persistent and he already thinks that Nysa and he are married, "I think I need to drop punches now" Ishan reacts with sarcasm and Nysa gives a side eye to him. They both giggle.

"Ishan, I do not know how to deal with him, you should come with me." Nysa pleads.

Ishan decides to meet Aryaman, whom he had heard a lot about but had never met in person. Aryaman was the person Nysa had been engaged to, and he appeared to be the ideal match for her. He was prosperous, reliable, and well-connected to rich-background people - a Perfect Asian Husband indeed! Aryaman had the crazy funds to support not only Nysa's ambitions but also her company's future initiatives. In comparison, Ishan came across as a simpler man, someone who loved profoundly but lacked the worldly advantages that Aryaman brought to the table. As they met at a restaurant over dinner, Ishan confessed his feelings and Nysa's consent to Aryaman, he appeared to be less understanding but after a few more conversations, he felt sorry to be third-wheeling. The meeting turned out pleasant, but there was an undercurrent of tension. Aryaman, the golden spoon boy- was very casual of a man, he appeared to really care about Nysa's pleasure, and he just needed the right words to understand... As Ishan listened to Aryaman discuss his aspirations, his vision for the future, and his complete support for Nysa that he had planned, he felt a stab of uneasiness.

Could he ever provide Nysa with the same level of stability and wealth as Aryaman?

This was a fine-to-handle situation until Ishan received a notification which was to make matters worse. Ishan had received an admission offer letter for his dream AI-led research project at Arizona University, US and this was not easy! It was his fourth attempt after several other rejections from various courses in Arizona, he secured one! Although he had different dreams for his life, he was still in his 20s, this was a part of his professional achievement and he wanted to pursue it. It was a dream come true moment in the year of intensive instruction and exposure that may change his career forever. But it came at a cost, he had to leave in a month as the dates and sponsorship were set. Right now, he was in a position where both of his future values were at stake, in front of him. The timing couldn't have been worse, Nysa was still healing and their engagement had previously been postponed. On the one hand, he had a dream: a chance to attend a prestigious school that may lead to opportunities he had never imagined. On the other hand, there was Nysa, the lady who had taught him the true meaning of love, resilience, and collaborative efforts. His thoughts strayed to her. Nysa was not just anyone. She was intelligent, determined, and gutsy, a lady who addressed life's challenges head on. Her laughter could light up a room for him, and her brilliance left him feeling both pleased and challenged. She wasn't someone who needed to be saved; she was someone who forged her own way. But Ishan enjoyed walking that journey with her, even if it was difficult to match, he was a man of his word.

He told Nysa he would be responsible for a life committed to her. That evening, following his encounter with Aryaman, Ishan left early with an excuse related to his work, holding the offer letter on his phone screen, he swung alone on a children's park which was near Nysa's house. He reflected on everything that how he loved Nysa, adored her more than anything, but he wondered if continuing in her life would mean holding her back. Aryaman could provide her with a life of stability and support, whilst Ishan's fate remained uncertain. However, he understood that love was more than comparing strengths and shortcomings; it was about cooperation and faith. Taking care of her happiness till death, could Aryaman do that? Ishan felt confident about this shot. Meanwhile Nysa spotted Ishan, swinging alone in the park, it was almost sunset and a breeze carried the distant laughter of children, tugging their steps toward a corner hidden by tall trees, soon to be leaving for home. The swings, an old faded slide, and a kaleidoscope station gleaming under the sunset appeared dull. Nysa knew something was wrong and Ishan was feeling uneasy or sad for some reason, her eyes lit up with wonder, and without a second thought, she headed toward the swings, her sandals kicking up bits of sand. Ishan noticed Nysa and welcomed her with a decent smile, she chuckled, following behind. "What are you, six?" she teased.

"Six and a half, thank you very much!" he grinned, plopping himself on one of the swings.

Her legs dangled as she struggled to gain momentum. Ishan shook his head, got down off his swing, and stepped behind her, giving her a gentle push. The laughter that spilled from her was infectious. He was feeling better that she was with him, she followed him instead of staying with Aryaman's at his so-rich-dinner table.

"You've got this!" he encouraged, watching her lean forward, kicking her feet to catch the wind.

Nysa tilted her head back, her hair catching the sunset. "You know, I've never been to an amusement park," she said, her voice was way more romantic now.

Ishan blinked in surprise. "Never? Not even once? How..like no..why so?"

She shook her head. "Nope. My childhood was pretty simple. No rollercoasters, no cotton candy... just books, maybe playgrounds like this and a few temple fairs."

He looked at her with amazement, Nysa was always full of surprises to him, she was so low maintenance, unpredictable but indeed the happiest human ever with the simplest joys in her life. And here she was, so present, glowing on an old rusty swing setting as if it was the best ride in the world.

"You're unbelievable," he expressed with a smile.

"I try to be," she winked at Ishan "Think I still fit on this thing?" Nysa chuckled as she leaped from the swing and headed straight for the slide. She climbed up and sat at the top, her legs awkwardly tucked in.

"Here I go..oooww," she muttered as she pushed off.

She lost her footing as the slide, in its old-rusty form, wobbled halfway. Nysa's arms flailed as she yelled for Ishan. Ishan was just standing at the right end, as if he knew she might fall, he knelt down on his knees to catch her before she fell, his black pants scraped the sandy base making it dirty.

"Got yaa," he grinned, breathless.

Nysa burst into laughter, leaning against him. "Look at your jeans, Ishan! Who needs a wash now!"

He glanced down at the dusty mess and shrugged. "I did..but worth it."

"You're ridiculous," she blushed.

"And you're Ms. Clumsy," he shot back playfully.

They dusted themselves off and returned to the swings, their laughter filling the quiet park. Ishan couldn't remember the last time he felt this carefree. It wasn't about grand adventures or extravagant plans; it was moments like this — simple, raw, and unfiltered — that mattered.

"Ready to head out?" he asked softly.

Knowing that Ishan would open up to her when the time was right, Nysa smiled and nodded yes. They headed back home, with sand stubbornly sticking to Ishan's pants. The next day, Ishan met Nysa at her house, showing her the Arizona offer letter, he explained everything to her, his feelings about meeting with Aryaman and his life post the acceptance into the program. Nysa listened intently, her expression unreadable. As they sat on a park bench Ishan murmured calmly, despite the agony inside. "I love you, Nysa but this decision is not solely about me. It's also important to consider what is best for you. Aryaman can give you everything you've worked so hard for. He's a stable, rich, and well-valued man. I am confident about our love but not about the stability that you need for your dreams."

"What I want is more than just stability and support; I want love, understanding, and someone who will fight for me no matter what. And it is you. You have proved it, Ishan! If you don't go and don't take this chance, how will you live after that? You will regret it, Ishan..maybe I will too..so, take this opportunity, everything and everyone after this is your life's test. So head to Arizona. Pursue your dream. I'll be here, waiting and building my own dreams until then. We will support one another, even if it is from a distance. "She explained calmly.

Ishan felt a sense of relief and gratitude. He did not make the decision, but rather they did as partners. He stretched for her waist and grabbed it tightly as his nose touched hers.

"We will make it work, Nysa. No matter what." Ishan whispered.

Nysa felt warm and grasped his face with her hands as he moved closer to her. Ishan swiftly took her neck, swept the hair strands that touched her face, and she closed her eyes, stretching her face to kiss his lips softly. Ishan smiled over her childish expression, as he felt her breath rising and kissed her cheeks moving next to her forehead, as they both giggled and called it a day by sharing some ice-creams.

Our Last Road Trip

CHAPTER TWELVE

The month that followed was a blur of preparations, they had negotiated their marriages and were to postpone some time away from each other before Ishan and Nysa could focus on their dreams. A delicate balance of enthusiasm and bittersweet expectations grew between the two. Ishan and Nysa spent their days juggling their various commitments while carving out time for one other. They talked about everything, dreams, worries, and how they planned to make their relationship work despite the distance that would soon separate them. Nysa, ever the planner, took care of some practical matters as she assisted Ishan with his travel documents, ensuring that everything was in order. Nysa got a weird-looking turtle to gift Ishan, she wrapped it well with a cringy gift wrapper, "What's this?" Ishan questioned her with a cute-curious expression.

"Some Feng-shui kind-of-a thing? Like good vibes, lucky charm!" Nysa expressed hesitantly as Ishan giggled, nodding a no.

"I know you believe in some core values but I do not what could have been the best for you so I got this from my choice. Someone in the market told me it's like a popular lucky sale. Um..." Nysa added.

Ishan smiled and packed it into one of his bags. She investigated Arizona's weather reports and packed some more tiny items that he could have missed. Meanwhile, Ishan attempted to lighten the atmosphere with his customary wit, cracking jokes about how he'd survive, pestering her about eating correctly and taking care of herself. But beyond the jest, there lurked an unspoken grief. Every shared glance and lingering touch held the weight of their remaining time together. A few days before Ishan's departure details were fixed-they felt the feeling of longing was approaching, and he decided to prepare something special to spend a very memorable moment with Nysa.

He planned a surprise date that he had diligently thought of, and called us to a place away from Guwahati where a young couple lived in their cafe, the café was less crowded but the owner-lady in the café appeared to be pregnant, someone had shared the location's idea to Ishan, describing that her cafe was a good stopover. He visited the place and came to know that she might need some financial help, so he took us there, prepared all the flowers on the café rooftop to make it more attractive, ordered a few more customisable, and we customised a romantic theme for Nysa and left it for their date night. The next day, Ishan explored the outskirts on his bike with Nysa, he gifted her a set of handmade rings. Each one was one-of-a-kind, made with care and love: a delicate dried-clay ring representing the malleability of their bond, a flower ring representing the beauty and fragility of their connection, and a simple leaf-made ring, a playful nod to how even the smallest things carried meaning when shared with her. Nysa felt deeply touched that how highly can a man think of you to do such efforts, Ishan expressed his love and she loved the moment she was spending with him.

Her respect and love Ishan grew as he added, "Wait for the final and special one, I had to struggle with the measurement but I did it! haha" With a mischievous grin, Ishan slowly put the rings onto her fingers while they waited for a break.

"When I come back, it'll be something even more special." He finished with a blush as he started the bike and wore his gloves, and his helmet and stretched Nysa's hand on his chest.

Nysa loved the chilly air that touched her cheeks, the freedom she had with him and ultimately the efforts he showed. She felt complete. The same evening, beneath a blanket of stars, Ishan revealed his romantic dinner plan for her as they headed to the café, he got a couple of dresses for Nysa to change. As he offered her to change, "Where did you buy all those from? And when?" Nysa was shocked.

"Maybe you want to look special or different, camper girl? I'll change and set some more into the theme. You can change your dress at the back, if you like any of them, my personal favorite is red by the way...and it was not much, just stalked your gram profile, Facebook and maybe LinkedIn, it's 21st century and I must know what my girlfriend likes. There are few options after my research, here" He smiled as he handed the dresses with a pair of black heels and a tiny makeup box to her.

Nysa was impressed; she loved how he was interested in her as she changed into the red dress, which had a flower design on the shoulder and some simple plates to it. She wore the long-length dress with some touch of makeup and headed out. The warm glow of the candles illuminated her face as he poured out his heart, he stood in front of her with a creamy white shirt and a matte dark grey trouser, his unbuttoned shirt revealed his sweaty, clean chest under his collar bones, which appeared so waxed, he came closer to Nysa as she was blushing a little, he held her hands to express her how much he loved her, how she had transformed his life in ways he couldn't express, and how he would carry her love with him wherever he went. With this, Ishan switched to his phone's camera "let's take one picture, please" he poised the phone in his hands, checking the angles. The candlelight bathes everything in gold, making her red silhouette dress glow against a white wall, she shakes her head, turning away.

"You know I don't look good in photos, Ishan." Nysa grows nervous.

"And did you know – Richard Avedon once said Beauty is not in face; beauty is a light in the heart he quotes, moving to catch her eye. "And in this light, the heart that is close to me is more beautiful than ever right now." Ishan quotes.

"Quoting someone famous won't change my mind, do I look easy to you?" she giggles, using her hand like a shield in front of his phone.

"Besides, I'm not properly ready for—"

"That's exactly why it's perfect," Ishan interrupts, lowering his phone slightly.

"It's so damn real.
You will always be this beautiful for me, no need for poses, no pretense.

Just you, being completely you.
The way the candlelight catches your dark brown hair right now...
Nysa believe me, it's like I have switched to a poetry in motion."

She rolls her eyes, blushing, but can't hide her smile. "You're unbelievable."

Ishan smiles raising his camera again. "Come on, just one. For a memory?"

"Alright," she sighs, turning to face him.

"Won't long," he says softly, already framing the shot.

The phone clicks, capturing not just her image, but the warmth of the moment, the gentle persistence of his artistry, and the subtle shift from reluctance to trust. Nysa expressed her feelings about him as they continued their dinner. She turned to face him, her eyes glassy and desperate, "Ishan... What if I'm not the person you think I am? What if I can't be everything you deserve?" Her voice wavered, the words tumbling out in a fragile confession.

He cupped her face tenderly, his thumb brushing away a single tear that dared to escape.

"Nysaa, I'm not here because of what I deserve. I'm here because I love you—for who you are, no conditions. I love you, for your strength, your kindness, and your heart and I can live every day interestingly like this, if it's with you. You've been through so much, yet you still stand here today. That alone is more than enough for me. I don't want to ask anything else from you but your presence is all."

His hands slowly slip down on her arm as he tries to lock his fingers with hers, he feels a ridge and looks down it was an old scar she told him about, when she desperately wanted to stop living, he realises how far she has come. She shook her head, the doubt still gnawing at her, craving affirmations. "But tell me why, Ishan? Why would you choose me, just look at me, I'm not sure if I am able to handle or reflect the love you'd give me?"

His lips curved into a gentle smile, and his heart cried a little as the scars were still visible but he decided to keep calm, his eyes unwavering as they met hers, he expressed, "Because I don't see your scars as flaws but they are growth. I see them as proof of your resilience, of the battles you've fought and won. I don't love you out of duty, Nysaa. I love you because my heart chooses to, every single day. And I'll keep choosing you, not because you're perfect, but because you're you."

With this going on, Ishan and Nysa decided to stay the night at the rooftop as Ishan introduced Nysa to the café owners and asked them about staying overnight. They agreed on a condition that Ishan and Nysa should leave before any customer finds them in the morning. They agreed and borrowed some bedding from the owner.

As Nysa helped Ishan to make the bed, she got a pen with her. Ishan was curious about what she might do with a pen, she grabbed his hand and drew a little flower ring on his hand, that was just a gesture for the ring that he gifted her. She expressed that she wanted to give him something but that's all she can do for now, and she kissed his hands. Ishan sits beside Nysa as she rests her head on his shoulder and he locks his fingers with hers, covering her body with a blanket. As he cherishes her face under the shiny moonlight, a slow old classical play on his phone and Nysa falls asleep on his shoulder while they are talking. Ishan kisses her forehead softly and closes his eyes. The next morning, the journey began with a bike ride through the winding roads of Guwahati.

They paused for some refreshing coconut water and sugarcane juice, their laughing mingling in with the sounds of the busy roadside stalls. They try some Assamese cuisine for lunch as their expedition led them to a remote waterfall, Nysa drove for the meantime, Ishan enjoyed the breeze as he held her tightly and closed his eyes to feel nature. The remote waterfall was hidden among thick flora, where the air was cold and their voices resonated against the rocks. They parked the bike and hiked a little to reach the beautiful waterfall which cascaded like liquid silver against the emerald-green rock face that was covered by algae, its misty spray creating a magical chilly-vibe where sunlight danced through the droplets. Trees around it flanked the waterfall, their roots clinging to moss-covered stones, while the thunderous sound of water crashing into the crystal-clear pool below seemed to whisper ancient secrets of the wilderness.

The scene was breathtaking - untouched, pristine, where nature displayed its most raw and magnificent performance. Tiny droplets hung in the air like suspended diamonds, catching light and creating an ethereal veil around the waterfall's powerful descent. Ishan climbed down the rocks to reach the waterfall as he removed his shirt, revealing his toned body frame, before he leapt into the glittering water. Nysa was taken off guard and found herself looking, her mind racing with the realisation of how much she would miss him. He acknowledged her look and smiled, inviting her to join him. As she resisted jumping just then, Ishan climbed up the corner and softly positioned his arms beside to lift her. As Nysa was caught guarded, Ishan lifted her with the help of his arms and slowly laid her in the water, as he giggled and grabbed his shoulder tightly, Nysa and Ishan eventually sat inside the cold flowing water. As they settled, Ishan grabbed her hand and pulled her closer strongly, trying to kiss her forehead softly.

"No matter where we are, I love it when we stick together," he said quietly, reciting a mantra in his mind for their togetherness as if to link their hearts even across the miles.

Later, Nysa climbed out of the cold flowing water and sat calmly by the waterfall collecting some amount of mud around a small rock, she formed a small heart from the wet mud, added a small wild leaflet on it as it dried, waited for the water to fall in silvery strands, and fidgeted with one of the rings he gave her. As the mud dried with the leaf stuck in the center, she brought it to Ishan, "It's my favourite," she said. Ishan started putting the flower ring onto her finger.

"Good to know my efforts paid off," Ishan chuckled.

Moving a moist strand of hair away from her face. The moment passed, their laughing fading into a shared silence, and then their gazes met. He approached slowly and tentatively, like if time had stopped just for them. She could feel the warmth of his breath mingling with hers, and her heart raced as their lips touched. The kiss began gently, delicate and exploratory, but as their emotions became more intense. The roar of the waterfall faded into the background, and the pounding of their hearts. Their foreheads lay together, and they both smiled in the little pause they made in between the kisses, the weight of unspoken promises hung between them. Ishan felt so sure about Nysa, picturing a life ahead with her in his mind, no strings no dramas, just them indulged.

It was their first proper kiss, yet it had the depth of a thousand seconds, a memory they would both cherish as they faced the challenges ahead. After enjoying their silence for a while, Nysa climbed up a huge rock, curled up her smooth back on the big rock, resting her head on another. Her honeyed glowing-like body moulded perfectly with the shape of her peach colored bikini, sunbathed in the beautiful weather. She started scrolling through her phone, her fingers moving slowly and her focus diverted from Ishan. Ishan watched her, amused yet slightly annoyed, he climbed up wearing his folded-wet dhoti with dark glammy shorts, to sit next to her, his body appeared as a warm glow settled over him, defining the edges of his body frame under the sun.

"Seriously Nysa? Screen time again? I'm starting to think your soulmate is social media, not me." He teased Nysa, nudging her arm.

Nysa didn't look up and giggled slightly. "Hmm, YouTube doesn't interrupt my scrolling with dumb commentary, so maybe you're right, I need to replace my informative, formal, fact-sharing boyfriend with the social media..haha"

"Oh come on, you're comparing a Google-like boyfriend and an entertaining app, here the ONLY common thing is entertaining.." he laughed. "Okay, guess the color of my eyes without looking up a filter to match it?"

She finally lifted her gaze, narrowing her eyes at him. "Dark Brown. Boring."

"Wow, see your attention to detail has improved by 1 credit..haha." He put a hand over his chest, mock-hurt. "Just a few seconds back when I was your attention, things were simpler. Now I've been ghosted by the internet, is it so?."

Nysa smirked. "Times change, babe. Social media trends faster than your comebacks." She leaned in closer to his arm, whispering mischievously. "But, I still think about you..."

Ishan giggles. "Touché. But if we're talking about trends, I prefer the classic one—face-to-face conversations - no.1 increases self-confidence and presentation skills, no.2 - gets the girl- job done!"

She rolled her eyes but softened, locking her phone. "Okay, fine! what's trending in the analogy world, Mr. Digital Detox?"

"This." He leaned in, brushing a gentle kiss across her forehead. "No filters, no hashtags, just us."

Her eyes flickered with warmth. "Hmm, it feels like a vintage boyfriend. I kinda like it."

"Well, don't trend-hop too soon," he warned playfully. "I'm sticking around."

Nysa grinned, resting her head on his chest. "Guess the digital world can wait for a while."

Soon they changed their wet clothes and left for home. Ishan assured Nysa that he was not abandoning her, but rather creating a future for them both. Nysa, as brave as ever, sought to hide her tears as she sat behind his bike, resting her head on his back for a while, knowing this was a step he needed to take. The night before his departure, they had a quiet dinner in Nysa's garden. It was simply just their favourite takeouts - dal tadka with pilau rice, but the moments were charged with meaning. After dinner, they rested on the couch, his arm across her shoulders and her head resting on his shoulder. They didn't say much, their intimacy did and the moment passed by. The stillness between them was filled with love, trust, and an unsaid pledge to remain.

Finally, the day arrived. Ishan had taken a break from his office, his boss turned out to be understanding as he was a great addition to the team but Arizona might bring something more to the team. Ishan bid goodbye to his colleagues. He was getting ready for his flight and Nysa was helping him remember everything, she carried a notebook along where she was crossing out the list of items he took, very very..keenly, carefully, and responsibly!

"Nysa? Can you help me a little?" Ishan calls.

A moment later, Nysa appeared in the room's doorway, her hair loosely tied back with a maroon clip, radiating the effortless beauty even in her pyjamas, Ishan was left breathless with her smell. She tilted her head with a smirk as she pulled him closer. "Can't even handle buttons without me, huh?"

Ishan smiled sheepishly. "Guess I've been spoiled by you. What am I gonna do without you? Come with me, please? Please? Little more please?"

Nysa stepped closer, her fingers deftly taking over the task. As she carefully fastened each button, their proximity stirred an unspoken intimacy between them. Ishan looked at her, his heart swelling with gratitude.

"Thank you but no, I have made my dream here, it's your time to work hard and no slacking! Report to your boss every day- that's me. haha," she said softly, her voice filled with meaning.

"No, thank you!" He kisses her forehead.

"For the buttons?" she teased, glancing up.

"For staying, understanding and signing up to endure this love with me!" he corrected, his eyes locking with hers.

Nysa's playful smile softened, and she paused for a moment and kissed his forehead. "Ishan," she began, "we've come so far. Don't you see? Everything we've been through—it's all led us here."

Her words hung in the air, pulling them both into the well of shared memories. They sat on the edge of the bed, and their laughter broke the emotional weight as they reminisced.

"Do you remember Dzükou?" Nysa asked, her eyes lighting up.

Ishan chuckled. "How could I forget? You were the most stubborn trekker I'd ever met."
"And you were the guy who got lost because you insisted on 'finding a better view,'" she retorted, laughing.

They fell into a comfortable rhythm, recalling the first time their paths crossed in the stunning landscapes of Dzükou Valley. Then, the conversation shifted to their earliest romantic moments.

"You know," Nysa said, nudging his arm, "I never thought you'd actually have the courage to ask me out after everything with Arushi."

Ishan sighed, a grin tugging at his lips. "I was terrified. I didn't want to mess things up with you, too. But then you walked into that office that day, all confident and sarcastic, and I knew I couldn't let you just be someone I admired from a distance."

Nysa giggled. "And here I thought you were a mess who just happened to be good-looking enough to tolerate."

"Gee, thanks," he replied, rolling his eyes.

Their laughter subsided, and the mood shifted again, heavier but tender. Ishan reached out, holding her hands in his.

"But seriously, Nysa. Everything about us—how we met, how we fought, how we've loved—it's been worth every moment. I wouldn't change a thing."

Nysa squeezed his hands, her voice steady but filled with emotion. "Neither would I. And soon, we'll be making another memory, once I'm back, hold on to my rings by then. Our wedding—it'll be the start of a whole new journey."

They sat there, lost in their shared past and the promises of their future, the bond between them growing stronger with every word and every shared look. Soon they reached the airport, Ishan's family was pampering and crying for him like he was a toddler, his mother was the most emotional among all of them, and Nysa managed to calm her down. Nysa held Ishan for longer than usual at the airport.

"You better not forget to call," she said, her voice shaking slightly.

"And don't let the time difference be an excuse."

Ishan brushed a piece of hair from her face.

'I will call you every day, Nysa. I promise! And when I return, we'll celebrate everything—your accomplishments, my growth, our togetherness and love too."

She nodded, not trusting her own voice. Instead, she placed a little notebook (It was her journal) in his hand.

"Read this when you're on the plane," she said.

It was full of memories, small notes, reminders of their love, and words of encouragement for times when he felt lonely or lost. As he went away, his heart heavy but resolute, he looked back to see her standing there, wiping her eyes and smiling through her tears. It wasn't the simplest path, but it was one they picked together.

Ishan and Nysa's physical distance strained their emotional intimacy because they clicked better when they could read each other's faces, and senses, and now it was a screen with texts where anything could be hidden, including any of their scars, reality, and trust.

Days passed, Ishan's good mornings and Nysa's goodnights turned into 'Hi and what's on?' As distance took over their energies and spirits, they grew miserable, they called once a day and blamed distance. None of them could grasp each other's lives and the only thing that mattered was their unbreakable love for each other. Nysa would try her best to connect Ishan with her new friends and events around, at days Ishan would also do the same and would share her pictures more than often about small things, festivals and college. It was hard for them to get used to screens and not be able to fully balance life , time and dreams, yet they were growing, it was a year long to go. As a few months passed, Ishan got engaged in the demands of his program, he kept working harder than he had ever before. Some days he remained up late reading over homework and presentations, while others he found himself navigating unanticipated cultural differences that left him feeling out of place. He video-called Nysa after his difficult days would pass and just dressed a fake smile on chats for her , so that she would not be worried about him. His face remained lined with tiredness, dark circles and his remarks lacked the warmth she was accustomed to. This became more often and now 5 months were yet to go.

Run To Me When The World Gets Meaner To You

CHAPTER THIRTEEN

Dear Heart,
She was tensed if I would always be there for her
and I genuinely want to be..
So what did you say?
Run to me when the world gets meaner.
Why?
The world would shadow us, lay thorns on us, rip us apart until
we choose to survive for ourselves but
when our hearts turn leaner, we would choose to survive for each other,
do the best for each other, prioritize each other and
the storms of choices would diminish,
Would you be able to hold her when she's falling, pushing you away for
your own good and
when the storms push you away too?
I'll be her strength, try harder and vow to nature to be hers - with
whatever I can..
So what did she reply to you?
Run to me when the world gets meaner...

Nysa called Ishan on his birthday,
April 3, 2015

Nysa's phone vibrated. She picked up, and it was Ishan. "I miss you, Nysa," he confessed. It was a phone late-night call for her, she felt nauseous but woke up from her bed and walked on her balcony as he continued. "But I don't know how to make this better. I'm trying."

"So am I. I called you 15 times. Where were you?" she whispered, tears streaming down her face, invisible to him. The pain of not feeling seen, heard, or understood was suffocating her now. Following a few seconds of shared stillness, Ishan began telling Nysa about his day, much like their usual routine, while Nysa remained silent. After a while, Ishan questioned her why she sounded so quiet. Ishan began telling Nysa about his day, much like their pattern, while Nysa remained silent. After a while, Ishan questioned her why she sounded so quiet.

"Ishan, do you even hear what I'm saying? " Nysa's voice broke in frustration. She had spent the entire day wanting to talk to him on his birthday, only to feel like an afterthought while he blabbered about his entire fun day.

"I'm listening, Nysa," he yawned. Nysa cut the call as she felt he was not interested and she waited for him to call back.

Ishan: Listen, I just finished a ten-hour shift today and met with my professor.
I am tired but I want to spend time with you, tell me what's going on?
Where do you think we were wrong?
And I am sorry if my over-excitement or stress ever made you feel hurt or held up.
Okay?
Nysa: Ishan, you're always drained to hear about my side, I'm worried about us, Ishan.
Do you realize how lonely I feel here?
I waited all day simply to speak with you for a minute without stress,
and when we do, you don't seem to care about my feelings.
(she replied to the text, tears welling up in her eyes.)

Ishan: I do care! I'm sorry Nysa, you felt this way, but..I'm doing this for us, remember?
I can't help but notice how intense things are here.
I Just work and live, expecting to see you next year and hug you forever.
I don't go to parties, I miss you in the festive streets, miss spending time with you.
As I see the dating spots, apps that my friends talk about,
It's just very hard Nysa, time, considering my situation I sometimes feel
.. taking out time is a lot now.

Nysa: I just need to know you are doing fine. Do you think I've got it easy?
Ishan.
Ishan?..

They get disconnected, and Ishan tries to call Nysa later that day, but she was asleep by then. Life tends to erect walls for them where there were once bridges, and for Ishan and Nysa, the days after the screen came between their sparkling love, it became like bricks being laid one by one between their lives. It began innocently, a missed call here, a delayed response there, a hint of overthinking. Insecurities piling and helplessness on sides. That evening, after their little disagreement, Ishan attempted to call her, but Nysa had already fallen asleep, overwhelmed by the weight of her thoughts. In the days that followed, the distance between them became wider. Ishan, buried beneath his rising job and personal duties as he was left alone by himself where no one looked after him, kept promising himself, "We'll talk later, I'll be home soon in a few months." However, later never seemed to arrive. Nysa, experiencing a small but undeniable distance, attempted to be patient, but the quiet became louder with each passing day, her little actions, and gestures seemed to drive Ishan's distractions and he tried to skip into a zone of himself. Ishan trudged through his days, a steady rhythm of meetings, deadlines, and unrelenting responsibilities. He was hopeful, always hopeful, that the chaos was temporary.

Just a few more months, he told himself, *and things will fall into place.* Yet, a part of him, quiet but persistent, knew better. He often found himself staring at his phone, scrolling through conversations with Nysa that had long since lost their warmth and rhythms. The realization stung: she was drifting. Her replies had grown shorter, her tone more distant. The once-vibrant connection they shared now felt like a pale echo, a memory that clung to the edges of his mind. Ishan knew it wasn't her fault. He had failed to strike the delicate balance between work, life, and love. There were times he wanted to call her, to explain, to say, *I'm trying, Nysa. I just need a little more time.* But the words never made it past his lips. Each day ended with him exhausted, making silent promises to himself to do better tomorrow. And yet, the guilt lingered. It gnawed at him during quiet moments, a sharp reminder of how he had overlooked her feelings. She deserved more—more attention, more care, more of him. But he believed, almost desperately, that this was just a phase. While these few months of their long-distance relationship appeared like a falling trajectory. Nysa would wake up to a text from Ishan, sometimes just a short "Miss you" or a picture of the sunrise in Arizona. Ishan tried to stay involved in her life, asking about her NGO-based work and sending occasional voice messages or mails when he couldn't find the time to call. Nysa, in turn, would send him pictures of her day or surprise him with a late-night call when she knew he was studying. But as time wore on, the cracks in their connection became more visible. Ishan's program grew more demanding. His schedule was filled with back-to-back classes, assignments, and networking events.

Even when he wanted to respond to Nysa's long texts or call her for an hour, he simply couldn't. He hated that his exhaustion was starting to seep into their conversations, making him sound disinterested or distracted. Nysa, meanwhile, started to feel the distance more intensely. She tried to keep herself busy with work, but the growing silence from Ishan's end made her overthink. Was he tired of her? Did he find someone else? She began to over analyze every delayed reply, every missed call. In her mind, the love they shared seemed to be slipping away, she could not dare to ask him anything as it would be a question of trust or patience between them, arguments might punch in and the emotional gap felt insurmountable. Nysa occasionally wanted to argue with Ishan because she felt insecure about this zero-attention game, and it was the least she could do to hear a lot from him and feel better knowing he was still battling for us. Ishan tried to reassure her from time to time.

"I love you, and nothing's changed. I'm just drowning in work right now," he explained during one of their rare calls. But his tired voice and hurried tone only deepened her insecurities. *Just a few months later,* he thought again, clinging to the hope that when the dust settled, he could make things right. He would have time to show her that he still cared, that she still mattered. But deep down, a quiet fear whispered, *What if she doesn't wait? What if by the time I'm ready, it's already too late?* Despite the doubts, Ishan held onto his hope, even as the weight of his choices settled heavily on his heart.

(1 month remaining for Ishan to return.)
Day 1 :
Nysa: Good morning! Did you sleep wellIshan: Morning! Slept okay, and stayed up finishing that project. What about you?
Nysa: I was restless. Couldn't stop thinking about how much I miss you.
Ishan: I miss you too, Ny. I hate that we're stuck.
By the way, I booked the flights home today, I'm excited to see you soon!
(Shares an attachment)
Nysa: Me too... but we'll get through this, right?
Ishan: Of course.We will,

You're my reason to work hard, to keep pushing and the biggest supporter of my dreams.

Nysa: Same. Don't overwork yourself, Ish.

Promise me?

Ishan: Promise. And you take care of yourself too.

Day 2:

Nysa: (deleted message)

Ishan: Hey, what's on?

Nysa: Nothing much. Just met some friends

finished my work at the office and went to a café.

You?

Ishan: I wish it was me with you, why them, not me?

Anyways

Just had a long lecture, then hit the library. This place still feels so lonely.

Nysa: Different how?

Ishan: Everything. The people, the food, even the weather, and I feel like my life's directed in some Hollywood movie.

Somehow, I am not getting used to this and I miss Indian food terribly,

terribly, but good for everything. I'll be home soon.

Nysa: Ishan, you're amazing. You'll adapt.

I believe in you. For now, let me spend time with my love of life.

Ishan: Thanks, Nysa. I needed to hear that. Cream and Espresso? Ew!

Nysa: No, it's Aloo Paratha with ghee and pickles..!

Ishan: Oh, you're cheating on your favorites huh?

Nysa: Sometimes, yes. I'm still not guilty. Also, guess what? I wore your ring today. Felt like you were with me.

Ishan: That makes me happy-ever-boyfriend. I wish I could hold your hand instead of just sending texts.

Nysa: Ah! Ishan...listen......okay, someday soon.

Ishan: Okay, I just gotta go for now! Keep texting, I will be back!

Nysa: I'll call you later then! Bye.

Day 3:

Nysa: (deleted message)

Hey, How was your day?

Ishan: Busy with my wife: Presentations, and kissing the coffee as much as I can.

Nysa : Wish it was me! So, how your friends and climate are treating you there, I bet the 'Phuchkas' here miss you a lot!

Ishan: I hope so! Friends are alright, just boring GDs and parties around.

The climate is full of my hopes..

I am missing Indian food too.

Nysa: Okay, I'm working late today, so I'll try to call you later. Bye for now!

Ishan: Sure, take care, love!

Day 4:

Nysa: Hi. How was your day?

Ishan: Exhausting. Presentations all day, and I still must prepare for tomorrow.

I might not be able to call or text..

Nysa: I had something to tell you, but it's okay. Later.

You sound drained. Ish, are you okay?

Ishan: Just tired. I don't want you worrying about me.

Nysa: But I do. I hate that I can't help.

Ishan: You do help, Ny. Just knowing you're there keeps me going.

Nysa: I feel like I'm losing you sometimes...

Ishan: You're not. You're the only woman I love, so never. It's just hard to balance everything.

Nysa: I know. I miss us.

Ishan: Me too. But this is temporary.

One day, we'll laugh about this, hold tight for me, a few days to go.

Nysa: I hope so. I love you, Ishan.

Ishan: I love you more, Nysa. Always.

Yet more than 20 days to go and their conversations showed how much they longed for closeness yet struggled to stay connected. Each word carried hope, love, and pain as they navigated the trials of distance. One night, after yet another conversation that left Nysa feeling unheard, Nysa sent a long text:

Nysa:Ishan, I don't think this is working anymore.
I can't keep feeling like I'm the only one trying, hurting, and remaining insecure. You're way too calm about handling things, bout us, you leave the conversations in between and I choke myself with curiosity/ overthinking with the questions that you leave unanswered.
I know it's gonna be the same when you return, you might have to focus on yourself and I know I love you, but I cannot stay on this sideline anymore, I'm hurting too much.
Maybe we should break up. Maybe I want to leave.
(deleted message)
(deleted message)
Thank you for everything,
I will keep loving you!

Later, Ishan read the message in disbelief, he knew it wasn't like her and she could never do something like this to him. He waited a bit and then he tried calling her, but she didn't pick up.

Ishan: Nysa, please don't do this. I know it's hard, but we can get through it.
Let's talk.
Nysa?
Hey, Please respond..
Nysa..?

But the damage was done. Nysa didn't reply that night or the next. And for the first time since they'd met, silence filled the space where love had once thrived. He kept calling her for hours on end, trying to reach her by email and letter, and days passed as his return date approached! This attempt to reach her was harder than expected for him because he never asked Nysa about her life without him, her life while she struggled to achieve her dreams, or how her childhood friends drifted away from her. His soul mocked him when he could not reach her and did not even know any of her friend's contact, her socials were just for a show, every person he tried to text through her social media was a fake identity in disguise of a friend and was not connected. As Ishan texted a few more mutual friends, they started projecting and throwing their opinions, this was like throwing a deer into a hungry lion's den. Ishan was already desperate, worried, and insecure, and the friends would make stories dragged from the dark or past that they found negative and would tell that to Ishan, this could make him picture Nysa wrongly because once his conviction about love has already been destroyed, what more could be toxic than the mind that stops believing. He reached out to her college friends through Facebook, but they had little to offer.

"She's been distant from us too, Ishan," one of them said. "Maybe she needs space."

The toxicity seeped into his head gradually, and although fighting hard for a few days, no response from her side filled the voids where his love and understanding formerly were. Every missed call, every brusque response, and every unsuccessful connection attempt added another brick to the wall that was forming between them. And while Ishan began to change as a result of his new life, Nysa felt trapped, burdened by her own troubles and the aching emptiness his absence had left. Ishan sat on his bed in Arizona, teary-eyed, staring at his phone screen and could not understand what was going on as everything fell apart in one day where he was not even ready to picture anything such. Nysa's absence, her words, and now her frosting silence hung on him like an anchor dragging him down. He had read her message several times, expecting to discover something, anything that suggested she didn't mean it. But as the days went on, her stillness became greater, and Ishan's anguish grew into grief. Just a week was left for Ishan to return.

He decided to text her mother, as he was determined that something was wrong or unsaid to him, and maybe this could be a hope,

Ishan: Namaste Aunty, I hope you're doing well. I'm worried about Nysa.
Can you please let me know if she's okay?

Hours turned into a full day, but there was no response as if the phone was untouched. As a last-shot effort, he called Ayush.

"Brother, I need a favor," Ishan stated, his voice breaking.

"Can you see if Nysa is at her place? "I just want to know if she's okay."

Ayush grudgingly agreed, but called back an hour later with devastating news.

"They moved out, I guess, sorry. The house appears vacant but I found a journal in her garden's mailbox, it had her name on it, I'll bring it over when you're back. Also, I asked the neighbor too...they had not seen Nysa and her mom in a while. I rang the bell and waited the whole evening in their garden, but no. What's going on, Ishan?"

Ishan's heart shattered as he told Ayush briefly about what had happened. Ayush was shocked and suggested, "Dude, see we love you too, don't be heartbroken, the one who is supposed to leave, will leave you. It's better you give up or you should come give one last try maybe. Because this appears serious nowadays it is normal to have such breakups. I hope she is fine, I will see if I find any news about her. Travel safely, until then."

The realisation that she was no longer in his life, but also physically unavailable, left him numb. He clung to his last scrap of hope: that she would show up when he got home. He envisioned her waiting at the airport, her eyes combing the crowd for him, eager to convey their love. But another part of him shouted a worse truth: What if she didn't? What if she was finished, and he'd lost her forever? Ishan wiped his tears, clutching the handmade rings she had once slipped back into his pocket. He whispered to himself, "If she's there, I'll do everything to make it right. If not... I'll learn to let her go." The days dragged on, and as his departure date drew nearer, the weight of uncertainty bore heavily on his heart.

(Ishan reaches Guwahati, Assam, India)

After a long flight back to India, Ishan walked out into the arrivals terminal, scanning every face in the crowd, hoping to find Nysa as she promised she would be there when he arrived. His heart pounded with anticipation, even as a small voice in his head whispered doubts. As the hours passed, the bustling crowd began to thin, and his hope waned. Still, he waited, standing at the same spot, watching every person who entered the terminal. By evening, the lights dimmed, and the airport quieted. Ishan finally stepped outside with his luggage, his heart heavy. Unable to leave, he sat down on a bench, staring at his phone, praying for some sign from her. The night crept in, cold and silent, and Ishan eventually drifted into an uneasy sleep, clutching the straps of his luggage.

Early in the morning, he was startled awake by the sharp ping of an email notification. He saw that Ayush was calling him from a distance, and as he blinked against the light from his phone, he saw that it was Nysa's name on a scheduled email. When Ayush got close to him, he asked Ishan to go home because everyone was waiting for him, including his desperate mother, and he was lying on the airport foot side, not answering any calls. Ishan followed Ayush and spoke behind him, Ayush understood the situation and drove him home. Ishan settled on the passenger seat as Ayush drove, his fingers shaking as he opened the mail from Nysa.

(Scheduled Mail From Nysa)

Subject: Ishan, I know you're back!

Dear Ishan,

By the time you're reading this, I hope you've reached India safely. You must be tired, and I hope you have successfully pursued your overseas dream.

I'm sorry, Ishan, I could not pick you up. But you performed great..admirably, remember, and I'm always proud of you. Rest well, eat a lot, and give it your all to a bright future! I just wanted to confess to you something but before that, just a reminder note here:

So, Mr.Ishan Raiyini, the reality is - some people stay because they learn to accept and then forgive. It's all about choosing to remember what the good part was and to let go of the negative aspects. I have high expectations from you-your journey toward growth, and I believe, even without me, you will be able to achieve what you want. It might hurt a little, but eventually, everything becomes past as the time ticks.

I know you can fight and die for the one person who loves you, and understands you but you also have a limit, grow up to accept that!

I'm more than grateful to be loved by a man who is you, you don't know what or how much it means to me, and loving you was so pure, so beautiful that the journey never made me feel unstable/unreal. Oh Ishan, I can never stop loving the fact that you're a man of acts, a guide, a real friend-partner, and an endless protector.You have understood me when none did, you have seen me through my worsts but I guess this is it now! I feel bad for not being able to return your gestures, for not being enough and for not staying. I should have told you that your Nagaland trip and how 'we' met was NOT a complete coincidence, (Chang was my cousin's friend- he told me about you and I fell for you from a distance from the moment I saw you..). I liked you from a distance and stalked you planned over a few of them but trust me falling for you was honest. My love is honest and so is this time. You never made me question 'what are we?', and had committed towards me like a pure soul without any conditions. However, it's time I leave my heart to you. Cause you wait for someone who you shelter hope with, shelter and expectation to return with and sadly, I cannot be that person!

The past few months have been... different, different than usual. Not better, not worse, just different. I've been thinking about us a lot, sometimes too much, and I've noticed things I didn't notice before, like how my wardrobe has changed from the colorful clothes you loved to more subdued colors, or how I suddenly prefer this new coffee brand over the one we used to drink together. I realized how your love was never conditional, never restrictive and you shared my pain, more than myself. A lot of events were intentional, but I suppose I've been adjusting and willing to love you more everyday, as I live more, until today. This is a very weird moment to express but there were a lot of moments and my imagination had witnessed a lot of possibilities where I found myself thinking about a peaceful life with our children! I was never ready for any such feeling but with you, it changed. You'd be a perfect father Ishan. I do miss you. I was missing us. I needed this time, though, to discover who I am without you, what I want, and to remind myself that I am more than just a continuation of our relationship. I just don't feel ready for anything and my body is leaving all the strength I need.

I've been struggling to concentrate on my work and balancing us. Even though it's a daily struggle, I cried overnights to settle everything and trust me, I couldn't. Even my health has not been decent – I went through saline, got admitted twice and the doctor said it could be worse in the future. On some days, I could not force myself to eat anything since the medications made me feel queasy (I missed you then). However, I'm getting by. I've even taken up yoga, which is beneficial, and seeing me try to strike poses would have made you giggle; it's not at all elegant.(I'm just writing this all in a letter cause I'm scared that I will not live anymore).

Ishan, I love you, but I had to be able to support myself and I don't want you to suffer with me through all this. It does not negate my fear but dragging you to this hell with me is not right. I almost lost my job in June and I could not tell you because you had your own busy side. I cannot picture myself here- a girl who used to camp outside, climb hills, and hike for hours, is now close to being bedridden. As time passed and we continued to communicate, I visited every place where we spent time together, and tried making the gulabi chai, everything was my favorite since you were there, a part of it. Nothing made sense about me anymore! I got lost while loving you, can you feel that? How strange!

Indeed, you are Zinc, Ishan - I was right about it. After the Nagaland trip, I was afraid of what would happen if we crossed paths again but here we are, unconditionally accepting, loving, and fighting for each other. Will we remain unchanged? Will I be adjusting or compromising my happiness in the frame of love with you? Would this still make sense? I know right, it's so not me but you still have time, to move on with your future. I am not happy with this relationship, Ishan..I am sorry!

Additionally, please don't let your overanalyzing derail this, but I had to say it. My rights, my heart, and my feelings are reserved for you including my caustic outbursts and coffee preferences. So, wherever I will be I will be fine but I know together - we will not be..sort of...! I've shared our common songs with you, I hope you like them. Take care of yourself, and don't try to find me, you will regret life! Live your best Ishan.

Always,
Nysa

(Shares a Song Playlist Link)

Ishan sat on the bench, reading and re-reading the email word by word, tears welling in his eyes as he slightly chuckled at her honesty. A weight lifted from his heart—she still loved him. She was still his Nysa, be it whatever, let the past begone, she felt lonely with his presence - ate him. Him being there through the screen which had become their temporary parts of lives and with time Nysa didn't let him divert irrespective of the reality that she was sick, wiping his face, Ishan continued to travel, as they reached home. He wouldn't wait any longer. He'd find her and make things right. Be it whatever. She had cried herself to sleep most nights, feeling foolish for holding onto the hope that things would magically fix themselves until she fell sick and Ishan did nothing. He felt ashamed that she couldn't let go because a part of her still believed in the love. He recalled how King Rama and Queen Sita are a timeless testament to the power of love to overcome physical isolation. When Sita was separated from Rama, their hearts were bonded by unbreakable faith, trust and passion. Rama's ambition to find Sita, as well as Sita's firm belief in his return, were driven by their unwavering faith in each other and their shared destiny. It was indeed a long distance but no notifications, no pictures, no letters only pure trust and the world had twisted so much today that trust is marketised on dating apps and can be brought over by texts or scrolling's.

Despite the distance, difficulties, and uncertainties, between the two souls (Rama and Sita) they never let doubt or despair cloud their love. The separation reminds us that love is more than just being present. Ishan knew it was all about resilience, trust, and a profound spiritual bond, just a mere distance cannot break them, not a chance when she had wrote she will still love him. Queen Sita bore her loneliness with elegance and dignity, maintaining her faith even in the darkest of times while King Rama, on his part, turned his longing into purpose, overcoming insurmountable difficulties to rejoin with her. The power of loving someone is invisible-invincible. Ishan had fixed his mind to be patient and look for Nysa.

Our Big Day

CHAPTER FOURTEEN

Dear Heart,
I wish I could see her again for the first time,
The echo of her name, the nervous hellos, that sweet denial stage and
ultimately falling for her over small stupid and normal things?
I remember that first beat..it was the rhythm of romance,
But see, she's not here with me anymore,
her memories have wrapped you in pain and
in another universe thinking that she could be near me,
kills you!
I could not do anything grand for her,
Nor could I build a castle, or write a book about her..
What should a normal incapable man in love should do in love's
embrace?
Cherish her soul, don't forget what you felt,
her fleeting trace, and stay with her memories,
submit to the love you committed and that's the grandest charm a man
can ever hold..
Is that enough?
Her soul knows it well!
It is.

Ishan's heart was racing as he returned home; he was quickly approaching the familiar corner of his lane, each step bringing him closer to home and the fear that he would not find Nysa there. He took a long breath to stop thinking about her for a while (which he couldn't), realizing that there's a time for everything and his family needs him to be happy. His fingers trembled slightly as they traced the old brass nameplate, smoothed by years of monsoon rain and summer heat. The experience was overwhelming: he inhaled the lingering aroma of cardamom chai, with his mother's coconut ladoos, which eventually brought tears to his eyes. The scents of incense sticks and the experiences can never be duplicated or replaced. He was home - not partially, but from his whole heart, every corner in his house reminded him of a tale, and every room held some affection for him. He greeted everyone warmly, but there was a distinct, heavy feeling in the air. His mother's normally upbeat manner seemed to be tinged with a quiet sadness. As they sat for tea, Ishan mentioned that he was planning to find time to meet Nysa, and she looked at him with a soft yet strained expression.

"You should visit the hospital where you once took her," she said gently, avoiding his eyes.

"Hospital? Why?" Ishan asked, his voice full of confusion and worry.

Her calm yet sorrowful expression made him even more uneasy. "Just go, Ishan. You'll understand." The following day, with uneasiness gnawing at his chest, Ishan called Nysa's mother, but there was no response.

As he drove to the hospital, his anxiety grew. He hesitantly said at the reception, "I'm searching for Nysa Sharma. She had previously been here.

"No, sir I don't think we have anyone like that.." A nurse responds from thc hallway.

"See, I am here to check that, it's urgent to me..she needs me miss!" Ishan begged in front of everyone.

The nurse inside the counter shared a gesture with the other nurse and nodded yes after taking a quick look at the records. "She is admitted here, yes."

Ishan's heart fell. In an attempt to get information, he blurted out, "I am one of her guardians."

He was guided to the intensive care unit by the nurse via a maze of white corridors.

Following the nurse through the hospital's quiet, sterile hallways, Ishan's steps faltered as the fluorescent lights overhead flickered faintly, casting a pale glow that mirrored the uneasiness in his heart. He was used to worrying, but this time it felt different—a deep, gnawing fear that clawed at him with every step; his palms were sweaty, and his throat was dry as though the air itself refused to give him breath. The nurse looked back at him with a mix of professionalism and quiet empathy.

"Her mother comes once a day to see her," she said, her voice low but clear in the quiet hallway, "but she can't stay long. There's a maid who usually stays with her, but..." With an almost contrite expression, the nurse paused. She's not here at the moment. I had no idea where she went.

Ishan's thoughts whirled negatively with guilt, fear and concern. What made Nysa's mother abandon her in this situation? How could anyone, much less Nysa, face this isolation while fighting something so destructive? His terror grew with each unanswered query. His heartbeat accelerated as they approached the intensive care unit, and the hum of equipment became more audible. Slowing down, he felt as though postponing the inevitable would somehow make it less imminent. The ICU's glass doors loomed ahead, offering a view of the world within, a place of silent pandemonium where life hung on the brink of existence. In front of a door, the nurse paused and looked up at him. Her eyes remained fixed. Her kind yet steady state seemed to be preparing him for what was to come. She said,

"She's in here."

For a moment, Ishan was immobile. His chest rose and fell with weak breaths as his hands clenched into fists at his sides. What would he observe? How would he respond? A glimpse of Arushi's wounds subtly passed through his mind alerting him about the worst he felt. He was overcome with regret for not being there sooner and for being so preoccupied with his own life that he had failed to see hers subtly falling apart. He finally plucked up the confidence to come forward. The faint hum of medical equipment and the antiseptic smell of disinfectant hit him as the nurse pulled the door open, and he saw her—Nysa. She was surrounded by wires and tubes, a somber reminder of her fight. Her face was hollow and pale, and the tubes and machinery all around her made her appear incredibly frail. Her once-bright presence appeared to have faded to a weak ghost of itself, as her chest rose and fell in feeble, irregular breaths. Ishan's heart broke into a thousand fragments when he froze in the doorway. He knew a Nysa who had argued with him, laughed with him, and carried herself with great independence, but this was not the Nysa. This person had waged a fight without speaking, and now she was on the verge of collapse, her fragility and suffering exposed.

His footsteps reverberated in the still room as he entered slowly. "How did I let this happen?" he mumbled to himself as he swallowed hard, the lump in his throat refusing to go away. With a clinical yet compassionate tone, the nurse stated, "She's fighting Crohn's disease, It's an inflammatory disease that has significantly gotten worse. She has experienced intestinal damage, severe anemia, and malnourishment. We're doing everything we can, but her health is critical," the nurse said hesitantly. Now it's almost the stage. As though reality itself were coming apart, Ishan sensed a change in the floor beneath him. Breathing shallowly, he supported himself against the wall as his knees nearly buckled. His thoughts were filled with memories of Nysa's subtle vulnerabilities, her stubborn independence, and her laughter.

His voice broke as he managed to ask, "How long...has she been here?"

"Something around 10 days in the Emergency but she has been visiting frequently, only Dr.Sarathi can tell you about her current condition, and she is in the next room." said the nurse quietly as she wanted no one to find out. Ishan was struck like a tidal wave by the weight of her loneliness, her suffering, and her stillness. As though reaching for her, he put his hand on the glass and took a step closer wearing a mask on his face.

"Nysa...why didn't you tell me?" he muttered, tears running down his cheeks. Nysa appeared to be a little different, he couldn't find the scar on her hand, her hair appeared lighter, and for a second Ishan felt so distant from her. He knocked on the next room where Dr. Sarathi was checking something on her screen, she invited Ishan inside. In the dimly lit office, Ishan sat opposite the doctor, his hands balled into fists on his knees.

"I'm Nysa's guardian, here's my ID, I have just arrived and want to know...How bad is it, Doctor?" He questioned, handing an ID to the doctor as his voice was firm despite the terror in his heart.

"What precisely is going on with her?"

The doctor checked the ID and recalled his name and signature on Nysa's previous medical records too. She sighed; the fatigue of breaking bad news was imprinted on her features.

"Ishan, Nysa's condition is critical. Her extreme stage of Crohn's illness has resulted in consequences, chief among them being sepsis. Her body has been overtaken by the infection, leading to systemic inflammation. Her organs are under a great deal of strain. As you should be aware, sepsis is a potentially fatal condition, and she has a considerable chance of going into a coma."

Ishan's throat tightened with breath. He asked for more information.

"Is she hurting?

"How likely is it that she will recover or wake up?"

The doctor lowered her voice. "She is currently stable but under a lot of sedation. We're doing everything we can to keep the infection under control and keep her organs healthy. But in situations like this, recovery is questionable. She will require 24-hour care and, to be honest, a miracle." Her words struck Ishan like a tonne of bricks. Hearing this strengthened his determination, even if his world had already started to fall apart. Reminiscences of Nysa flooded his head, including her quiet strength, her fiery energy, and her laughter. This was not how he could lose her.

His firm words circled his mind, "I'll stay here," broke the lingering silence. "I won't be leaving. Work, commitments, and other things can wait. I won't let her deal with this because she needs me. Sensing the resolve in his voice, the doctor nodded, adding, "Having someone who cares deeply for her nearby can make a lot of difference."

Ishan sprang to his feet, his determination unwavering.
He headed back to her chamber.

As though reaching for her, Ishan put his hand on the glass and took a step closer. The world around him blurred; the sterile white of the hospital room dissolved into the overwhelming ache in his chest. Inside, Nysa lay motionless, her fragile frame connected to machines that sustained her life. The rhythmic beeping of the heart monitor became the cruel metronome of his guilt, each sounds a reminder of his neglect. He sat by her bedside, his trembling fingers entwined with hers. Her hand was cold, her once vibrant warmth replaced by a chilling stillness. Ishan's mind spiralled into a storm of regret. How did it come to this? She had been his light, a spark of life in his monotonous existence, yet he had let her dim while he chased fleeting shadows of ambition and obligation. He gazed at her pale face, the hollow contours that hinted at the battles she had fought in silence.

"I thought you'd always be here," he whispered, his voice breaking.

"I thought there would always be time."

The thought clawed at him relentlessly, how he had taken her for granted. His spiritual pursuits, his philosophy, and his excuses now seemed diminishing. What was the point of enlightenment if it blinded you to the ones who mattered? Love wasn't eternal by default, it needed tending, care, and presence. And he had failed her. He stared at the monitor, the steady rhythm both a comfort and a torment. For the first time, he truly understood the fragility of time, the weight of lost moments. She had been slipping away, and he was too caught up in his world to see it. In that shadowy room, with only her breathing and the buzz of machines for company, Ishan grabbed an empty glass, poured some water, and drank it all at once.

After a few minutes of looking at her, he fell asleep alongside her, making a vow—not just to her, but to himself that if she woke up, he would change, stick to her, and understand her. But if she didn't, he would carry this pain forever without looking back or changing himself for anyone else. The shadows of his selfishness loomed large, swallowing him whole. And for the first time, he was truly afraid of the inattentive man he had become.

What the..?

CHAPTER FIFTEEN

Dear Heart,

Life has unfolded backwards, everything I felt, experienced and learnt fleeted in no time,

I chased a dream and paid a price,

Doesn't' everyone pay a price for their dreams?

They do but what if a multiverse holds my past, my memories and dreams with a better embrace where I never lose anything?

It's a mirage powered by greed.

Why do you fall for it?

Imperfections and failures are your test to learn and fix while you grow..

Would I live again, the way forward?

Can I start everything afresh?

No

Then what am I supposed to live for?

Your consciousness, conscience and to give love.

Why should I always give?

Because you are not selfish, you know what purity is and you are a man of your actions,

Giving is the major reason for human existence, if everything is about you then why not let the world

diminish and live by yourself.. only the art of giving defines the part of humanity in you..

Ishan? Ishan...Ishu..? Ishan wakes up to a sweet voice calling his name with a hint of frustration.

"Nysa is calling you.
She needs you to speak to her parents about your wedding." Ishan's mother explained in a louder voice.

Ishan wakes up and finds himself wet ..with sweat, as he looks at the time and feels shocked. As he checks his mail, there is nothing new, and the mail Nysa shared is not there anymore. The first rays of sunlight poured into the open hall, illuminating the faint patterns of Sanskrit inscriptions on the wall. Ishan stirred from his makeshift bed, his body stiff from the uneven surface, a soft tune of classical music *Zindagi Ke Sath* by *M.Rafi* diverted his senses. Rubbing his eyes, he noticed an elderly pandit, clad in a simple khaki dhoti and a handcrafted Pashmina shawl, walking calmly toward the exit. The man had an air of wisdom about him, his steps slow but purposeful. Ishan's eyes fell on the wall where the pandit had been standing moments ago. The Sanskrit letters seemed freshly written, their elegance and precision mesmerizing. Confused and curious, Ishan sat up.

"Pandit ji!" he called out, his voice cracking from sleep. None replied.

Ishan scrambled to his feet, his heart racing. He opened his mouth to say something, to ask who the pandit was or what he was doing there, but before he could utter a word, another pandit stepped out of the hall and into the morning mist. Ishan hurried to follow him, but as he reached the door, Ayush's voice called out groggily from behind him.

"Bro, what are you doing? It's barely morning. Come back!."

Ishan froze, turning back to see Ayush sitting up, rubbing his face and yawning.

"Ayush, did you see him?

The pandit who was just here?"

Ayush frowned, looking around the empty hall. "What pandit? There's no one here except us. You've been dreaming or something. Sleep!"

Ishan felt a chill run down his spine. "No, I wasn't dreaming. He was right there, writing Sanskrit on that wall outside this room." He gestured toward the wall and it was blank.

Ayush stood up, walked over to the wall, and squinted. "I don't see anything new here, man. Just the same wall that was here before."

Ishan's head swam with questions, how could Ayush not see it? He had been so sure of what he saw. The inscriptions were vivid, the pandit's presence undeniable. But now, standing in the silence of the hall, doubt began to creep in.

Ayush clapped him on the shoulder. "You've been overthinking too much lately, bro. Maybe your brain is playing tricks on you. Come, let's get some chai."

Ishan nodded a 'no' absentmindedly, but his mind was racing. Who was the pandit? What did the Sanskrit writings mean? And why was he the only one who could see him? As Ayush left, Ishan felt something was very different. He was still sleepy and the classic song made him extra comfy to enjoy a nap. Everything had felt so real, almost unbearably. After a while, Ishan woke up when the soft murmur of voices around him intensified. He blinked, trying to make sense of his surroundings, gripping his mind back to reality, his body felt lethargic and his mind heavy. He was lying on the old, comfortable sofa in his room, far from the cold, sterile atmosphere of the hospital intensive care unit. He was shocked! He woke up, saw the Pandit ji, and now this...the air was filled with the distinct buzz of activity as the sunshine poured through the lace curtains. His mother was rushing about, giving directions for what appeared to be a complex ritual preparation. His father, who was often multitasking, was pacing while talking on his phone in hurried, clipped tones. His pals were all over the place, giggling, decorating, and coming and going with bright marigold flowers and glittering curtains. The fragrance of jasmine and marigold filled the air, mingling with the soft sound of sacred chants that echoed through the space. Chaos reigned; However, it was the sort of disorder that seemed alive. His attention was drawn to a blur of rose pink before he could fully comprehend his location. It was Nysa, hurrying towards him with her dupatta sloping haphazardly and her lehenga glistening in the gentle early light. Her eyes were bright with a mixture of worry and annoyance, and her cheeks were flushed.

"There you are!" she said, her tone piercing yet tinged with indisputable affection.

"I have searched all over for you! You're here, of all places, napping as if nothing were happening while everyone else is racing around. Are you even concerned? Glaring at him as if his absence had resulted in a great catastrophe, she crossed her arms.

Ishan, still confused, sat up. His voice was raspy as he whispered in confusion, "Nysa?"

"What's happening? Were we not? Why does it appear so unfamiliar, like every inch of my sorrow is fixed right here." The hospital's recollection hung over him like a shadow as he walked away. Yet here she appeared, vibrant, brimming with vitality.

"Stop daydreaming!" Nysa yanked him to his feet with a snap.

"There is too much for us to do. Everyone's waiting, so hurry up." She remarked, half pleased, half annoyed, "How are you able to sleep with all of this chaos?"

As his senses gradually returned to normal, Ishan took another glance around and gulped some cold water in a hurry. He seemed to have walked into a completely different life, which was bizarre. The dread of her disease and the weight of the hospital room had disappeared. It was a vivid, overwhelming, and somehow reassuring moment. His mind rushed back to the hospital, to her tiny form, to the sound of her hard breathing.

"This can't be real." Ishan's thoughts were racing as he gazed at her. However, how? You were, Nysa. Unable to force himself to pronounce the words," he paused.

With a humorous inclination of her head, she questioned, "What can't be real?"Ishan stumbled back, his mind whirling. Had he entered a different reality?

Was there a cosmic grace here? Or had his desperation created a horrible illusion? He turned to face Nysa, who was grinning curiously at him while adjusting her dupatta and jingling her bangles.

"Ishan, you're behaving weirdly. Did you have a head injury while you were asleep?" She asked.

To be sure she was there, he wanted to reach out and touch her hand, to feel its warmth. But he was anchored by terror. He didn't want to break it if this was unreal. He didn't want to wake up. The questions he dared not ask made his head hurt. Was this a present? A dream? Or a sight of another world, where a more compassionate course had been selected by fate? A slight smile appeared on Nysa's face as she pulled him towards her. Perhaps it was a dream, or perhaps it was something more, a chance to experience the delight of life once more, a glimmer of hope. He decided to follow her for the time being, as Ishan got closer to Nysa, and his heart was pounding. Everything about her appeared too genuine, to be true, from the familiar gleam in her eyes to the subtle glitter of her light bridal jewelry. His mind was confused, trying to make sense of everything, while Nysa was just in front of him. Her bangles jingled quietly with each movement as she turned abruptly and drew closer before he could speak.

"Ishan, you're impossible," she muttered, her voice wavering between irritation and something more profound. She reached for his collar and kissed his neck softly drawing him in. The weight of a mile's worth of distance of emotions poured into his breath as her lips touched him. The sounds of the busy family and hawan faded into the distance as the world around them became blurry. Ishan's body seemed to betray him, reacting to her touch intuitively, while his intellect screamed for clarity, leaving him bewildered. Nysa softly whispered against his ears, her voice cracking a little, "I missed you. You have no idea how long I've been waiting for this. For you?"

Before he could respond, she began unbuttoning his shirt with deft fingers, her smell drove him crazily close, and her movements led to an intensity that matched the chaos in his mind. Ishan's hand shot up, holding one of her ankles gently, halting her actions. His voice was a mixture of bewilderment and amazement as he said, "Nysa. This... doesn't make sense."

Ishan read from her face, the warmth of her touch and the sincerity in her eyes made everything seem true, but the persistent doubt in his chest would not go away. He whispered, more to himself. She stopped for a moment and glanced up at him with a mix of annoyance and kissed him for a bit longer while his shirt remained unbuttoned and her hands slid down his abs. Her puzzled expression perplexed him even more when he stopped her hands by interlocking his fingers with hers.

"Ishan, what's not making sense?

That I cherish you?

That after all this time, we're finally together?

"But when I last saw you, you were..." Unable to express the memory of her frail body in the hospital bed, he trailed off. Nysa's face softened as she cocked her head. "You overthink things. She put a palm on his cheek and remarked, "Always stuck in your head. Just be with me right now, right here."Nysa's enigmatic smile and whispered "Does it matter?" left Ishan torn between the surreal beauty of the moment and the lingering echoes of reality. Nysa turned towards a large mirror, her hands trembling as she adjusted the delicate necklace resting on her collarbone. As she briefly expressed, "You know Ishan I have always wanted a small wedding where the people we love in our lives would be blessing us and this preparation, this welcoming feeling to start a new life, especially when it's you.. it's perfect. You know.."

She continued to talk about their future and her imagination, Nysa's reflection betrayed the storm swirling inside her—nerves, doubts, the weight of her past clawing at the edges of her joy. She wasn't sure if she deserved this moment, this love yet she spoke. A wave of thoughts followed her heart-What if she wasn't enough? Ishan found her there, his presence quiet but grounding, like an anchor in her sea of chaos. However, he was more unsure whether to surrender to the dream or fight to wake up, and the line between truth and illusion blurred further, leaving him on the precipice of longing and doubt. He pushed her softly, distant from him, Nysa continued to chastise Ishan for his "legendary level of weirdness" while he rubbed his eyes. Some energy was flowing through the room, yet something wasn't quite right. Nysa stood there, looking at him as he saw a strange banner on the wall, waiting to be hung, he googled it, as it appeared like a ridiculously corny tagline in Sanskrit, underneath, "Daiva, Daiva Yugmah,(divine couple) blessed on earth!" He murmured, "What the—?"

He tried recalling his memory as he left the room, away from Nysa, he pulled Ayush from a crowd of aunties and started explaining him that he had fallen asleep off next to Nysa in the hospital room, surrounded by the sterile smell of antiseptic and the sound of her heart monitor. Holding her delicate hand and making silent vows to be by her side was his final recollection. He had fallen asleep, exhausted and anxious, a weird calm descending upon him among the turmoil. The sound of bells and shankh (conch shells) greeted him as he awoke. Although he was in his room, his bed was decked out as if it were for a special event. The ceiling was adorned with marigold strings, and the window let in sunshine that was filtered through colourful paper cutouts."

Ayush interrupted.

"Bro, she is your fiancé, how can you even think of her being sick! Cheap dude. Let me go to the aunties and you go to your future aunty. I love attention." Ayush leaves thinking he was joking.

Ishan noticed the same Pandit Ji who had just given him a lecture on life and spirituality before he could comprehend this madness. Now, the elderly man was quietly making a huge hawan and drinking tea while idly reciting mantras. He approached him after wearing his white and gold kurta, folded neatly on the chair next to him, and rubbed his eyes, certain that he was still dreaming, but the noise outside was getting louder—laughing, loud Punjabi music, clinking utensils, and happy voices. Ishan's mother was overseeing decorations and telling him to get ready.

"Ishan! You'll be late! How can you be so careless on your wedding day? Get ready properly." He whispered, his heart racing and his eyes fell upon a large poster on the wall that read, "Ishan Weds Nysa."

"Pandit Ji?" Ishan stumbled in nervousness. "Weren't you... at a temple? Why are you here?"

Pandit Ji smiled wisely at him. "Setting lives on the right path—doing what I do best." After giving a mysterious wink, he resumed lighting the hawan fire.

It became more bizarre. A giant family portrait of Nysa's family stood on one side of the room; they were far too happy to be in his living room. Hovering close by, his mother was still directing traffic like a drill sergeant, giving the decorators orders before abruptly turning to face him.

"Ishan! Get ready and stop being a statue! For crying out loud, you are the groom!

"Groom?" His voice became more frightened as he whispered something beneath his breath.

"What's happening? I am. He slapped himself in a dramatic gesture, desperate to get out of this bizarre carnival. Hard.

He rubbed his cheek and winced. "All right, I had that feeling. I'm conscious. However, what is this?

Nysa rolled her eyes and reappeared next to him. "Are you going to quit behaving like you're in a Christopher Nolan film? Ishan, this is real. Now get dressed! You're embarrassing me."

Ishan continued to rub his cheek, whispering to himself, "This is the most costly practical joke ever, or I'm dreaming." Perhaps I ought to attempt self-slapping once more.

The weight of what could have been weighed heavily on him—a parallel reality in which her absence was his love of life faded, her laughter had diminished into quiet white sheets, and her touch was but a memory buried beneath the weight of loss. Yet here she was, alive, bright, and achingly genuine. The prospect of losing her had changed his very molecules, instilling in him a profound spiritual knowledge of love's vulnerability. He looked for his mother, who was still decorating and now putting up some garlands. Ishan stood next to her and called her with a strained look, assuming he was worried about getting married or overanalyzing the situation, his mother pulled him aside.

"What is wrong with you Ishan?" She asked with a hurried expression.

"Maa, there is a lot happening right now, but I know my presence here is important, I don't know if I am ready to be involved here or maybe all these ritualistic preparations, colourful garlands, and the wedding.. it feels like too much, we could have just signed court marriage for now.." He questioned her.

"Ishan, the court dates are for tomorrow and so is your final wedding, today, we are just doing the *hawana* for you better lives ahead. Also, both of your planetary positions, lunar calendar (tithi), and birth charts (Kundlis) directed the auspicious date of tomorrow at noon..go ready now, I think 'you are' drunk! She scolded.

Ishan stood still zoning out and looking at the *hawana* preparations, the pandit ji appeared mysterious to him but he was experiencing extreme uneasiness. Nobody related to him or understood what he was trying to say; he was a joke to everyone, and nobody was concerned about anything other than the wedding and his welfare!

"Ishan.."
His mother called him softly as she looked at him.

"Remember when grandma taught you about the Bhakti tradition? You told me about this..that she emphasised the importance of divine love, but earthly love, too, required worship, presence, care, and acknowledgment. She also told you how Lord Krishna's counsel to the gopis, particularly to Radha rani, emphasised that love was a selfless surrender, a bond that brought divine delight into mortal lives. See the way children use this term 'love' is way cruel and easy, I'm proud that you didn't and I am proud that you grew up to be a man of your word."

He felt a stab of shame that everything was fine until she left him. He was not able to collect or balance his mind, and his love for Nysa.

"If someone neglected or failed to cherish the love in front of your—family member, wife, or a friend—they were essentially oblivious to the riches offered by the universe. Godly devotion, or bhakti, is essential for liberation, but it is the love shared with those around us that binds us to life.. Neglecting it would be like standing before a deity and closing one's eyes. We need money to survive, but sliding into a cycle of earning and spending without regard for Love, whether spiritual or earthly, is equivalent to being non-living." She continued.

"Maa, these feelings and emotions are so unique to each individual that they must be honoured, and I agree that love should be viewed as a sacred offering, as it is the truest expression of devotion but maa, I am not able to understand where I am standing right now? How am I supposed to accept everything?" He expressed in a louder voice.

She looked at him and wondered what went wrong with him, "Are you in your sanity? You should start getting ready if you don't understand what is going on, I'm here to tell you – go get changed first." She commands Ishan in an angry tone.

Ishan was about to ask his mom further about what was happening with him but Nysa's voice cut through the tense vibe of the mother and son, her light and overly cheerful call.. "Aunty ji! How are you? You're glowing and crashing today huh..!" she chirped as she approached them, her presence radiating a forced energy that immediately unsettled his mind, and his heart was beating faster. Ishan stiffened his chest uncomfortably, his jaw clenched. Nysa looked different—not in appearance but in demeanor. Her smile was wider than usual, but her eyes didn't carry the warm glow that he used to admire. There was something painfully artificial about her, as though she were playing a role, trying too hard to get his attention.

His mother caught up in Nysa's presence, beamed. "Hello, Nysa! My little princess, you've brightened up our aura," she said warmly, completely missing the undercurrent of tension.

However, Ishan couldn't meet Nysa's gaze. The questions gnawed at him like sharp edges—what was real and what wasn't? What had happened after they returned from the airport? The gaps in his memory felt gaping, and he needed answers. Nysa took a step closer, tilting her head childishly with a smile as if expecting him to react.

"Ishan? Hello hero?" she teased, her voice attempting to bridge the invisible chasm between them.

He remained stone-faced, withdrawing further. "I need to try on my kurta," he muttered, dismissing both of them and turning sharply toward the door.

His mother's eyes flickered with concern. She leaned toward Nysa, whispering, "Did you two fight? He's been like this since he came home."

Nysa forced a smile. "No, Aunty. He's probably just tired or nervous about all of this." But there was a crack in her voice that betrayed her feelings.

As Ishan walked away, thoughts clouded his mind. Am I matching the events right? I returned from the airport, the conversation between us was just now, there were strange gaps that he could not recollect in his mind—none of it added up. He clenched his fists. Another thought popped up, but why is she acting like this? And why does it feel like I'm missing something vital? He walked towards the corridor where less people passed by, and sat down wondering if even Nysa was really like a Zinc to him, averagely adjusting but a unique person who bonded with his soul releasing a unique but crucial reaction. However, it wasn't just his heartbeat that kept him connected to her; it was as if every fibre of his being, every molecule, and every breath lived just for this moment with her. He imagined a future that was defined not by fear of loss, but by the bravery to love totally, deeply, and unapologetically. In her presence, he realised that love was more than a feeling; it was a power that transcended time, and added reason to one's existence itself. He was spiritually and molecularly in love with her—a love that was woven into his very being, he kept untangling this feeling as soon as he grew mature.

His thoughts shifted between the profound and the intimate thoughts about loving Nysa, realizing how love and dedication were connected, a lesson replicated throughout the rich fabric of Sanatana Dharma. His mind wandered to the narrative Shiva and Parvati, in which Parvati's devotion prompted her to cross lifetimes to be with Shiva, emphasizing that love—whether for a spouse, family, or the divine—is an essential component of our destiny. But what was more bothering was, how many more Zinc-souls could end up like them. As Ishan stood in the bizarre turmoil of a life that made no sense, his mind raced. What had brought him here? Was this a complex trick his mind was doing, a dream clouded by fatigue, or had he had a bad drink? The jagged edges of reality seemed distorted as if he had been transported to another realm where time was hazy and reason was non-existent. A split thought hit Ishan, sharp and sudden—a pang of insecurity. *Did she ever care? Was I just a fleeting chapter in her life, a name she didn't even bother to mention?* The weight of that doubt pressed against his chest, bitter and suffocating. He tried to rationalize it, but the fragments of their memories mocked him, refusing to be neatly boxed away.

Love had always been a maze for Ishan, but with Nysa, it felt like navigating shadows. She was there and not there, present but elusive. Her silence had planted a seed of doubt that now grew wild in his heart. Was her isolation a shield from hurt—or a sign that he had never truly mattered to her? Yet it wasn't only the disconnected setting that unsettled him. It was Nysa. Or rather, Nysa's thought. Since she left his life, he had carried that familiar anguish like an unseen wound, and it still tore at him. Despite his repeated attempts to contact her, he had always been met with stillness, as if she had vanished into thin air. Even her closest friends, Vani and Alia, had become little more than echoes of worry, tangentially connected but never totally committed to her, as his hold on hope had weakened, thread by thread. Nysa, though? She had always been a mystery shrouded in loneliness. There was no denying that she was solitary, quiet, and ensconced in a bubble of aspiration. She didn't ever mention Ishan to her friends, never had many people with whom to confide, and lived in seclusion like a shadow pursuing her ambitions. His fists clenched involuntarily with regret, shame, insecurity, and guilt of not even being able to offer her a constant stressless friendship. The part of him that sought closure battled with the part that still loved her fiercely. Was it even romantic love, doubt stained his mind's edges. And yet, he couldn't let go. *I need answers,* he thought, swallowing the lump in his throat. The lines between insecurity, love, and obsession blurred dangerously, but one thing was clear—he had to confront Nysa, even if it unraveled him in the process.

In the meanwhile, looking at him sitting and zoning out like a street boy, his mother gently smacked him on the head with a ladle before he could test the notion. Mr Bakshi walked in, he approached Ishan, "Congratulations, champ! I'm proud of you, getting married is great!"

"Mr.Bakshi, this doesn't make any sense," Ishan questioned him in a tense tune.

"What or How am I supposed to know this? No marriage makes sense to me, I'm here to bless you, it's your choice and to enjoy the puchkas, haha!" He presumed Ishan was joking and he walked away towards a small food stall outside.

"Please stop zoning, Ishan! Go get ready now! Time is approaching," his mother notified and walked into a room behind his back.

"At least they used a decent picture of me for the poster if it is." Mr. Bakshi wandered off towards the corridor, murmuring.

"This can't be real," Ishan walked towards the changing room, to eventually checked the time and date on his alarm clock as he made his way to the changing room, which left him stunned because nothing of the sort had occurred....

(to be continued..)

262

May this saga remind you to heal again and let you note that in every kind of heartbreak, or in the embrace of letting someone go - there is always growth.

Dear Readers,

This page is for your self-reflection.Feel free to reflect on what you think or how you feel.